The Promise
JM Dragon

The Promise

JM Dragon

Affinity
eBook Press
NZ
2016

The Promise
© 2016 by JM Dragon

Affinity E-Book Press NZ LTD
Canterbury, New Zealand

1st Edition

ISBN: 978-0-947528-16-4

Editor: JoSelle Vanderhooft
Proof Editor: Alexis Smith
Cover Design: Irish Dragon Designs

Acknowledgments

The inspiration for this story came from my love of old movies as in the good old black and whites of the 30's and 40's and one movie in particular, ah but to be so innocent again in what love has to offer.

I'd like to thank my beta's Mel and Nancy for your help in improving this novel, we do all make a great team.

Thanks to Jo for a great edit and the catches you made from my English to American were awesome.

Always my thanks to the Affinity management team and the wonderful supportive authors who live under the Affinity umbrella.

Dedication

For my friend Sally, who has had a rough time of it in the last 18 months' health wise. Keep getting better I'll continue to send my best wishes to you for a full recovery.

Table of Contents

Also by JM Dragon

Do Dreams Come True?
The One
Letting Go
Circus
Falling into Fate
The Fixit Girl
In Name Only
Death is Only the Beginning
Lonely Angel
Echo's Crusade
A Window in Time
Waterfalls, Rainbows and Secrets
The Dragon's Halloween Collection
Incantations – A Collaboration
Affinity's Christmas Collection 2010
Christmas Collection 2011
Christmas Collection 2012
Christmas Collection 2014

Define Destiny Series
Define Destiny
Haunting Shadows
In Pursuit of Dreams
Actions and Consequences
All Our Tomorrows
Two Steps Forward One Back
A World of Change

When Hell Meets Heaven
Fatal Hesitation

Prologue

Claire Tremont throttled back the engine of her Ferrari F12 Berlinetta to answer a call via Bluetooth. "Grams, it's been ages. How are you, and more to the point, why are you calling me in the wee small hours?"

"I needed to be back in the city for a meeting early this morning, and the red-eye was the only flight available. I arrived home an hour ago."

Claire rolled her eyes. "Ah, the terrible red-eye flight."

"Darling, are you free Sunday for lunch?"

"Sunday lunch is always tight. I do have a hectic social life and Racheal is very demanding." She grinned.

"Hmm, you girls and the demands of the social world, I want to see Racheal too."

"Okay, okay, I'll...no, we will be over on the weekend."

Claire negotiated a tight turn onto Fisher Street and drew to a screeching stop outside Checkers Club. "Grams, I have to go. What was it you said you wanted? Right, right.

Racheal is leaving for Europe on Monday for three months, so I can do that. Yep, love you too, Grams."

She was about to hang up when her grandmother spoke again. "Sure, yes, it's a promise, Grams. I promise a whole month of my time."

With the call finally ended, Claire stepped out of the car and locked it, then threw a glance at the gaudy neon lights flashing in front of her. She smirked at the long line waiting for entrance to the club and moved to the right and the VIP line, which was empty with only a couple of hours before the club closed. Most of the VIPs turned up after the official closing time.

"Ms. Tremont, a pleasure as always. Stella said the champagne is on you tonight."

Claire tilted back her head and winked at Binky Sykes, one of the bouncers. His beefy body made him look like he could tackle twenty bulls. But if you saw him with his puny boyfriend making mincemeat of him in their regular verbal sparring matches afterhours at the club you might think again.

"Darn, I thought I'd nailed that bet about Reggie getting laid. Is Howie still studying hard? Which classy place did he go to in the end? I've forgotten." Claire walked past the line with a jaunty glance at the staring eyes.

Binky chuckled. "Yep, majoring in plastic surgery. Only another six months and he's fully qualified. Got to say my kid brother has all the brains. He's been accepted to Dartmouth, an Ivy League college. Still can't believe it myself." Binky shook his head, and his shaggy hair appeared to move as if it were infested with something.

"Hey, if he can get into an Ivy League college it's more than I could do. One day you are going to have to bring him to meet us. We'll be good. Who knows when we might need his particular skills for all those chin and tummy tucks in the future? See you later, Binky." Claire waved and entered the club.

The music boomed out as she strode past the people filling the entranceway and walked up the stairs to position herself on the balustrade that enclosed the dance floor. She narrowed her eyes as someone below caught her attention, then moved in sync with the petite, buxom blonde who was strutting her stuff to an oldie beefed up by the DJ, "Hippy Hippy Shake." Wow, did that woman's hips shake, not to mention the rest of her.

As the music stopped, Claire glanced around. As usual, the club was packed with barely enough room to circulate. Turning her gaze back to the blonde, she grinned as the woman sashayed off the floor.

Within minutes the blonde arrived on the upper level and slid across the vinyl seat of one of the booths.

Claire made her way over to it. "Do you dance professionally?"

Green eyes snared hers. "I might. What's it to you?"

Claire negligently leaned against the wooden frame of the booth. "I thought so. You are one sexy dancer. Want to dance with me?"

The green gaze seemed to x-ray her inner being. "The last song of the evening is my favorite and sums me up."

Claire laughed and held out her hand. "I'll take my chance. Though I've never been here for the last dance. What is it?"

"'Wild Thing.'"

"Perfect. I'm Claire. Wild Thing, do you have any other name?"

"Avery."

They entered the throng of the dance floor.

†

Claire struggled to walk to her car and unlocked it after two attempts at pressing the button on her key chain. *I must be dog-tired. I feel like I've had a gallon of booze.*

She snaked into the driver's seat and turned the ignition. The deep purr of the engine as it came to life was music to her ears. She glanced at the apartment building she'd exited, then at the dashboard clock—4:00 a.m.

On automatic, she set the car in motion and sped up the road, her natural GPS taking over, as her brain seemed somewhat befuddled.

Her thoughts were filled with the young woman, Avery. She was, for sure, a wild thing and was up for anything in bed. Claire's alarm on her watch had alerted her to the need to get out of Avery's place. Racheal would be wondering where she was. Pissing off her fiancée, even if they did have an open relationship, wasn't in the cards days before Racheal left for Europe.

Claire grinned as she negotiated a corner. *I can have all the uninhibited fun I desire when she's gone—can't wait.*

The faraway noise of bells punched through her thoughts. She passed them off as another part of the city in the distance. She continued forward and was amazed when she saw red lights flashing in front of her.

The blast of a train's whistle, parallel to her was the last thing she recalled as she plunged into oblivion.

Chapter One

Melissa Jackson walked steadfastly toward the curb and watched the relatively quiet flow of traffic pass her by. In New York City that was a rarity; however, she was in a middle-class area where most were at work. The neighborhood wasn't exactly a rat run connecting to a more popular district. People didn't come here unless they had business or lived here.

She glanced at either side of the road twice and took a chance the large, white transit van heading her way was going at a pace she knew she could beat and stepped into the road. She stumbled into a hole, twisting her ankle and landing on the street. Disorientated at the unexpected fall, she frowned and looked at her feet just as the blare of a horn alerted her to the oncoming traffic. Then amazingly strong arms gripped her and pulled her out of danger.

"That was a close call." Melissa looked up into concerned, pasty brown eyes. "Thank you," she mumbled, smoothing down her exclusive purple Mark Alexander overcoat, which now had earthy patches in several places.

"I figured you tripped on that cracked part of the road. Did you hurt yourself? I've seen a few people do that. It should have been fixed months ago. Glad I could help though."

Melissa heard what she thought was sincerity and turned to her savior, a woman who couldn't have looked any more nondescript. She had the plainest features, and that long nose could definitely do with help. Her brown hair matched the color of her eyes, and she could benefit from a gym to shed those extra pounds around her hips.

"I'm so grateful too. Please, where did you come from and whom do I have to thank for saving my life?" Melissa asked with a smile.

"Kris, Kris Lake. I wouldn't say 'saved your life' exactly." She shrugged. "I work for Pritchard Insurance." She motioned with a finger toward a row of buildings. "It's my lunch break. I decided to treat myself to a coffee and savory muffin at Maggie's Bistro, well two actually. I wouldn't have been here otherwise." An engaging grin accompanied Kris's explanation.

Melissa liked the sound of this woman's voice and most importantly the inflections. They were honest, and that was refreshing. "Well in that case, even more reason to thank the fates for sending you my way. How would it be if I bought you lunch today—my treat?" A frown cast over Kris's face. "I insist, and besides, you were going to lunch, correct?"

Kris nodded. "I can't let you pay. I did what anyone else would do under the circumstances."

Melissa inwardly shook her head. *If only you knew the circle I live in, you'd change your mind.* "It's a thank-you from a very grateful old woman. Please, I'd like to, and believe me, I can afford it."

Kris shuffled from one foot to another for ten seconds and then stopped. "You don't look that old, but thank you, I'd enjoy the company." She gave a wide smile.

That smile had Melissa reflecting on her previous description of this woman. She was beautiful in a way that some would call soul-deep.

Melissa took Kris's arm. "Lead on, my new friend."

†

Kris settled into her usual chair at table sixteen in Maggie's Bistro and smiled at the people around her, mostly regulars. She didn't need to see the single-sided menu to know what she wanted and rocked in her chair. The woman she had helped had gone to the bathroom. Today hadn't been such a good day at work, but at least her noble deed had saved the day.

"Hi, Kris. Same as usual?" Kris watched the older woman weave in and out of the tables rather awkwardly. Obviously her ankle was giving her trouble.

Kris looked at Perry, the waitress. She was around fifty-five with a ready smile and hundreds of stories to go with the tattoos she wore with pride. "Yep, thanks, Perry."

Perry prepared to leave as she scribbled down the order.

"I'm with someone today, she's…well, coming now,"

Perry glanced in the direction of Kris's gaze and frowned. "I know her from somewhere. Who is she?"

Kris bit her inner lip. "Well, I—"

"Ah, I'll have mint tea, and do you have a double-chocolate cookie?" the woman decisively spoke as she approached the table

"Sure." Perry scribbled on her pad.

"Excellent." Melissa sat down.

Perry left, looking decidedly perturbed.

"So, Kris, this is a lovely place. I have to admit that though I've been in this area many times, I've never partaken of the local eating establishments."

Kris digested that statement and exhaled slowly. "I hope you don't think this is too forward, but I told you my name—"

"My manners. I'm so sorry, Kris. Melissa Jackson. I forget sometimes that people…. I want to thank you again. You said you worked for an insurance company. Do you enjoy the work?"

Kris picked up the glass of water on the table and sipped it. "I did, but at the end of the month, I'll be looking for another job. All this Internet insurance business made Stan, the owner, decide to retire and shut up shop. No point in selling the client list. It's been dwindling big-time for the past two years."

"Do you have other work to go to?" Melissa asked, staring into her eyes.

"No, I'm thinking of going home." At Melissa's expression of curiosity, she added, "I'm originally from Broome. My dad is a carpenter at the largest construction company in town. I'm the only child. Guess going home to Mom and Dad isn't as bad as living on the streets in New York. I don't have any savings. The rent and basic living expenses take all my salary."

"You don't sound happy about going home."

Kris looked down at her glass, then shrugged. "I'm not. I left because my parents didn't understand my orientation." She sucked in a deep breath and took a chance. "I'm a lesbian. I can't for the life of me think they have changed their minds since I left ten years ago. Sorry, I shouldn't have—"

Melissa took her hand in a warm grasp. "I'm glad you did." She gave Kris an intense gaze. "My granddaughter is a lesbian too. Her parents weren't impressed at first, but when she introduced them to very wealthy, prestigious clientele in her circle of friends, they changed their tune." She sighed heavily. "Claire has had a tough time for the last eighteen months."

Kris was intrigued by the conversation and the woman named Claire. They were at least a respite from her current problems. "Do you mind if I ask why she's had a tough time? You don't exactly look like a person from a family who would fall on hard times." Melissa's clothes would have taken two months or more of her salary.

Melissa cocked her head and stared at Kris. "Hmm, perhaps. However, money does not buy happiness, wisdom, or health."

"I'm sorry I...." Kris knew her cheeks were red from the blazing heat that surged through her face. *Damn, I can't finish a sentence. She'll think I'm an idiot.*

Melissa smiled. "I like you, Kris. You are not only forthright, but sympathetic. It is refreshing in this day and age. Claire was in a rather horrible accident; a train hit her car. She's very lucky to be alive. It's not, of course, what she thinks most of the time, but we are working on that aspect. Depression is a terrible thing."

Kris's eyes widened. "She was hit by a train! Whoa, I'm so sorry. I think I'd be depressed as well."

"Yes, well, my dear, Claire was responsible for the accident. She'd indulged in excess. I never understood why her life took that direction." Melissa dropped her gaze.

Kris saw the tears forming, and she reached across and touched the older woman's hand.

"Younger people don't always understand," Kris softly said.

"'Younger,' my, I wish. Claire was thirty-three! She knew better."

Perry returned and deposited their beverages on the table. "Be right back with the goodies." She winked at Kris.

"She likes you," Melissa said, stirring her tea.

"No, no. She's just being friendly. It's part of the job. Most people don't even notice me." Kris shrugged, depositing a sachet of brown sugar into her coffee and stirring vigorously.

"Does she call you by name when you come into the café?"

"Well…yes."

"You don't come every day or even every week, right?" Melissa insisted.

Kris frowned. "Well, no. I only come in here as a treat. I can't really afford anything else. Today was special. You can't let life get you down, right?"

Melissa grinned. "No, you can't and—"

"Here you go, ladies. Your goodies." Perry placed their food on the table.

"Thanks, Perry." Kris smiled.

"Perry?"

The waitress looked at Melissa, and Kris did the same thing.

"Yeah?"

"You won't remember me if I come in the café again, will you? My friend here uses your establishment infrequently, so why do you remember her?" Melissa stared at Perry.

Perry frowned and then slapped a hand to her brow. "Oh now I remember you. You're Mrs. Jackson, who helps the women's mission on Smith Street, and when I mean help, I do mean that big-time. My sister—"

"Thank you, my order looks perfect." Melissa waved Perry away.

Kris watched Perry leave. She looked uncomfortable as she muttered, "Enjoy."

"What was that about?" Kris asked.

"Nothing, my dear, nothing. I may have a proposition for you. Would you be willing to listen?"

Kris picked up one of her muffins, and before she took a bite, she replied, "Sure."

†

Kris stroked Knight's sleek, black hair as he lay across her lap. She gazed blindly at the TV screen. If anyone asked her what the program was, she wouldn't have been able to answer. Her fingers tickled Knight's ears, and she smiled as he purred gently and snuggled closer, wanting more.

"She offered me a job for a month, Knight. Not long in the grand scheme of things, but the pay is more than I get in six months." She dropped her head and nestled it close to Knight's head. "What do you think, puss?"

Several purrs later, Kris spoke again.

"Dad taught me carpentry. He said if I put my mind to it I'd be better than he was." Kris shrugged and laughed. "Yeah, and I took that advice to become a carpenter." She scanned the apartment. "I know I refitted the kitchen cabinets and they look good, but that was out of necessity." The midnight-colored, shorthaired cat simply gazed at her. "Knight, you are no help."

Knight jumped off her lap and ran to the kitchen window. Kris dutifully walked to it and opened it. Knight gave her a cursory glance and vaulted out onto the small, enclosed balcony where his litter tray and playthings were located. She half closed the window and sighed heavily.

"Melissa said Knight will be taken care of in a superior cattery until I come back, but I'd need to see it first." Kris scratched the side of her head and frowned. "I love Knight. He's my only family. I need to be sure this place is good enough. If everything checks out, at least this option is better than going to my parents'. They hate pets. I'd have to find him a new home—never going to happen." Kris drew in a huge breath.

That's it, decision made. I'm in.

Chapter Two

Claire threw the remote on the floor and stood. She glanced around the single-floor apartment in the basement of her parents' home in Central Park. Not that anyone outside of the multimillionaire crowd would call her home a basement. It had been remodeled to include a bathroom, kitchen, two bedrooms, and a large open-plan area.

To Claire it was a prison.

One she had made herself, true, but nonetheless, a prison.

The doorbell chimed. Claire grimaced and rolled her eyes. *I guess an unwanted visitor is better than that crap they call TV today. Reality show after reality show. Whatever happened to good old-fashioned fiction?*

The chime rang out again.

"I'm coming," she snarled.

She walked toward the door, then swung it open and glared at the person on the other side. "Grams?"

"Well, I have to say by your expression you are not happy to see me," Melissa Jackson replied with raised eyebrows.

"Sorry, Grams, it's not the usual day you visit. Anything wrong?" Claire waved her grandmother inside.

Melissa glided into the apartment and looked around. "Don't you ever tidy up? This place is a pigsty and that's being unkind to the pigs of this world."

Claire frowned. Sure there were a few clothes scattered around the place, and yes the dishwasher was full and pots were filling up the sink, but she had been about to set the machine in action.

Defensively Claire picked up an errant sweater and held it, twisting the fabric through her fingers. "Yes, you caught me on cleanup day, that's all."

"Well, you know the word at least." Melissa turned to face her.

"You have that expression on your face, Grams." Claire frowned.

"I do, good you recognize it. You made me a promise before the—" Melissa gestured toward Claire "—accident. Do you remember?"

Claire pouted. "Not really. Was it important? Oh, silly me, you are here now, so it must be. What did I promise?"

"That you would give me a month of your time to help me resurrect the disused cottage at Seasons." Melissa sat on the only chair that didn't have an item of clothing on it.

"Grams, I'm a cripple. I can't help you." Claire turned her back on her grandmother, stalked over to the kitchen, and slammed the electric kettle on the counter, then switched it on.

No reply. Claire gazed in her grandmother's direction. "I can't keep that promise."

Melissa gave Claire an intense stare and shook her head.

"What does that look mean?" Claire said.

"I was nearly killed yesterday."

"*What?*"

"Nearly. That's the important thing; details don't matter at this stage. It brought me to my senses about life, at least some of the things I hadn't followed through on," Melissa said. "You took the pity-party way out, and I'm taking the opposite."

Claire pursed her lips and scrunched her nose. "Okay, I'm game, but making you a promise a couple of years ago surely can't be the only thing that's on that bucket list."

"No, but you are the most important part of it. Darling, we have both diced with death earlier than we would want. That must mean something." Melissa sank into the recliner.

Claire scowled. "Yours was a genuine accident, mine was stupidity." She looked at her virtually lifeless right arm. "I got taken big-time. I suppose it was inevitable."

Melissa nodded. "Make that tea and we will talk. What do you have to lose? Believe me, the daytime shows are horrendous. Whatever happened to old-fashioned entertainment that made you feel good?"

Claire chuckled. "Got that right, Grams. Okay, I'm prepared to listen. What's so important?"

Melissa laughed. "Darling, this is going to be the best decision you have ever made in your life. I met a wonderful young woman and she saved me…."

†

15

Carl Tremont poured a glass of single malt whiskey and turned to his wife and daughter. His features contorted as he advanced toward them. "She's mad. Claire isn't in a fit state to do manual work." He sat in his favorite Swiss recliner, one of the few presents from his wife in the last forty years that he actually enjoyed.

"Carl, that's rather harsh. Darling, don't take any notice of your father. Mother was trying to help, I'm sure. However, I agree. Claire, manual work on the cottage isn't really you, now is it? Never has been your forte, really. You're a party girl and what with...."

Carl shot his wife a glare. "Your mother needs to be institutionalized, Anna. I've mentioned that she's been more irrational than normal in the past year. Claire isn't going. End of story. If she wants to work, I'll organize a desk job putting stamps on envelopes." Carl took a drink from the crystal glass he held.

"Carl, that's rather menial. Can't she take up her old job as one of our executive salespeople? She knows some very influential people," Anna said.

"Look at her, Anna. Are we going to sell a property if she's the face of the company?" Carl flicked Claire a look. "Sorry, kid, but it's business. Besides, you could get it fixed, but oh no, you have a stupid mindset that you need the scars to remind you. What about the fact you can't hold a cup of coffee in your right hand as the reminder? Your hand isn't a problem; we can get around that."

"Always knew you understood me, Dad." Claire dropped her gaze.

"Yes, I do; you take after your mother's side. Who the hell wants a reminder of an infidelity?"

"Haven't a clue what you mean, but I'm going to Seasons and help Grams out. Hey, she actually thinks I'm useful, unlike you two." Claire stood and strode out of the room.

Her quiet words rang out like an explosion.

Anna turned to him. "Really, Carl! Now you've made it worse. She's going. You know how stubborn she is." Anna sank into the brocade sofa and sighed. "That's your side of the family."

Carl shook his head and took another sip of his drink. "I'll guarantee she'll be home within a couple of days, and that's being generous. Besides, what can she possibly contribute to a renovation?" He reached for the *New York Times* and buried his head in the property section.

"You could be more sympathetic. Look at what she's been through."

Carl lifted his head and narrowed his eyes. Anna was the only woman he had ever loved enough to make a commitment; the family money hadn't hurt either. They'd met in college and both had similar aspirations except for one thing—children. Still, one had sufficed to keep her and the family happy, and then he'd had a secret vasectomy. Damn, what a dead loss the kid had turned out to be. A party girl and a lesbian to boot.

Now she's a cripple both in mind and in body. Damn, I should have forced her to have that surgery to fix those scars. It's going to cost a fortune to fix them now.

"Like I said, she can work for the firm when she gets back. It's about time she did a decent day's work." An interesting listing caught his eye. "Anna, 13 Craddock Avenue is up for sale again. I'll give Jed a call. I know the right person for that loft conversion." He stood and headed

17

for the door. "We'll go out for dinner. Let's celebrate our next sale."

Anna frowned. "But we haven't even begun negotiations."

"I feel lucky." He left the room.

†

Claire flopped down on her bed and heard a spring pop. She glanced at her body. At one time, her physique had been strong and toned. Now it was thin and weak. "Just like me." She spoke to the lemon-sorbet-washed wall and ran the fingers of her left hand through her blonde hair, which could only be termed a shaggy mess.

She closed her eyes as tears rushed forward, trapping them like a dam.

"Dad's right of course, but when isn't he? I'm no use to anyone. What was I thinking agreeing to Grams's suggestion? I'm not the woman I was when I made that promise, even if I can't remember it."

Claire opened her eyes and saw nothing but the shimmering tears that obscured her vision. When she blinked enough times to clear her sight, her eyes caught a silver-framed photo on the bedside table. In it two women raised a glass in a toast, smiling.

"I miss you, Racheal. I wish I hadn't been so foolish to think that I didn't have to pay for my behavior." She turned the frame facedown. Then she fell back onto the bed and sobbed for the life she had ruined—hers.

Chapter Three

Kris clapped her hands against her cold cheeks and stared at Seasons. The taxi had dropped her off at the eight-foot black gate adorned with four red symbols: flower, sun, leaf, and snowflake. She'd almost told the driver to turn back since the place looked way too imposing and grand for the likes of her.

After going through the gate, she gazed upon the turreted mansion called Seasons and was overawed. It was immense. Who could possibly have a family large enough to fill all those rooms? She nervously bit her inner lip as she scooted toward the front door and rang the bell.

Waiting, she scratched the back of her neck and looked down at her small suitcase. As she was about to ring again, the huge, white door opened.

Kris sucked in her top lip as she came face-to-face with a dour expression the likes of which she had never experienced before.

"Yes."

"Hi, I'm…well, I'm…." Kris frowned and wondered if this was the place. "I…."

"Ms. Lake, I presume. Mrs. Jackson told me to expect you."

"Yes, yes, that's me. Kris Lake. I wasn't sure if…." Seared by a harsh gaze, Kris stopped talking.

"I'm Mrs. Rank, the housekeeper. Please come in, and I'll show you to your room."

"Thank you, but I kind of expected to stay at the cottage. This is too grand for me." Kris swallowed hard, her cheeks growing hot as she averted her gaze.

"The cottage isn't livable. That's why you have been employed."

Kris stared into dark pools of brown that were almost black. She didn't want to stay in this house, at least not alone with this woman. She figured all her nightmares would come alive at once if she did. "Yes, yes, but I thought I'd be staying in the cottage and not having to bother anyone." Kris held her breath.

"You will not be a bother unless you make yourself one. I've a pot roast almost ready. Are you hungry?"

Kris was amazed at the offer and decided there and then as she nodded that she would make no more assumptions about people. "Thank you. To be honest I'm starving, haven't eaten since a piece of toast at six this morning. I had to put Knight in the cattery early, it was hard for us both," Kris rambled.

Mrs. Rank turned and gazed at Kris. "You like cats?"

"Well, never thought I would." She giggled. "Knight took my heart when he turned up as a stray on my balcony and has been with me since then. That was five years ago. I guess I'd end up a cat woman if I could afford it."

Mrs. Rank nodded. "Then you will be very welcome here. Seasons, and especially the cottage, likes people who love animals. Please come inside, Ms. Lake, and I will show you Seasons as I've known it from childhood."

What an odd thing to say that the house and cottage know you like animals. Kris gave a tight smile and gawked at Mrs. Rank. She was a plain woman and at least sixty, perhaps a little acerbic, yet something else, yes something else—

"Are you going to come inside?"

"Yes, sorry." Kris entered, and as she did, felt the overwhelming sensation that this place fit her like a glove.

†

Kris leaned back in the kitchen chair and rested a hand on her belly. "Wow, Mrs. Rank, I've never tasted pot roast that good before." She smacked her lips.

Mrs. Rank nodded, threading her fingers together. "A family recipe from my late husband's mother's side. My mother-in-law implied it was centuries old but with updated ingredients by each generation."

"Goodness gracious, how wonderful. I don't think there's anything in my family like that." Kris shrugged. "I wish there were." She had picked up the melancholy note in Mrs. Rank's voice and flashed her a beaming smile. "Maybe one day you might share it with me... if we get to know each other better, that is. I figure that family recipes need to be remembered."

Kris furrowed her brow. *Lame. Why did I even say that?*

Mrs. Rank stood without replying. She pointed to the teapot. "Do you care for tea or coffee?"

"Tea please, thank you. Please, can't I help? I don't want you to wait on me." Kris frowned.

"Perhaps when Ms. Claire and Mrs. Jackson arrive you could help with the preparation of meals." Mrs. Rank prepared the tea at the kitchen counter.

"Absolutely, anything to help." Kris bit down on her lip and said, "I've never met Claire, but Mrs. Jackson said she was in a terrible accident. Do you know her well?"

Mrs. Rank's back stiffened. She did not reply and continued with her task.

Crap, I wonder if she knows she's a lesbian and doesn't like that. Puts me in the crapper.

Kris heaved a sigh of relief as Mrs. Rank finally spoke as she laid the tea things on the table. "Ms. Claire is spoiled. She has never understood the true meaning of life or the joy that could come from it. She's a taker, like her parents. I have not seen her since she broke the heart of one of our ladies in town."

Kris was lost for words and sipped on the tea the older woman had set in front of her. It was good. "People change, maybe she has."

"Perhaps, but it would take a deep love that eclipsed everything else for that to happen." Mrs. Rank stirred her silver spoon in the dark liquid in her cup. "Now you, on the other hand, have so much potential."

Kris scratched the side of head. "Really? You think so? We've only just met. My parents once said that when I was fourteen, but I disappointed them."

Mrs. Rank stared intently at her, and Kris was mesmerized.

"You need the right place, the right time, and the right person—we shall see if it comes to fruition."

Kris opened her mouth to speak but stopped when Mrs. Rank stood.

"Let me show you your room. Tomorrow Mrs. Jackson arrives, so you'll want to be fresh."

Kris looked at the time. It was barely 7:00 p.m. "Thank you, sure." She quickly took another sip of tea, stood, and followed Mrs. Rank out of the kitchen.

†

"It's been a long time, Ricky, a very long time." Shirley Rank starred at the photo on her bedside table of a young man in military fatigues. He smiled broadly.

Shirley's heart raced as she looked at picture. They had been married barely two weeks before the Army shipped him to Vietnam. The picture had been taken a few hours before he left. She recalled his words.

"Shirl, you know I'll be back. Heck, who would dare ever separate us? Remember the promise." Ricky Rank grinned and pulled her into his arms.

"I don't want you to go. I have a feeling—"

Ricky laughed and placed her at arm's length so they could see each other.

"Guaranteed to come back safe and sound, right? It's what you said, and you are never wrong. I remember you saying that the day we met at Seasons."

Shirley looked around. "It isn't Seasons, Ricky. We need to go back, back to where we met, and then perhaps I will feel how this really transpires."

Ricky released her and threw his arms out to his sides. "I will not be a deserter. How would that look? How would I feel? Better yet, how would you?"

Shirley drew in a deep breath.

"Neither one of us could live with the nametag 'deserter,'" she sagely replied.

"There's a but though, right?"

Shirley shrugged. "I'm going to be waiting until the end of time for your return. You know that, right?"

Ricky grinned, hugged her close, and kissed her soundly.

"They're saying the war's almost over. About time, I say. I love you, Shirl. No one is more beautiful in my eyes or ever will be. That's a promise."

Shirley sank into the hug.

"I love you."

Shirley sat on the edge of her bed and shook her head.

"It's almost time, Ricky. I feel it in my bones. I want this legacy to continue, and when it does, I can move on with the rest of my life until we are together again."

Chapter Four

Melissa glanced at her granddaughter, who wore a sullen look. Not uncommon. She'd seen it on many occasions when things hadn't gone her way. However, Claire had willingly agreed to this without too much prompting, so why was she looking like a sourpuss? Melissa sighed.

"Are you okay, Grams?"

"I'm good. I was thinking, that was all."

"Care to share?"

For a split second, Melissa took her eyes off the road and smiled before returning her vigilant gaze to the traffic. *My, how her face changes when she's animated—even with those scars.* "Hmm, sharing with you? Not really." She chuckled. "Claire, I want you to be nice to the young woman I've employed to help you. Do you think you can do that?"

"Sure. What is her name again?"

"Her name is Kris Lake."

Claire laughed. "Interesting name, I hope she lives up to the hype. Is she attractive?"

Melissa ground her teeth—her dentist was going to charge her heavily for the abuse. "That young woman saved me from a terrible accident. I think beauty is in the eye of the beholder. You of all people should appreciate that now." Melissa spoke the truth; sometimes it hurt. Glossing over Kris's less than attractive features wouldn't help the situation. "Do you have a problem with people who aren't considered, in your social set, beautiful?" In her peripheral view, Claire shuffled in the seat. "Yes or no."

"Once maybe I did, and I know others do. My parents for example and—"

"Racheal?" Melissa immediately added and wished she hadn't.

"Yeah, Racheal and our closest friends. I understand," Claire bitterly replied and slouched.

Melissa smiled as she continued to watch the road and saw the gates looming that led to their destination. "Seasons, my love. Here you will find the real you as you are today. Other people's opinions won't matter. Besides, I think this will help you enormously. Being cooped up in your basement apartment was good in the beginning, but not now."

Claire sat upright again. "Grams, it doesn't matter where you are or what you do. At some stage other people's opinions matter. Isn't that life?"

Melissa laughed and stopped the car as they reached the gate. "Darling, you are learning, except ultimately only one person's opinion will matter. It comes down to a promise."

Claire frowned. "A promise? Okay, I'll buy in to that. Not actually sure what you mean, but then you have always come up with odd explanations. I love you, Grams. Thank you for taking me out of that hellhole I called home. This will be good for me, meeting new people and old ones, even if I can't remember them."

My darling, I'm sure that's what aggravates you the most, your memory loss. Well, it's time to make new ones. Melissa chuckled. "Good to know. When love comes with a promise, you will have endless riches of the heart."

Claire shook her head. "Who said anything about love? I'd rather have riches in the bank balance."

"Claire, I love you dearly, but you have a lot to learn. Make me a promise that you will actually try to be happy while you are here."

Claire shrugged, then grinned. "For you, Grams, anything. Even being nice to a stranger named Kris. I remember someone called Mrs. Rank, but the rest is foggy."

Melissa smiled. "Shirley Rank is a fixture. Seasons wouldn't be the same without her. She can be quite... unexpected, and she adores you."

"Hmm, now you have my interest." Claire grinned.

"Well, your interest can wait. We haven't updated the gate to automatic, so you'll need to open it." Melissa grinned at her granddaughter.

Claire groaned. "And I thought we had money." She climbed out of the car.

Melissa watched her walk proudly to the gate, then bit her lip as Claire struggled to open it with her good arm. "This will be great for her, I know it. I just know it," she whispered and gave Claire two thumbs-up as the gate opened.

Claire shrugged and trudged toward the car.

"Seasons, here we come," Melissa said brightly once Claire was back in the vehicle, and they drove through the gates.

"Damn, this means I have to shut them too." Claire frowned.

"No, darling, I'm not staying long. I have a dinner engagement tonight at the golf club. I'll be back late but will see you in the morning for breakfast before I head home." Melissa drove toward the main house.

She placed her foot hard on the brake and drew up to the house, with squeal of tires preventing the front end of the car from colliding with the steps leading to the main entrance.

"Grams, you really need to brake earlier. You almost ended up in the front door." Claire released the panic handle.

Melissa disengaged the engine and opened her door. "You are not the only one in the family who likes to drive dangerously." Her heart dropped like a stone as she realized how insensitive that must have sounded.

Claire grinned and climbed out of the passenger side. "I was only teasing, Grams. Hey, now I know where my need for speed comes from. Dad will be pissed. He thought it was from him."

Melissa sighed softly in relief and shook her head. "Your father is the only man I can guarantee will never get a ticket in his lifetime. My goodness, a tortoise travels faster than he does."

Claire chuckled. "Yeah, I feel sorry for the Merc SLS he drives. God, what I wouldn't give to drive that."

"It's a manual, a little difficult in your current circumstances." Melissa immediately regretted her words, silently chastising herself.

"Hey, Grams, at least that's one thing he can't blame me for if something goes wrong with his car when I'm gone."

"So very true, my darling."

The door to the house opened and Mrs. Rank appeared.

"Hmm, not so sure I'll not get blamed for all manner of things with her," Claire muttered.

Melissa laughed. "Shirley, how lovely. You remember my granddaughter, Claire. She's all grown up since you last saw her when she was seventeen."

"Mrs. Rank, how wonderful to see you again. You haven't change a bit." Claire shook the older woman's hand.

†

Kris watched the sporty-looking car virtually drive through the front window. A squeal of brakes halted the collision.

Two women were in the front, one she knew, and the other only by her first name.

"My gosh, I wonder what Melissa's granddaughter is really like. Mrs. Rank was lukewarm about her." Kris drew in a huge breath. "I'll like her unless she's opinionated. I hate that."

A few moments later, both got out of the vehicle, and the younger woman shook Mrs. Rank's hand.

She was surprised when Mrs. Rank didn't drop Claire's hand. *Hmm, that's interesting.* Kris took advantage of the moment to check out Claire and noted that she looked familiar. Exuding confidence, her face from the side view was beautiful with its pale complexion and soft, warm features.

"I bet she wows everyone she meets."

Kris gasped as Claire turned to the house. Lifting a hand to her mouth, she let out a cry of sympathy. One side of Claire's face was flawless, the other ravaged by scars, her lips on the left side dropping into an almost sarcastic expression. *How cruel life can be.*

Then Claire cast her gaze upward and caught hers. Kris shrunk away from the window and retreated to her room.

†

Claire looked around the lounge and drew in a shallow breath. *It looks familiar, but I can't place it, and I should. Damn, I hate this memory loss.*

"Looks good, Mrs. Rank." She turned to the housekeeper.

"Thank you, I do my best. I have your old room ready," Mrs. Rank said, pointing to the hallway.

"Actually I want to meet Ms. Lake. I assume she is here?"

"Claire, behave," Melissa softly growled.

"Grams, I'm being nice. It's always polite to meet people as soon as you arrive. It would be awkward if we met at breakfast without being introduced."

Melissa frowned.

"I will find her for you, Ms. Claire." Mrs. Rank turned to leave.

Claire's temper flared. "Forget it. We'll meet tomorrow. I'm tired."

"Of course, of course, Ms. Claire. I have salmon for your dinner. Do you want it served in your room?" Mrs. Rank shuffled and twisted her fingers together.

Claire was frustrated at her lack of control. *Damn, I hate salmon, always did. Don't have the heart to tell the old soul as she's made the effort and she does look familiar in a good way.* "Can it wait until tomorrow, maybe lunch?" Claire smiled.

"Yes, yes, of course. I'll make those preparations. Excuse me for a few minutes. I need to check something in the garage."

"Absolutely." Claire smiled and turned to her grandmother as Mrs. Rank walked off. "And?"

"And what?" Melissa smirked.

Claire narrowed her eyes. "You have something to impart before you leave me in this mausoleum."

Melissa chuckled.

"Funny, Grams, sure. Out with it."

Melissa hugged her tight. "I love you. No matter what people say about you, inside there is a very special person waiting to explode. Keep the faith, darling. I'll see you tomorrow morning before I head for the city."

Claire growled. "Hmm, this must be someone important. Do I know him?"

"No, actually no. Love you." Melissa grinned and gave Claire a peck on the cheek before she disappeared out of the front door.

Guess it's me and.... Claire looked around. She was alone. "Damn, who gives promises these days and keeps them? Me obviously."

†

Melissa was about to open her car door when she spied Shirley at the side entrance of the triple garage. She headed in the same direction, shouting for Shirley's attention.

"Shirley, I'm sorry about Claire. She can sometimes have irrational mood swings."

"Oh that's perfectly all right, Mrs. Jackson, I understand after such a horrific accident." Shirley smiled.

Melissa nodded. "That's the right word for it too. I still to this day can't understand how she came out of it alive."

"She still has things to do in this life; that's why she was spared."

Melissa shook her head. "Hmm, thank God the train was slowing for the track change to the station or it would be a different story."

"As I said, she still has work to do here."

"You always were optimistic, even after your Ricky died, I envied you the strength of will to keep going. I'm glad you were there for me when Graham passed. The way you cared for me is the reason I believe Claire staying here is the best thing that can happen to her right now." Melissa frowned. "What do you think of Kris?"

Shirley gave her an intense stare and nodded. "Perfect choice. I'll take care of Miss Claire and Miss Lake...I promise."

Melissa smiled and hugged Shirley close. "Thank you, my friend. I will see you at breakfast." She turned away and then swiveled back. "How is the family? Are any little ones on the way?"

Shirley's expression became sad as she shook her head.

"It will happen, I feel it in my bones. Bye, Shirley."

Melissa strode off in the direction of her car.

Chapter Five

Kris awoke with the sun streaming in from the French window, which was slightly ajar, allowing a tepid wind to flow into the room. The scent of the sea tickled her senses. She crinkled her nose, relishing the aroma of nature at its best. It was so far removed from her small apartment in the city and the gas fumes that choked the air.

She glanced at the round, black, stainless-steel travel alarm clock. She'd set it for six thirty; it was only five forty-five. Regardless, she sprang out of bed and looked out the window. Startled to see a figure standing in the middle of the lawn, Kris pursed her lips and frowned. From this distance, she couldn't distinguish if it was a man or a woman. Their back was turned and they were dressed in black, slim-fitting trousers and a bright red, cable-knit sweater with, contrarily, flip-flops. A black baseball cap hid Their hair.

Perhaps it was a gardener surveying what work was needed that day, or maybe a neighbor. On second thought, a neighbor wasn't probable at this time of the day, as the property was at least a mile from the next house. Or it seemed that way when she'd traveled here.

For a few more seconds, she remained at the window and wished she hadn't seen the figure turn, and their gaze catch her own like a missile. There was no mistaking the feminine profile, and from this distance, it was an arresting one.

"Claire." Kris snuck back into the shadows of her room and sighed. "She's gonna think I'm crazy, or worse, a pervert who watches people when they aren't looking."

She headed to the bathroom for a quick shower, having promised Mrs. Rank she would help with breakfast. The thought made her nervous.

†

Claire sat at the breakfast table, resplendent with polished cutlery and every imaginable bread and fruit concoction. She'd chosen a seat that overlooked the view of the sea. While she sat, a fleeting memory engaged her. Grams had said that as a child, Claire had apparently coveted the view, but her father had always assumed that place. *I guess it was the privilege of the head of the family.* The image faded.

"Ms. Claire, how wonderful. You are an early riser."

Claire smiled as the housekeeper scurried into the room.

"Always. Can't seem to change a habit of a lifetime. Believe me, I've tried."

Mrs. Rank gave her one of those looks that might seem like censure but in fact was understanding. The housekeeper was a strange duck. She was always reliable no matter what—even if she didn't approve. Claire didn't know how she knew that, but she did.

"This is wonderful. Kris is an early riser too. We've made pancakes, Canadian bacon, and eggs. Do you want everything or…the salmon from last night?"

Claire almost choked on the juice she'd just sampled. "Maybe lunch for the salmon. Everything else, absolutely." Claire looked behind Mrs. Rank. "Where is Ms. Lake?"

"Oh, she said she wasn't hungry. I believe she headed for the cottage to get started on her task. It will be interesting to see the old place habitable again. It hasn't been since—"

"I'll have coffee with my breakfast. French. Do you have it?" Claire said, bored with the conversation, yet wanting to know why Kris Lake didn't stay to eat or at least be sociable. They were supposed to be working together.

"Of course, yes, I'll make some." Mrs. Rank nodded and left the room.

Claire stared at the sea, which ebbed and flowed on the shore, lost in the memories of what could have been. She couldn't remember much from her past—just snippets. She felt oppressed by the fact she felt sure her self-destructive path had begun here at Seasons and had involved a woman.

"What the hell was her name?" She scratched her forehead, unable to recall the woman and the event she was sure began the downward spiral that had been her life until the accident. Now she had no life.

"What do they say? Everyone eventually gets what's coming to them. Guess I did," she muttered and snatched a warm whole-wheat roll and bit into it. The door opened and she turned, half expecting to see Mrs. Rank.

"Grams, what are you doing up? In fact, what are you doing here? I thought—"

Melissa held up a hand. "I always come home. It's the right thing to do. Besides, there is so much activity in this household so early, who can sleep?"

Claire chuckled. "I'll give you that, Grams. Your protégé is at the cottage already."

Melissa glanced at her watched. "It's barely seven. What about breakfast?"

Claire shrugged. "Guess she wanted to make a good impression."

"Claire!"

"What?" Claire sipped her juice.

Melissa shook her head. "Kris doesn't need to do that. As far as I'm concerned, she has already made a marvelous impression on me. Where is Shirley?"

"I wanted French coffee."

Melissa gave a heavy sigh and then smiled as Mrs. Rank appeared pushing a heated food trolley. The aroma of sumptuous bacon, eggs, and pancakes along with a steaming coffeepot announced her arrival.

"You are a star, Mrs. Rank." Claire allowed the scent of the breakfast to infiltrate her senses.

"She's always been that way, Claire. You were just too insular to notice," Melissa said.

"Whatever. Let's eat." Claire winked at Grams and gave Mrs. Rank a thumbs-up.

†

Kris stood with hands on hips, taking stock of the wooden cottage with a large veranda/deck area. She looked up at the second story and saw three windows. It was a substantial cottage. It could easily house a family. It certainly needed some love and care but not exactly as much as she expected. The yard was a nightmare of overgrown trees and a tangled mass of foliage.

Rubbing her chin, she muttered, "A few of those shutters need repairing. Major paintwork and probably the hinges need oiling. I can do this without help in the time given."

She stroked a hand over the gnarled timber of the front door. It sent a tingle down her spine.

"Dad always said a true carpenter felt the good stuff when they touched it. Pity I didn't meet your expectations, Dad, but at least you taught me how to recognize quality." Kris shrugged and turned the doorknob. It didn't move.

"Darn." She stepped back and frowned. "I should have asked Mrs. Rank for the key."

She sighed and cast her glance to the hillock, knowing the ocean was on the other side. It was tempting, far more so than the inevitable meeting with Claire. A shudder went down her back.

"I'm such a wimp. I should go back to the house and enjoy that great breakfast. Oh no, silly me, I chose to ignore the delicious food, with bacon to die for. And for what? An inanimate structure. I must be mad."

A faint groan drew Kris's attention. Her eyes darted to every corner of the area, yet she saw nothing. Her gaze then settled on the front door of the cottage.

"If I didn't know better, I could have sworn you heard me," she said to the house. "Ridiculous, of course." She ran a gentle hand over the door's top panel and smiled. "Sorry, just me being... me, I guess. I'll give you a promise to bring you back to your old glory. As long as you don't spook me like that again. Deal?"

Kris chuckled softly at the absurdity of her words. Yet as she said them, a warmth filled her with expectation and hope.

She turned toward the path that led to the seashore. "I might catch a shrimp or two for my breakfast." Then she giggled. "No net. Next time, then."

†

The tide was going out, and the wonderful smell of seaweed freshly thrown on the sandy beach created happy recollections of childhood. Her dad had even gotten his feet wet in the lapping waves. He never swam with her but kept his eye on her while she frolicked in the water... good times.

Kris looked at the shingle made up of millions, maybe billions of shells over time. Darn the simple but effective way the brain brought back memories long stored away, maybe even forgotten.

She smiled and moved along to the edge of the shore. The clarity of the water was remarkably good as she ran back and the sea moved forward. For the next minute or two, she had a cat-and-mouse session with the most dominant force on the planet and laughed as she made an error in judgment and water flooded her canvas shoe.

"You never can second-guess Poseidon's playground." She chuckled as she shook her left shoe, then the right.

"So very true. I've never seen you here before."

Turning in surprise, Kris bit her lip and said nothing.

"Oh, we have a silent daughter of the sea. I can deal with that. Do you do this often?"

Kris shook her head.

"A woman of few words. Not easy, but I can work with that. I'm Fern Delancy. You are?"

"Kris Lake," she gasped out.

Kris stared at the woman in gym clothes who reminded her of a middle-aged Sophia Loren; dusky skin and deep brown eyes with tied-back, chestnut hair completed the beautiful image. She had the most melodious voice Kris had ever heard.

"Well, Kris, it's good to meet you. Are you staying close by?"

Fern continued to jog in place.

Stupid, stupid, she's gorgeous and talking to me and I'm making a fool of myself. "I'm living at the Seasons for a month. Mrs. Jackson asked for my help."

"Oh is Melly here? She's lovely. Got to say you are a bit young but... hey, whatever floats your boat."

Kris frowned. "I'm helping to restore the cottage. I don't know what you are insinuating. Mrs. Jackson *is* a lovely, kind woman."

Fern shrugged. "Sorry, my mistake. Melly has a reputation in certain circles."

Kris sucked in a deep breath. *I'm not going there.* "Do you live here, or are you on vacation?"

"I live here. Have the grandest house in the Pegasus Development; ask anyone." Fern grinned, holding out her hand.

Kris reluctantly took it and didn't like the moisture left behind, though the grip had been tight.

"Why not take in Curiosity Bar when you want some relief from the hard work. I'm there most nights." Fern winked and with a wave ran away, taking the seashore route.

Kris watched as Fern ran. She was a competent runner. Her eyes wouldn't leave the woman's tight ass, and that made her blush.

"At least she didn't ignore me. Most women who look like that do unless they want something." Kris looked around and saw no one in sight and chuckled. "Thank God no one else is here or they would think I'm mad talking to myself.

"Right, if I can't find shrimp, then a clam will be welcome. Where are you hiding?" she announced as she waded into the surf near an outcrop of rocks.

Chapter Six

Claire screwed up her eyes as she stood in front of Grams.

"Hey, I object to that expression." Melissa winked.

"You should, leaving me here for a whole month with Mrs. Rank and a total stranger! This is almost worse than my parents' solution to my solitary existence. In fact, it is! You actually care about me. Yeah, business in the city, you told me. I guess I should have listened more carefully to what I promised." Claire shook her head and turned to look out of the window and at the remarkable view in front of her.

Melissa placed a hand on Claire's shoulder. "I love you, care about you, want the best for you, and would, given the right circumstances, die for you."

Claire pursed her lips. "Whoa, that's too much info. I'm glad Mom told me of your love for theatrics, or I'd have fallen hook, line, and sinker for that one."

"Your mother knows nothing. Head buried in the sand like a—" Melissa threw up her hands "—ah yes, an ostrich."

"That's a bit cruel, Grams. She's your daughter." Claire stomped off in the direction of the patio door leading to the lawn.

Melissa laughed. Then walked over and stood next to Claire. "I'm going to give you a piece of advice you refused to listen to as a teenager."

Claire scowled. "You think I'll listen now?"

Melissa smiled.

Claire shook her head and forced a smile. "Love you, Grams. Whatever advice you have, give it, though you know I'm not one to take it easily."

"I know, darling. In fact, what I'm going to say might freak you out a little." Melissa grinned. "Perhaps not. You youngsters don't know what freaky is. I could tell you some stories anyway."

"Grams, get on with it, or you will be here the full month with me."

Melissa grinned. "Silly girl. Life, my darling, is full of hope and lots of expectations and promises. Along the way, we stumble sometimes of our own accord; other times fate makes its intentions known. At this moment in time, Claire, you are being given a rare opportunity, one that will change your life forever."

Claire frowned. "Go on."

"There is one promise that will determine your fate. I think here and now in this place you will reach that point."

Claire wrung her hands together and softly whistled. "Got to hand it to you, Grams, you would win an Oscar with that statement. Ever thought of writing a book?"

"You'll find your future here, Claire, I promise." Melissa smiled. "From an unexpected source. It might even be Shirley."

Claire rolled her eyes. "Yeah right. More likely the reticent Ms. Lake. God, she doesn't look like a Kris, more like a Violet."

"That's very rude, darling. I hope you treat Kris with as much respect as you do me. In fact, I insist." Melissa shook her head and walked toward the door.

Claire turned and sucked in a short breath. "Grams, I'll be good, I promise. You really like Kris Lake, don't you?"

"I do, and not because she saved me from an accident but... something about her resonates inside me. A good thing, I might add. Just promise me you won't scare her away."

Claire looked at her weak arm and frowned. "Can't promise she won't be spooked." She moved it slightly, and the fingers barely responded. With her good hand, she traced a finger over the disfiguration on her face. "However, I will not verbally do anything to upset the woman."

Melissa smiled. "That's my girl. I'll be back in a month unless you need me in an emergency. Now let's track down Kris and introduce you properly."

†

Kris moved her toes in the surf and smiled as it tickled. She held her head up as the early morning sun shone directly on her skin. It burned slightly, and as she turned her head, she gasped.

"Melissa... I... I wasn't expecting to see anyone."

"Sorry, my dear, we didn't mean to sneak up on you." Melissa edged forward and placed a gentle hand on her shoulder. "I wanted to personally introduce you to my granddaughter. I was disappointed not to see you for supper last night and at breakfast this morning. You do know it's the most important meal of the day?"

Kris forced her lower lip between her teeth and then wish she hadn't as the granddaughter stared directly at her. *Why does she look familiar, at least the good side of her face?* "I… I was tired." *Totally lame, and what about this morning?*

"I understand that," Melissa said.

"What about breakfast? You couldn't possibly be tired then, could you?" Claire interrupted.

Kris struggled to answer. Claire had a voice that demanded attention, as did her general presence.

"Claire!" Melissa scowled at her granddaughter.

"I'm sorry, that was rude of me. It's just that being here with all this lovely expanse of ocean after the city, not to mention the magnificence of Seasons, I was overwhelmed," Kris said. It was true, but how could she say she was scared to death to meet Claire? Even more so now—she remembered this was *the* Claire Tremont. Kris wasn't that out of touch with what was going on in the lesbian scene. She subscribed to one of the local club newsletters, which described Claire and her fiancée as the in people, or at least used to.

Kris thrust out her hand. "I'm pleased to meet you, Claire."

Claire cocked her head and frowned, grasping the proffered hand. "Good to meet you too, Kris. I believe Grams has given us a task to complete in a month."

"Yes, she has." Kris nodded.

Claire shrugged. "Not sure how much help I'll be." She lifted her right arm, supported by her left hand. "However, I'm game if you are?"

Kris heard the words, and as they sank in, she released the unconscious breath she had held since Melissa had given her this role. At this moment, everything seemed to fall into place. How odd was that? "Trust me, one arm is as good as two if you are willing." Kris stopped dead. "I'm sorry—"

"No." Claire grinned. "That's the first time someone hasn't been condescending on meeting me initially. You and I, Kris Lake, will get on well." Claire turned to her grandmother. "Grams, do you think Kris and I can complete the work?"

Melissa smiled. "Never thought anything else or I wouldn't have paired you together. Well, my dears, I have to be back in the city for dinner. I'll leave you two to become better acquainted."

Claire hugged her grandmother close and kissed her cheek.

Kris smiled and was surprised when Melissa hugged her too. Melissa whispered in her ear, "Take care of my little one. She seems all brash and confident, but deep down she's looking for that special something to anchor her life." She pulled away.

"Right, ladies, when I get back you'd better have some great progress for me." Melissa grinned at them, waved, and headed back toward Seasons.

Kris watched her go and almost ran after her. The idea of being alone with Claire overawed her. *I can do this. She isn't an ogre.* Sucking in a deep breath, she valiantly smiled and turned to Claire.

"Do you want to see the cottage?"

Claire, her eyes still on the retreating figure, muttered something.

"I'm sorry, I didn't hear that."

Claire abruptly faced Kris. "It wasn't important. Yes, please show me the cottage. I haven't been there that I recall, but then my memory isn't that good anymore." She directed her gaze at Kris.

Kris sighed softly and smiled. "A bit rundown, but not insurmountable. We can do it."

Claire frowned. "You think *we* can?"

"I know *we* can. Follow me." Kris smiled and then began to walk the way she had come from earlier.

Claire didn't immediately follow. Instead she watched Kris Lake walk away. The woman was unremarkable; in fact, *plain* and *slightly overweight* came to mind.

She looked at her useless limb and snarled at the impossibility of her being a help to anyone. How embarrassing could this get? Except it didn't really matter. Kris appeared nice in a homely sort of way. Spending a month here wouldn't be the worst few weeks of her life. Nope, probably some of the best, she suspected, after the last couple of years.

"Are you coming?"

The words weren't demanding or even annoyed. *They sounded more like an invitation, so why am I wasting it?* "Sorry, be right there." Claire shrugged and followed in Kris's steps on the beach. She grinned. *I loved doing that as a kid.* The memory, however brief, was welcome.

Chapter Seven

Kris and Claire stood next to each other surveying the cottage from the overgrown garden.

"Wow, you think we can make this shipshape in a month?" Claire asked.

Kris shifted her position to look at Claire. "Of course. It really isn't as bad as it seems, trust me." Grinning, she headed to the porch.

Claire reached out and clutched Kris's arm.

Kris, startled, stared at her.

"Is it safe?"

Kris laughed. "Perfectly. My dad is a carpenter by trade, and he taught me a lot. This is a wooden-framed house; I promise you will be safe. Doesn't look like any dry rot to me."

Claire frowned. "No one has ever promised me that before."

Kris smiled at her. "Really? Well I'm going to say it to you now, and please believe it. I know what I'm doing."

"Then I will. So, what brings you here, other than Grams's persuasion? Any friends or lovers left behind?"

"No." Kris bit her lower lip.

"No one?" Claire frowned. "Really. Wow? Not even a best friend?"

Kris walked toward the door. "I've never had a best friend."

"Everybody has a best friend, in kindergarten, high school, and beyond. Everybody knows someone they can call that," Claire said.

"Guess I'm different," Kris replied. "Did your grandmother give you the key to the cottage?"

"No. I assumed you had it." Claire placed her hands in her slacks pocket.

"Darn, I'll go back and ask Mrs. Rank." Kris turned and began to walk toward the main house. "Oh, there's a ridge behind the cottage that has breathtaking views over the ocean and the town's inlet. See you in ten minutes." Kris left.

†

"Well, she didn't even give me time to say I'd go." Claire shook her head as Kris appeared to skip along the path toward Seasons, her sandaled feet crushing the grass. Stroking her chin, she smiled. *I vaguely remember the ridge. Grams said we spent most summers when I was a kid here. Oh well, Kris seemed pleased to tell me. I wouldn't have had the heart to tell her I knew the place had she given me the chance.*

"Me, a heart? Who would have thought it?" she theatrically spoke to the old cottage before tentatively stepping onto the old wooden deck. Several moans and groans accompanied her weight on the plank and she grinned. "Hmm, I do that in a morning too."

Claire peered into the house through one of the nearest grime-covered window panels. She scrubbed the glass with her hand, and an area swirled in front of her that allowed her to see into the cottage. It was dark and uninviting, clearly needing some tender loving care. Solid objects covered with drop cloths to keep the dust out littered the room. *Some hope of that.* The place didn't look as if anyone had entered the property for years. When was the last time she had…? *Okay, no access to that memory.*

The squawk of a bird drew her attention toward the overgrown area to her right. A lanky tree of distinctly odd proportions stood to the side with as much foliage as her armpits—none. A lone, sparrow-like bird stood proud on the highest branch. It was pretty, with an orange yellow breast and black head and speckled white on black wings. It twittered at her again, and she shook her head and turned away.

The commotion above her continued in earnest.

"What's up with you, buddy? Haven't you found a worm for breakfast yet?" Claire feigned a scowl, then chuckled.

She fumbled in her pockets and drew out an oatmeal cookie. Mrs. Rank had insisted she take something with her from the breakfast table. Dutifully Claire had wrapped the cookie in a paper napkin and intended to dispose of it rather than eat it. *Oatmeal tastes like gravel. How can anyone like it?*

She broke off a part, crumbled it in her hand, and threw it at the foot of the tree which, remarkably, was reasonably clear of overgrowth.

The bird immediately swooped down and began to eat the crumbles.

"Everything has its worth in this life—even a horrid cookie." She stepped down from the deck and the bird flew into the shrubbery. "Not quite friends yet, hey, buddy?" She headed to the side of the house to go to the ridge.

Several times twigs and tangled reeds struck her, so her progress was slow. Having only one arm to push ahead was awkward and frustrating. A twig snapped in her face, and the sting had her cursing.

Eventually she reached the safety of open space, and her heart swelled at the sight before her. Water as far as the eye could see entranced her. She drew in a breath at the simplicity of nature and the sheer wow factor. Even the pesky vegetation that had attacked her had merit in its own way.

A massive flat stone was in front of her, and she sat on it.

As the beauty in front of Claire spellbound her, thoughts of her parents rushed like the sea coming into her brain. Her father in particular. Other than the business, golf was the only pastime he entertained. As she found out later in life, flirting with women young enough to be his daughter was another one of his dalliances. *What a loser.*

The aggression she had always harbored toward him soared inside her, and her cheeks grew warm. She looked down at her hands. She sighed, expressing the breath she hadn't realized she had been holding.

"You found it. It's marvelous, isn't it?"

The joyful sound of Kris's voice allowed Claire to relinquish her anger, and her body relaxed. Moving her head, she looked at the woman who was standing about three feet from her.

"I did. Yes, it's just as great as you said."

Kris held out a set of keys, her face wreathed in a grin. "Want to explore the cottage?"

The excited words had Claire purse her lips slightly. The woman seemed to revel in the simplest of things, allowing herself to become part of this innocent world even if it was for only a month. "Wouldn't miss it."

Chapter Eight

The lock grudgingly gave as Kris turned the key, and the creak of the unoiled hinges irritated her eardrums.

"Seems no one has been here for years," Claire said.

"Yeah, Mrs. Rank seemed reluctant to give up the key. Would you believe it was on a chain around her neck? I think this place has a special significance for her."

They entered the cottage and the dust bunnies scampered around, filling the air with floating particles as the breeze entered.

"Smells a bit, doesn't it?" "Musty, like one of those secondhand bookstores." Claire moved to stand beside Kris.

Kris raised her eyebrows. "You don't look like the type who goes to old bookstores."

"Really? What type do I look like?" Claire inquired.

Kris bit her lower lip. "I'm sorry, I didn't mean any disrespect."

"None taken. In fact, I'll have you know when I was in college, I frequented one of those stores for months. With a hot older woman behind the counter. No healthy lesbian worth her salt would have passed up the chance to have her notice you."

Kris laughed. "And did she notice you?"

"Everyone does, right?" Claire waved her good hand theatrically over her face. "But no, she didn't. Those darned musty books were her life, at least while I was in college. What about you?"

"I didn't go to college."

"Really? I'm surprised."

Kris walked past the furniture shrouded in dusty sheets and stopped at the arch leading to the kitchen area. "Wow."

Claire followed. "Okay, I'm game. What's the wow for?"

"This has a kitchen area more advanced than the one I have in my apartment. A bit of elbow grease and it will look great. Have you seen that oven? I'm in love."

Claire laughed. "In love with a cooking range, my, that's some competition."

"Look at it, Claire, it's beautiful. I know it's vintage 1930s, but with a cleanup, I bet we can make her enamel shine like it did in the old days. Don't you just love black and white?" Kris ran her hand over the dull exterior of the appliance.

Claire scratched her head and looked at the range. "Sure, we can do that, but don't we need to update the main building first? Not that I'm an expert."

Kris turned to her, blushing. "Sorry, I bet you think I'm stupid."

"Never call a person stupid until they do something stupid. As in me." Claire traced a finger over a jagged scar above her right eye. "Being excited about things isn't stupid, it's enjoyment. I wish I had your outlook. Perhaps I'd be in a better position than I am now." She sighed heavily.

Kris stared at her. "I don't know you, Claire, but I admit I know of you from the local tabloids. You don't know anything at all about me. I figure that for a month we can just be two people who want to make a special woman happy by helping to renovate the cottage. Let's leave our pasts behind us."

Claire stared at Kris and frowned before blinking several times. "I wish I'd met you years ago, Kris. You are so pragmatic."

Kris smiled. "I'll go with pragmatic. Come on, let's explore some more."

Chapter Nine

Claire hadn't laughed so much in years. Kris's gentle manner and excited curiosity as they scrambled around the old cottage was catching, even with its creaking floorboards, hinges that required a liberal application of oil, and the dust. Almost as much dust in the place as grains of sand on the beach. The cottage inside needed more attention than the outside from her observations, and it was going to take good old-fashioned hard work to make it spic and span. She looked at her right arm.

Hmm, that might be tricky, but I'll give it my best shot.

"Did you have a good morning, Ms. Claire?"

Claire nodded as Mrs. Rank stood in front of her. Talk about sneaking up on someone. Absently wiping away a cobweb from her hair, she looked at Kris's retreating back heading toward her room.

"Absolutely, Mrs. Rank. When was the cottage last lived in? And I don't mean when the family used it. That's not living in it," Claire asked, her eyes still following Kris until she disappeared around the bend upstairs.

Claire was so engrossed in Kris she only caught the odd word from Mrs. Rank's reply. She was surprised to see sadness dwelling in every contour on the housekeeper's face. "I'm sorry, Mrs. Rank, I didn't quite catch that."

"Never mind, Ms. Claire. I have a lovely crayfish salad for lunch. It's ready when you are."

Claire bit her bottom lip, wanting to know what Mrs. Rank knew about the cottage but figured she had time to find out. "Wonderful. I need to freshen up first. All that grime, you know. Let me know when Kris is ready to eat and I'll be there."

Mrs. Rank crossed her arms over her ample breasts. "Kris is helping me to shop in the town over lunch."

Claire clenched her fists, feeling irrationally angry that Kris wasn't joining her for lunch. "I'm eating alone? Do you think that's fair?" she pouted.

Mrs. Rank shrugged and clucked like a chicken. "Absolutely not, we can't have that. I will inform Kris that we shall go shopping after lunch."

Claire held up her hand. "No, no, it's fine. Go shopping. I need to do some emails and private stuff. How about we all make sure we have dinner together? Can we have beef instead of seafood, please?"

"Why of course, Ms. Claire. What time?"

"Six is a good time to have a glass of wine before we have dinner, I think. Oh, and while it's just the three of us, we are equal. No exception and… Claire is good enough for me." She saw twitches cross Mrs. Rank's expression. She certainly had trouble with the request. "Are we in agreement?"

"Yes, yes of course, whatever you say, Ms.…Claire."

"Great start. Okay, I'll go wash my hands and face, and then I'll be back for lunch on my own...by choice." Claire winked and Mrs. Rank colored slightly. "Oh, and I can't call you Mrs. Rank."

Mrs. Rank shuffled around a square foot for a few seconds, then announced, "Shirley. Yes, Shirley. My husband loved the name. It's what attracted him to me in the first place."

Claire became thoughtful. "He was hooked on you too, right? Not just the name?"

Shirley nodded. "Not just the name, you are right."

Claire smiled. "I like happy endings. I remember you once helped me with a puppet show for my parents. They hated it of course, were bored out of their skulls, my dad in particular. Still, you made me feel better. Can't remember why, but you did." Claire shrugged and turned toward the stairs. *Wow, I'm doing well with the memory here.*

"It was important for you. A child should feel good about their actions if they are trying to please, even if the recipients don't appreciate it. I certainly did." Shirley smiled, her thin lips growing taut.

"For a few moments you were the surrogate parent I kind of wished for," Claire replied in a trembling voice.

"Thank you. I'm honored you thought that."

Claire hesitated.

"Are you going shopping with us too? I'm looking forward to my first real visit to the town. I only passed through when I arrived." Kris closed the gap between them and the stairs.

An unusual warmth flooded Claire as she smiled at Kris. "Not today. Soon though. Don't spend too much."

Kris chuckled. "I don't have much to spend, so highly unlikely." She turned away and then back again. "Are you going to be okay on your own?"

Claire bit her bottom lip at the concern in Kris's voice. "Yes, absolutely. Will you bring back some of Mimi's rhubarb-and-apple pies for dessert tonight?"

Kris grinned. "I'll find Mimi's for you and do just that. See you later, then?"

"Absolutely," Claire slowly made her way up the stairs to her bedroom.

†

Kris breathed in the salt-encrusted air that greeted her as she walked along the main street of Chartres. So much healthier than a city filled with the fumes of ever-increasing traffic, and she felt safer too. Not just about the lack of vehicles hogging the road, but personally too. In New York City, she was constantly on the watch for pickpockets as she waited in the throng of bodies waiting to cross the road. Here there were fewer people. Sure, it was a Monday morning and most who'd stayed the weekend would have gone back to their main residences long ago, but the luxury of not walking into people felt great.

Kris stopped at a crossing, and as she glanced around, her gaze alighted on a young woman who was maybe around her age. The woman stood outside the very store where she was going to buy the pies Claire requested. Her stance was relaxed. The carved hiking cane she held on to fascinated Kris the most.

Who uses that in beach terrain? Strange.

She looked both ways, noted the speeding car and stopped, then quickly crossed. As she walked the few steps to Mimi's store, the woman hadn't moved.

Kris looked at the cane, her eyes dwelling on it for a ridiculous amount of time. *She'll think I'm nuts.*

"Don't you just love the smell?"

Kris flushed in embarrassment as the woman stared at her. "Why…why yes, I do. Truth be told, this is the first time I've ever been here. My…friend wanted rhubarb-and-apple pie for dessert tonight and said this was the place."

"Certainly is, and your friend has great taste. Pies are something most people ignore nowadays, a bit old fashioned. Fancy cupcakes are the modern trend."

Something instinctively likable about the woman attracted her. Coming here had been a good call. "Not that keen myself, all that frosting." Kris chuckled.

"What a great laugh you have. It's so genuine. I'm Jess Smith." She thrust out her hand.

Kris, surprised by the sudden movement, grasped the proffered hand. "Kris, Kris Lake."

"Lovely name. You're new here, right?"

Kris laughed. "Yeah. How did you guess? Oh I know, you haven't seen me around here before…then again, I did say I'd never been here before, and that's the big tell, right?"

Jess turned fully to face Kris and smiled, exaggerating her dimples. "Exactly right. Are you here for the short stay or long haul?"

"A month. I'm helping to restore an old cottage. It's a new challenge. I'm looking forward to it. What about you?" Kris asked.

Jess shuffled, and her body disguised by a long overcoat appeared to lean on the cane more.

"I'm a fixture." Dark eyebrows wriggled and deep blue eyes caught hers.

"I envy you. I wish I could stay here forever. I love it and I've barely been here a couple of days."

"Are you free to have a coffee? Millie's does a great one complete with a Belgian chocolate cookie. I'll understand if you don't want—"

"Thank you, I'd love to. I'm waiting for someone. She's having her hair done and won't be ready for at least another hour."

Jess laughed, and Kris allowed the gentle sound to surround her. It was one of the most calming noises she had ever heard.

"A tint, right? Not just a cut?"

"How did you know?" Kris laughed.

"Oh, an educated guess. They have specials on a Monday. Let me lead the way."

Kris grinned. "I'm closest, let me."

"No, they know me and we will most definitely get a good table." Jess maneuvered around Kris and opened the door. As soon as she did, a server grabbed it and grinned.

"Hey, Jess, you took longer than normal to decide. What's it going to be?"

Kris held back at the server's words. *Very personal.*

"I'm taking my time, Josie. I have a friend joining me today. We will have the cookies no matter what, and don't scrimp, I'll know," Jess said.

The server, in her late twenties, with a slim build and of medium height, responded with a cheeky smile that negated the beaky nose "Hey, I know you have special weapons, not a chance. Let me have that coat."

"Thanks, Josie."

Jess took off the garment, and Josie took it before walking away.

Kris followed Jess, who seemed to know exactly where she was going and was pleasantly surprised at the Reserved sign on the table. "You definitely come here often."

Jess didn't reply immediately, which surprised Kris. Her new friend methodically made her way to the table and sat down before placing that fascinating cane to the left side of her chair.

"I definitely come here often. In fact, every day at this time. So you will know exactly where to find me if you want me." Jess shrugged.

Kris sat opposite Jess and clasped her hands together. "I do, thank you."

"Okay, Cane Girl here wants a large latte plus her cookies. What can I get you?" Josie appeared, pad and pen in hand.

Kris quickly replied, "Same. Please."

Josie chuckled like someone who smoked at least twenty a day. "Perfect."

Kris watched Josie leave and then turned to Jess, who was staring at her. "I was fascinated by you at the window from across the road."

Jess grinned. "Yeah?"

"Yeah. Not to put a dampener on this, but the cane in beachside territory? Then I worked it out."

Jess's expression became pensive. "The conclusion was?"

Kris hesitated and then said, "You are one of those people who are happy in their skin. Is that true?"

"Yes, I am now. Had a few hiccups along the way but, yes."

"We have coffee coming, then I want to know how you do it."

"Do what?"

Kris sighed. "Be the most confident woman in the room, and yet...."

"Yet?" was the terse reply.

"You tell me," Kris said.

"Does it matter?"

Kris reached across the table and clutched Jess's hand, "No. As a friend I'm interested, but if this is all you want to say, I'm good too."

"I can feel you are a good person, Kris Lake. Thank you for entering my life. I have a feeling we will be good for each other."

Kris squeezed Jess's hand as the server brought their coffee. "Me too. For the first time in my life, I'm happy here. I feel it's the place."

Jess grinned. "Then let me tell you about the regulars around here. I'll get to me eventually."

Kris laughed. "Works for me, but remember I only have an hour."

"Oh, it could take me a decade."

They both laughed, and the customers around them smiled approvingly.

Chapter Ten

"I'm going to meet Jess Smith at Mimi's in a couple of days. She's so nice, Mrs. Rank. Do you know her or her family?"

Shirley placed a packet of flour on the shelf and turned to the woman who was just like her, or at least would have been back in the day. The social lines were less defined these days. "You know she's blind?"

"Yes, she told me it happened in the Iraq War. Does that matter to a friendship?"

Shirley shrugged. "Perhaps not. What about Ms. Claire?"

"Claire? How will this affect her?" Kris frowned. "I won't shirk the work I've been hired to do, if that's what you are thinking?"

"Not that, my dear. Never mind."

"Mrs. Rank, if you think I need to stay away from town and just keep focused on the work at hand, I will. But surely making a friend here couldn't do any harm?" Kris murmured.

"None, my dear, none. Jess Smith is very fortunate that you enjoy her company. Now I need to think about dinner and you need to get about your business. Dinner will be at seven prompt. Although according to Ms. Claire, drinks are at six."

Kris nodded and left the room.

Shirley watched her leave and placed her hands over her lower face. She sighed heavily before looking upward and shaking her head.

"Is love ever simple?"

†

Kris rested back on her haunches and surveyed the small area of enamel that now began to show its true color—bright blue. She gazed at the monster oven and grinned as she wiped a hand across her face before rocking forward and beginning another patch. Time consuming but worth it in the end. She'd bought special cleaning materials just for the job when she went to town. The other items on the list she and Claire had made would be delivered the next day by lunchtime. Not wanting to waste any precious time, she'd taken the provisions to begin this job. Besides, what else did she have to do, other than take walks on the beach? Not that the thought wasn't deliciously decadent, but Melissa had trusted her with this renovation, and she was going to do her very best to make it happen.

With a satisfied sigh, she got back to her task in earnest. It was only two thirty, and if she continued at the speed she was going, at least a quarter of the oven would be done before she had to leave and clean up for dinner.

†

Claire made her way down the staircase slowly, glancing through the picture windows showcasing the view outside. A memory flashed forward, and she grasped the rail at its power. She gazed unseeingly out of the final window detailing the approach to the house.

Gravel crunched and dust exploded in a mist as the Trans AM convertible skidded to a stop. Long legs and a thin, almost emaciated body stepped out.

Claire watched in fascination from her vantage point on the staircase. As always the woman outside looked marvelous in full flow, and Claire felt moisture building between her legs in anticipation. Then she schooled her features as the doorbell rang. She quickly ran down the few steps and opened the door.

"Hmm, I didn't expect you, my love. No Reedy to do the honors?"

A tickle of laughter followed the comment.

"Everyone is out, including Mrs. Rank. I wasn't expecting you," Claire said with a frown.

A slender finger trailed down her left cheek and sent electric pulses through Claire's body. Now she was on fire. "Oh, but you want me here now, don't you?" A hand snaked over Claire's T-shirt and pulled at her right nipple.

"I...I sure...." Claire groaned, her body definitely not in tune with her brain. "What if my parents come home early?"

The door closed behind them, and before she had time to think, her body was pushed gently against the wooden door. Kisses trailed down her face, down her neck to the hollow between her breasts, and then she was gone.

Claire's hands grabbed at her lover, tugged at the flimsy dress she wore and pulled it fluidly over her head. Her breath caught at the sight in front of her.

"Wow, no underwear."

"Only for you. I wanted to be ready."

Claire's hand was placed on her lover's mound, and immediately Claire found her clit and began massaging it until a howl of excitement erupted. She used her other hand to plunge inside and moved in rhythm with the body she lusted after.

Her world spun as hands snaked inside her shorts and she was experiencing the same sexual pleasure.

"Claire, is anything wrong?"

Claire dragged herself out of her daydreaming and stared at the interloper to her thoughts.

"No, of course not. I was just thinking."

"I'm sorry."

Claire frowned and walked the few steps to the ground floor. "It isn't a problem, Shirley. So you're back from your shopping expedition, and might I say your hair looks lovely."

Before Claire's eyes, Shirley came alive and preened like a peacock at the compliment. Then her cheeks turned a rosy shade as she smiled.

"Thank you. I like having my hair done once a month, even though no one but me generally sees it. A habit, I guess." Shirley tentatively touched a curl that rested against her forehead.

"We should all do something for ourselves once in a while. Besides, it makes us feel better, doesn't it?" Claire nodded her approval and looked beyond the housekeeper. "Is Kris back?"

"We arrived an hour ago. She went to the cottage, I believe."

"Without me? Oh." Deflated, Claire furrowed her brow. *Why didn't she ask me to go with her? Yeah right, because you would be so much help.* She dropped her gaze to her right arm and scowled.

"She said she will be back in time for dinner and drinks at six as you suggested. Can I get you some coffee?"

Claire shook her head. Then made a decision.

"I'll drop by and see what she's doing. Grams wanted me to be productive while I'm here, and checking out emails in my room isn't what she would call that. I'll see you in the dining room at six, unless you want—?"

"No, bless me, no. I have everything in the kitchen under control."

Claire shrugged and opened the front door, her eyes uncontrollably going to a mark on the doorjamb. It was faint, but nonetheless if you knew it was there, you could see it— scratch marks.

"See you later, Shirley." Claire shut the door behind her, thinking, *Now just who was that woman?*

†

Traversing the undergrowth she had encountered earlier that day, Claire cursed at the nettle scratching her ankle. She bent to investigate the area and saw the small pink blob inflame. Where was the famed dock-leaf antidote when you needed it? Although she knew if she closely surveyed the area, she would find one. But it was only a minor irritant, so she pushed on.

A few minutes later the roof of the cottage appeared, and as she closed in on the building, she could hear singing. It was indistinct, and somewhat off key, but joyful. The melody was happy, and she smiled. *How could hard labor be a happy chore? Guess I'm going to find out.*

Moments later, she stepped on the deck, and the groan was audible but not as intense as the first time. "Guess you're getting used to us, hey?" Claire grinned and opened the creaking door.

Normally she would have expected any occupant to look up and see who was entering the building, but that wasn't the case with Kris. She was so engrossed in her undertaking and singing that she obviously failed to hear her. Claire simply watched this unusual woman at her task.

After a couple of minutes, Claire felt she was being rude and cleared her throat loudly. Still no response. *Maybe she's listening to an iPod.* Searching Kris's ears, Claire couldn't see any evidence of those pesky earbuds that always seemed to fall out. Walking closer, she tried again.

Kris spun around and gasped. "Oh."

Claire pursed her lips to avoid laughing at the comical expression on Kris's face. "Hey, I see you're ahead of me." She pointed to the cleaning materials.

Kris stumbled to stand and screwed up her face as she did. "Damn, I'm getting old. My knees are creaking."

Claire smiled. *I like this woman. She's so refreshingly honest.* "You and me both. These days I refrain from kneeling for any length of time. Why didn't you find me? I would have helped."

Kris's cheeks flamed. "I'm sorry, Claire. I thought you might be busy with your emails and stuff. I know how popular you are. Besides, the vast majority of the materials we need won't arrive until sometime in the morning."

Claire cocked her head to one side. "That's the second time you've said you know something about me. For the record my popularity is exaggerated, especially these days."

"I'm sorry." Kris averted her profile.

"Just where exactly did you glean your information about me? I'm not being critical, merely interested." Claire waited for the reply and saw several nervous twitches on Kris's face.

"The *Lesbian NY Underground* monthly newssheet. I subscribed to it when I came to New York. Silly I guess," Kris quietly replied.

That gossip rag. Crap, I'm going to have my work cut out convincing Kris I'm not everything they made up about me, even if most of it is probably true. Jude never did like me. "I know the editor, Jude Kingston. She set it up in the nineties and it has its moments," Claire said. "What did they say about me that you remember?" She leaned against a cloth-covered object that felt like a chair.

"Oh, I can't really remember. Just stuff." Kris looked Claire in the eye and raised her eyebrows. "Well, you were engaged to another socialite, Racheal Nevin. She's very beautiful," She gushed.

Yep, Racheal was very beautiful; is. "And?"

"After your accident they say it's over, but no one is prepared to officially confirm that."

Claire drew in a ragged breath. "Anything else?"

Kris frowned and bit her lower lip.

"I can take it, Kris. Besides, it is better out in the open." Claire's hand gripped the chair.

"Well, they implied you were a womanizer even when you were engaged. You've been photographed with lots of women since I've been receiving the subscription.

You love nightclubs and fast cars, and I heard a quote that you loved fast women," Kris reluctantly replied.

"I guess that makes me some kind of rake in your eyes. Not exactly someone you'd want to be around." Claire caught Kris's gaze and refused to let it go until she had an answer. She thought she could already guess the response, except Kris's green eyes never wavered.

"Truthfully, I prefer to make my own opinion of a person. If that's all right with you?"

The innocent confidence in those words made Claire's heart swell, and she nodded. "I'd prefer that too."

They stood there for a few moments in silence.

"So, what have you been doing?" Claire asked.

Kris grinned. "Did you know this oven is blue?"

Claire chuckled and placed a hand to her forehead. "Why bless my soul, no. What significance does that have?"

Kris grinned and began to relate her theory.

Chapter Eleven

A week passed and the cottage was taking shape. The buildup of dust and grime was scrubbed away, leaving the outside of the cottage looking if not respectable, then at least giving an idea of what needed to be done to make it so. Kris's assessment that the shutters needed repair was accurate. Several hung precariously from one hinge, making them squeak like frightened mice when a breeze blew. The decking was sound but needed a good covering of oil to bring it back to its original glory. The windows themselves now gleamed, to allow vision inside the building.

I did that. Claire smiled in satisfaction at the knowledge she was actually making a difference.

The interior was a little trickier, but at least they had swept the floor and cleaned the kitchen table. The sandwiches Shirley would bring over at twelve thirty sharp meant they didn't share their meal with spiders and sticky cobwebs. The stainless-steel sink that at some stage needed replacing was clean and served its purpose.

"Penny for them," Kris said.

71

Claire stopped her surveying of the building and smiled.

"Free of charge to you. I was just thinking you were right about the condition of the cottage. My parents should employ you to look over properties before they take them on. They have purchased some stinkers in the past." Claire wiped her hands on the torn jeans she wore for working on the cottage.

"Really? I thought they were real estate agents, not owners. At least that's what I've read about them." Kris turned a bright pink.

Claire mused over that comment. "A bit of both, or at least they did in the past. Things changed about ten years ago, and now they are mostly agents."

"In that case, they haven't got an opening for me, have they?"

Kris smiled as Claire walked over.

"With you on the team, they could start their portfolio again. Changing the subject, what do you think?" Claire pointed to the windows at ground level.

"Great job, Claire. They are gleaming inside and out. Told you they would." Kris placed a hand on Claire's shoulder.

Her touch sent a shiver down Claire's spine. An unexpected reaction, and she frowned. "Hmm, so what have you planned for me next?"

"Well it's almost—" Kris nervously glanced at her watch "—twelve thirty. Shirley will be here in a minute. Do you think we should ask her to join us one lunchtime? It must be lonely always being on your own."

Claire shrugged, annoyed at her initial response to Kris's touch. She knew Kris had heard the less than friendly reply and probably wondered what brought it on. Maybe having Shirley and her predictable conversation would be a good thing.

"No." The explosive negative reaction surprised Claire. It was the opposite of what she was thinking.

Kris blinked rapidly. "Okay, I was just thinking…well. Is something wrong, Claire?"

Claire bit her lip. "No, sorry. Of course she can join us if she wants. Ask her when she gets here, and tomorrow she can bring lunch for all three of us."

"Oh, I forgot to tell you. Tomorrow I won't be here for lunch. I'm going into Chartres and having lunch at Millie's. The day after that for sure." Kris beamed.

"On your own?" Her eyes took in every nuance of Kris's expression. *She looks happy about having lunch in town but…who does she know? How could she know anyone? She's only been here a little over a week.*

"Silly, no." Kris smiled. "When I went into town last week to order the supplies for the renovation and helped Shirley—"

"So it's Shirley you are having lunch with?" Claire muttered. *She called me "silly." Who does she think she is?*

Kris chuckled. "No, Shirley is visiting…actually I'm not sure what she's doing. It's something along with the weekly shopping, I think. Remember, you wanted those apple-and-rhubarb pies from Millie's?"

"Yes," Claire ground out.

"I met a really nice woman. We got talking and shared a coffee. We arranged to meet for lunch tomorrow. I'll only be gone about two hours and I can bring back more pies." Kris smiled.

"I don't care about any damn pies," Claire shouted.

Kris flinched and stared at her. "There is something wrong, Claire. What is it?" She placed her hands on her hips.

Claire ground her teeth—her dentist was going to be rubbing her hands in glee if she damaged her crowns. Her irritation about Kris's rendezvous was totally off the scale, and she didn't know why. If she and Kris were lovers, she would understand it in part, not that having multiple partners in other relationships, even with Racheal, had ever bothered her before.

What the hell is happening to me? I've spent too much time alone since the accident. That must be it.

"Sorry, I'm sorry, Kris. I'm tired. I think I need to rest," Claire softly replied. "I'll see you later." She quickly walked down the three steps to the garden area and headed off toward the house.

"Claire, wait."

She ignored Kris's appeal. Just as Claire turned onto the main path to Seasons, Shirley appeared with a wicker basket.

"Oh, are you having lunch at the house?" Shirley asked.

"No, I'll see you at dinner." Claire stomped off toward Seasons.

"Was it something I said?" Kris murmured, getting over the shock of Claire leaving so suddenly. *Maybe she was tired. I forget she's physically impaired, but to me she isn't.*

Her stance shifted as she glanced toward the overgrowth and the trodden-down long grass Claire had walked through. The sound of a breaking twig had her looking expectantly into the vegetation. *Claire's coming back.* Then Shirley appeared and Kris disguised her disappointment with a tight smile.

"Is it lunchtime already?"

74

"Yes, twelve thirty as always. Claire is heading for the house and said she doesn't want lunch. Is something wrong?"

Kris smiled, though her stomach churned. "To be honest, I don't know. She seemed okay one minute, then the next...." She held up her hands.

Shirley sniffed the air, placing the basket on the deck, and looked around. "You told her that tomorrow you are seeing someone else."

Kris almost fell over at the remark. "How did you know? At least that I said I was having lunch with a new friend?"

Shirley shook her head. "One day you will find out. I told you it might not be a good idea."

Kris frowned at her mysterious tone. "That's ridiculous. It's only lunch and Claire can come along if she wants. She left before I could say that." Kris shook her head and sat down heavily on the deck next to the lunch basket.

Shirley stopped a foot away from her. "You are both doing a good job here, and I hope this won't jeopardize anything. It's important for both of you, although you probably don't know it yet."

Kris whipped her head upward and looked at the older woman. "I don't understand."

"Of course you don't, my dear, but you will soon enough. Believe me, you will—I know."

Cryptic remarks were never a strong point for Kris. *I hate riddles and was terrible at working out anagrams.* "What have we for lunch today, Shirley?" That was the easy way out. Puzzles always gave her a headache, and she'd rather not have another one. Claire was enough of a headache.

"Beef and sour pickle on rye, potato salad, corn cobs."

Kris silently groaned. *It's everything Claire likes. I guess the potato salad and corn cobs are okay.* "Great. Thanks, Shirley. Do you want to join me?"

"No, no, I'm afraid sour pickle doesn't agree with me. I'll see you at dinner." She gave that tight smile she was famous for, at least to Kris. She looked around again and then said good-bye and left.

Kris watched her leave and summoned up the enthusiasm to open the wicker basket. Sure enough, the odious beef-and-sour-pickle sandwiches, but as she ventured further, she found a greaseproof paper package with a couple of shrimp rolls inside.

"Oh you are wonderful, Shirley. I swear you are a clairvoyant." She grabbed the package, opened it, and bit into the roll with gusto.

†

Claire sank on the bed in her room and groaned.

What an idiot I am. What does it matter that Kris is having lunch with someone else? She's a means to an end. A promise I made and will endeavor to complete for Grams. What difference does it make if Kris makes a friend or two here? She deserves it. Ah, but what if this friend isn't what she seems? Kris is so naïve.

With Claire's thoughts in turmoil, she closed her eyes and her stomach rumbled.

Damn I'm hungry too, and I left a lunch for what? Stupid jealousy. Idiot, you are not jealous, not in a sexual way, anyway. She doesn't come close in the beauty department to Racheal or other women I've dated.

Claire opened her eyes wide.

"Maybe Shirley has seconds." She got up from the bed and wandered over to the window.

Sure enough, Shirley was making her way toward the house. "Hmm, I'll wait a few minutes and go down and ask for a baloney sandwich. It will suit my thoughts—a load of horseshit." Claire shrugged. "Kris can take care of herself. Why should I be concerned?"

The statement reverberated around the room. Claire frowned, reached for her phone, and began to tap rapidly on the screen. As she pressed the Send button, trepidation fluttered in her stomach, and it had nothing to do with hunger.

She jabbed the End button. "I'm an idiot." Leaving the room, she decided food would help her chaotic emotions.

†

Kris used the napkin to wipe her lips, and then folded it neatly before placing it back in the picnic basket. Smiling, she touched the coarse wicker and trailed her hand over the leather straps that held the cutlery, cups, and glasses in place. Not that they had used the glasses, she thought with a chuckle. They were purely for effect; who had wine at a midday picnic?

They probably aren't even glass.

She pressed her forefinger and thumb together, then flicked the rim of the object. It gave off a high ping. "Wow, it is real and sounds like crystal too. I've never used crystal glasses before. I thought it was a myth about the sound— awesome."

She unwrapped the small tablecloth, which she'd thought was a large napkin the first time she'd seen it until

Claire gently corrected her. *Stupid to use it just for me.* She knew Shirley would wash it after one use.

The food, perfectly catered on a china plate, had been made especially for Claire. She guessed the less elegant sandwiches were almost an afterthought. Not that it mattered; the housekeeper did make the effort to accommodate her tastes, and that was the most important thing.

She placed the utensils she'd used inside the basket, closed the lid, and hooked the toggles securely to make sure it stayed shut.

Kris stood up from the kitchen table and looked around. The old stove, her pride and joy, was pristine. This morning she had even playfully suggested they make dinner on it one evening before they left. Claire had given her a genuine laugh instead of a tolerant one. Claire said she was good with a wok and maybe she should cook, but a fire extinguisher would need to be at the ready. They had both burst out laughing, and Kris was sure they had connected in some deep, fathomless way that was difficult to explain.

Kris opened the door and walked onto the porch. "Those windows do shine. I could even do my makeup in them if I ever used any." She shrugged. "Time to do more. Claire will be back, I know it. She's not a quitter." She began to collect the items to paint the decking.

Chapter Twelve

Claire didn't return to the cottage that afternoon. In fact, she had her dinner in her room. When Kris asked Shirley what was the matter, a headache had been the explanation. It could be true, but somehow she didn't think so. Concerned but not sure what to do about it, Kris decided to respect Claire's decision and had a quiet dinner with Shirley. As they progressed to coffee, Kris decided to ask what the older woman had meant earlier that day.

"I know you said it might not be a good idea for me to meet Jess. Is that the real reason Claire isn't having dinner with us? Although I confess it's a crazy notion." Kris gave Shirley her full attention and could see every flicker on the other woman's plain features.

"Claire is a complex person. I do not second-guess her. If she said she had a headache, then I'm sure that's the truth." Shirley's neutral expression didn't falter.

Kris didn't know what to make of Claire or Shirley. In the time she had been at Seasons, she felt like this was the place she needed to be and the people she needed to be with. Right now, she was wondering if her loneliness and lack of prospects had created that picture in her head. She wasn't in Claire's league nor did she come from the right financial background to be her friend. Shirley, although she was the hired help, was part of Seasons and the family. Kris was nothing more than a temporary worker, without the prospect of a long-time relationship with the family and, in particular, Claire.

"I'm the hired help. Right, I understand that, but why do you make cryptic statements about it being important that Claire and I...? She doesn't care if I meet someone else. Why should she? If it's because I might shirk my duties, that's not going to happen," Kris stated dramatically and then stood.

Shirley remained seated and poured another cup of coffee without a flicker of emotion.

Kris sighed heavily and shook her head. "I'll load the dishwasher before I go to my room. I'll see you in the morning. Good night."

As she reached the door and began to turn the handle, Shirley's nasal voice drifted toward her.

"It's more complex than that, my dear. Seasons has a history of bringing people together and equally tearing them apart if they don't follow their destiny."

Kris turned abruptly, her eyebrows arched at the statement. "Destiny? You think Claire and I have a destiny together? Does she know this? She'd have hightailed it back to New York if she did." Kris wiped a hand over her mouth. *Okay, this is ridiculous.*

Shirley brought her coffee cup toward her lips, and before drinking from it, she placed it back on the saucer. "As I said, Claire is complex. It will be up to you, unless you think me crazy?"

Kris had to tamp down the urge to laugh at the question. *Damn straight she's crazy. But who is crazier, her for the words, or me for listening?* "No, I don't think you are crazy. I haven't known you long enough to make that judgment call." Kris smiled. "Besides, aren't we all crazy at some stage in our life? Good night."

"Good night, Kris, sleep well."

Kris gave her one last look as Shirley sipped her coffee. *Weird, that's all I can say about today—weird.* She opened the door and left.

✝

Jess giggled like a sixteen-year-old as Kris related her passion for an old stove. "Really, you are turned on by a piece of metal. Granted, there is fire in there to make you hot, but...." She grinned.

Kris laughed too. Jess made her feel relaxed because she wasn't purporting to be something she wasn't. "Don't be silly. Not turned on, exactly, but she's a wonderful piece of equipment. Maybe before I leave, you can come over to the cottage and feel it for yourself."

"Well that's an invitation I'm not going to pass up. You do know that Seasons has a reputation, don't you?" Jess moved her hand slowly to her coffee mug and drew it to her.

Kris watched in fascination as Jess clasped her mug. If you didn't know any different, her disability wouldn't be evident. The deep blue of her eyes disguised the fact the orbs were sightless. She always had a bright smile, and it gave her an ethereal look that went with her elfin features.

"As you didn't ask what that reputation was you must know already. Guess you should as Shirley Rank still lives there," Jess said with a smile.

"What?" Her daydreams disappeared as she tuned back into the conversation. "Shirley? You know her?"

Jess chuckled. "By reputation."

"She has a reputation? Please tell me more." Kris cupped her chin in her hands and leaned her elbows on the table.

"No, I'd rather know more about you."

"Spoilsport." Kris released her chin and sat upright. "I told you about me last week. Now, you are less of an open book."

Jess sighed.

"If you don't want—"

Jess slipped her hand across the table and touched the little finger of Kris's right hand. "Okay, I can do that. I told you the gruesome details of my accident."

"Yes, a landmine in Iraq, and you came home here afterward. That was…2009, right?" Jess's hand trembled, and she gently drew Kris's hand into a firm grip.

"Yeah, right. I was in the hospital for a while but eventually came back here to Chartres. Where else would I or could I go? Family roots and all that stuff. I tried living by myself."

Kris eyed Jess. She looked distinctly uncomfortable. This might have been a bad idea. "Sorry, Jess, I'm way too inquisitive. Tell me about Seasons instead."

Jess stared at Kris, and she could have sworn her new friend could see her, but that wasn't possible. "I live with Mary—my big sister—and her two kids. She's a widow.

Steve, my brother-in-law, was killed in a boating accident three years ago, and she was finding it hard to make ends meet. No life insurance, but at least the house is paid for. It's a derelict almost. Maybe we should have you over to our place after you finish at Seasons." Jess chuckled.

"You have nephews or nieces, or one of each?"

Jess's whole body jolted. She straightened up and excitedly reached for her pocketbook and withdrew a wallet. "I know this looks strange, a blind person carrying photos she can't see, but take a look. The eldest is Annie. She's ten and Kim is five. Great girls, even if I say so myself." Jess proudly shoved the wallet toward Kris, which she took and gazed at the grinning children who were standing next to a swing in a park.

"Little blondies, and their grins remind me of you." Kris felt sadness for the youngest, who had never really known her father. Jess laughed and retrieved the wallet as Kris placed it close to her free hand. "Must be tough for them all."

"Yeah, it was, but kids are very resilient. They move on quicker than adults. Mary sometimes breaks down and cries for Steve. What can you do? She loved the guy. It must be hard to lose someone unexpected like that."

"She has you now to help."

"Well, she has my money anyway. I don't really contribute that much. How could I?" Jess waved a hand over her eyes.

"You sound like Claire." Kris rolled her eyes. "Sorry, I didn't mean to sound disrespectful, but you don't seem the type not to contribute."

Jess shook her head. "Here I was going for the sympathy vote and you caught me."

Kris laughed. "I knew it."

Silence settled between them for a few moments. "Saturday evening, are you doing anything?" Jess smiled at her.

Kris considered the question. "I guess it depends on the timing. I'll be working until around six, and then usually we have dinner with Mrs. Rank at seven. Why?"

Jess hesitated.

"And?"

"I play piano and sing at Chartres Golf Club on Saturday evenings. If you were free, I was going to invite you. I have several breaks during the evening, so you wouldn't be on your own all night," Jess quietly said.

"You sing and play piano. How awesome, Jess. What time do you start?"

"Eight until midnight. If you can make it by six thirty I'm sure I can swing us dinner in the restaurant. What do you say?"

No one had ever invited Kris to a function where she knew the entertainer. In fact, she'd never been out before on a dinner date. *Is this a date though?* She scratched her left eyebrow, deep in thought.

"No reply. Bad idea? I guessed it might be. I'm not exactly Alicia Keys, but I can promise you I'm not tone deaf."

"It isn't that, Jess. Can I call you later once I've checked in with Claire and Mrs. Rank? You probably think that's crazy." Kris shrugged.

"No, I don't think it's crazy. It's thoughtful. They might have plans and not have told you yet—right? You have my number. Call me, even if it's last minute."

"You are wonderful. I'm so glad we met. I think we need more coffee now. We've been so engrossed in chatter it's gone cold." They both laughed, and Kris scraped back her chair. "I'll go order again, my treat."

As she walked toward the counter, she considered the possibility of going out on a date with Jess. It felt good. Jess was nice and they got on well. Perhaps things between them were meant to be. Fate had a way of stepping in and showing you another path when you needed one.

Chapter Thirteen

Claire looked at her watch and pursed her lips. Where was Kris? She'd said she was just having lunch, not taking the whole afternoon.

The chirp of a bird sounded familiar, and she looked at the tree outside the cottage and then to a spot three branches up—sure enough, her new buddy was perched watching her.

"Missed your treat yesterday, didn't you?" She withdrew an oatmeal cookie and crumbled it with her good hand, then sprinkled it at the bottom of the trunk. She stepped back a few paces and waited.

Her new best friend flew down confidently and began to peck at the pieces strewn on the ground.

Claire watched the bird, which she had researched online and discovered was a male Baltimore oriole. Shirley would be giving her deepest scowl if she knew Claire had given the cookie to the birds, or rather this bird.

"Enjoy it, little fellow. Can't guarantee this will last for that much longer." Her phone buzzed, and she took it from her pocket and looked at the caller ID—Racheal. She stared at the screen. Irritated by the tone, she pressed the Decline symbol.

Claire looked up through the tree's branches and saw the sun trying desperately to send its bright rays through the dense foliage. A bit like her situation with Racheal.

"I miss you, Racheal but...."

A rustle of vegetation indicated someone was around. She turned to see who the intruder was.

"Claire, sorry I'm a bit late. Shirley, would you believe, was delayed at the post office. She wouldn't tell me why, but she looked upset. Do you think maybe you could go and check if she's okay? She might confide in you."

Claire looked at Kris. *Why on earth would she think Shirley would confide in me?* "Oh, it might be something or nothing. As far as I know, she doesn't have any close family, so it can't be someone has died." Claire regretted the words as soon as they were out of her mouth. The shock on Kris's face mirrored her own. "Okay, I'll go. Did you enjoy your lunch?"

She didn't want to watch Kris's features so closely, but she couldn't help herself. A smile traveled not just to Kris's lips but seemed to emanate through her whole body.

"Yes. Jess is so talented, Claire. Would you believe she's a singer and piano player? I've never met anyone who can play an instrument. It's way cool. She asked me out Saturday to watch her play at Chartres Golf Club. Do you mind if I go? I don't want to leave you with Shirley if you prefer me to be with you."

Claire held herself motionless. Her eyes moved to her best buddy perched on a branch.... *Yeah, I'll call him Buddy.*

"Look, if I'm out of line about wanting some free time, I will decline." Kris frowned. "I'm not a slave here though, so I figured Saturday night you wouldn't care either way. Do you?"

Do I? Claire pondered that. Not only was her body impaired, obviously her thought processes were too. *This should be a no-brainer. I don't care. Who is this woman who can make me feel torn?* "Go. As you say, it doesn't matter to me. I take it being a Saturday night she's taking you out to dinner too?"

Kris shrugged. "Yes, if I can make it by six thirty. Do you mind if I stop working at five? It will give me time to have a shower and arrive at the golf club by that time."

Claire gazed at Buddy, who was still tucking into the oatmeal cookie. *What would you say, Buddy, if you were in my shoes? Yeah, easy, right. Kris doesn't matter in my long-term, and if she did...it's as a friend. Friends are good for you, and I've never had one like Kris.*

"I'm glad you've found a friend. Why don't we stop at four, and that will give you lots of time to get ready for your date."

Kris shuffled from one foot to the other for a few seconds. "I'm not sure we can call it a date, Claire, but I'm hopeful," she tentatively said.

Claire nodded. "I'll check on Shirley. What have you got in store for me this afternoon?"

Kris smiled. "You are wonderful, Claire, thank you. Sorry I can't be so generous. It's the bathrooms for you to scrub."

Claire groaned. "Maybe I'll take a sick day."

Kris laughed, and Claire realized she liked that sound. It made her feel good and she'd missed it yesterday.

"Okay, slave driver." As Claire turned to walk away, she lifted her good arm and mock growled in her best Terminator impersonation. "Bathrooms don't go away...I'll be back!" Kris's laughter followed her up the road toward the main house, and her whole body was lighter for it.

†

Claire loudly cleared her throat as she entered the kitchen area. Shirley hadn't been in any of the main formal rooms downstairs. The kitchen area was the best bet, she figured. She felt as if she were taking a step back in time as she entered through the swing door, just like she felt in the cottage. Though this room was more fifties style. Bright yellow greeted her like the morning sun, and she frowned.

I wonder if I ever noticed this before. When I was a kid.

A large refrigerator dwarfed all other equipment, except for the range. It was similar to the one in the cottage.

"Kris must have fallen in love with this first." She shook her head, smiling. Cabinets of all sizes filled the outer walls. A breakfast bar, which probably was more a preparation area back in the day, took center stage. Claire glanced around but saw no sign of Shirley. "Hmm, I wonder where she is. Not sure I want to go to her room."

A flicker of movement from the window leading to the kitchen garden caught her eye. She headed in that direction and opened the door. Shielding her eyes from the sun shining directly at her, she furrowed her brow to make out if Shirley was there. A large tree drew her attention. It was twice the size of her tree near the cottage and had a wooden seat encompassing the trunk. Shirley sat there, her head in her hands.

Damn, Kris was right, she is upset. Maybe I should leave. What can I do?

Then Shirley's sticklike figure moved. She looked up and she headed toward Claire.

"Claire, did you need something?"

Claire was certain the hand that whipped across Shirley's eyes brushed away tears.

"No, not really. Actually, Kris thought you were upset and she was worried about you...so am I. Can we help?" Claire wanted to turn away and go back to cleaning the bathrooms. It was so much easier than personal problems.

Shirley sniffled.

"I can't call myself a good listener, Shirley, but over the last few days actually I've found I have hidden depths. Besides, if you don't tell me tonight at dinner, Kris will interrogate you in the nicest possible way."

Shirley stared at her as if she were a stranger.

"Kris is a lovely girl, very comforting and astute." Shirley sighed heavily. "A dear friend of mine died a month ago, and it brought home to me again that life isn't forever."

Her words were matter-of-fact almost, emotionless even. Yet her stiff and awkward body language told a different story. Claire moved to within inches of Shirley and pulled her gracelessly into a hug.

"Sometimes it's good to talk to a stranger."

"But you are not a stranger," Shirley softly said.

Claire shrugged and released the older woman to arm's length, stepping backward. "Tell me, please. I promise I won't tell anyone unless you allow it."

"Calvin, dear Calvin was a good friend. He made me realize Ricky was the one for me."

Claire didn't understand. "That was a long time ago, right? Did you see him often or keep in touch? Sorry to be insensitive, but your husband has been dead for a while."

"Yes, Ricky has been gone forty years. I haven't seen Calvin for about that time."

Claire disguised her surprise. "He meant that much to you? I see."

"You don't, not yet. You will soon. He brought us together, my husband and I, you see," Shirley softly replied.

Claire shrugged. "I'm sorry for your loss. Guess it's too late to say, 'Have time off for the funeral.'" She was perplexed by Shirley's cryptic words and wondered what she meant. *Weird, like Kris said.*

Shirley caught her in an intense gaze, and Claire's heart lurched.

"Go where your heart travels, my dear. There you will find your true destiny. Believe in love, and it will provide you with the truth of your soul. Calvin, Ricky, and I saw the truth."

Crap, this is way too deep for me. "Good to know, Shirley. I'll explain to Kris you lost a dear friend." Claire attempted to reenter the house, but an arm prevented her.

"Life is all about knowing who you are and accepting what you can bring to a relationship. Forget the past; live for the future."

Claire sucked in a deep breath. *There she goes being weird again. Hmm, I might have to speak to Grams about what she's talking about.*

"Tonight we are having pizza. I'm going to call it in. Shirley, relax or, if you can't do that, take the rest of the day off. Do you like pepperoni?"

"Thank you, I love pepperoni. May we have a seafood pizza too?"

Claire chuckled. "Absolutely."

†

Kris gazed at the shutters, which were next on her list. This mini-renovation project was going well, she thought. Claire had, remarkably, turned out to be amicable. Not that she had any frame of reference about her other than the society tabloid, which made her out to be a rich party girl without a care in the world except for whom she bedded next.

That wasn't how she saw Claire. Nope. In fact, she figured they might even be friends—not best friends and all, but a friend with whom Kris could perhaps keep in touch in the future. She hoped so. New York was a lonely place, at least for her.

She walked over to the stepladder in the far corner of the decking. As she moved it, the wood beneath her feet creaked with every step. "You'll be the final job, my friend. Can't have us scratching and scuffing the new paintwork I plan to give you." *No, that was wrong.* "We, yes, we will give you." Her heart warmed as she thought of Claire.

Claire's disability was obvious, and she struggled with many things everyone else took for granted. *Probably has difficulty with shoelaces. That's why she wears slip-ons. Even so, she's valiantly tried every task I've given her and only had that one tantrum yesterday. It was bound to happen, and now she seems fine.* Recalling Claire's narrowed eyes as she went back to talk to Shirley, accompanied by that flippant reply about the bathrooms, Kris grinned.

She picked up the stepladder and walked back to the first shutter on the first-floor level. This was going to be a piece of cake, but the upper floor might be a tad more difficult. *I'll have to think on that.*

After resting the ladder against the wall for extra support, Kris climbed up the first three steps, giving her access to the highest set of screws. From the tool belt around her waist, she selected the appropriate screwdriver and began to dismantle the shutter. Within a couple of minutes, she was at the final screw, but it was stubborn.

"Darn screw. Just come out, why don't you," she beseeched the object.

"Oh that sounds interesting. Haven't used that term to describe a screw before, but there is always a first time." Claire laughed as she stepped up on the deck and joined Kris.

Flustered, Kris placed her hands to her face and then grinned. "I've taken eleven screws out and no problem. Typical, the final one wants to protest. What gives?"

Claire shrugged. "Oh, must be that butch stance you have with the tool belt and all. Probably scared the hell out of the final screw and it doesn't want to out itself."

Kris laughed. "Well putting it like that, what do you suggest?"

"Love the tool belt. I have to say it suits you. However, for a sensitive coming-outer, maybe it needs a gentler touch. Allow me." Claire held out her hand for the screwdriver.

"Don't be silly. If I can't do it, how do you think you can?" Kris cringed. "I'm sorry, I didn't mean that you weren't capable."

"Hey, say it how it is, Kris. You're right. Normally I wouldn't try except…."

"Except?"

"Grams provided me with a power kit, and I know there is a reversible drill there, so it may prove useful."

Kris was confused. "You have power tools?"

Claire chuckled. "Of course. You think I could do work like that on my own steam?"

"Why haven't you used them before?"

Claire solemnly replied, "Because I haven't needed them yet, and I can say to Grams I did it under my own steam. Right?"

She is everything I thought before and more. "Got that. Right. So, pray tell, where can we find these tools?"

"And I thought you were so butch you could do everything with your own hands." Claire laughed.

"Most of the time. Not that you will find out, but occasionally I need help. Well, Claire Tremont, are you sharing?" Kris smiled and Claire returned the grin. *Yep, Claire isn't what the tabloids said. No way.*

"You do realize that once these are down it's up to you to sandpaper them for painting, and you might, if you beg very nicely, have the opportunity to do just that." Kris chuckled.

"Hmm, hard taskmistress, but what can a healthy lesbian expect from a woman who wears a tool belt?"

They both laughed as Claire pointed to a molded plastic case hidden in the corner of the kitchen vestibule.

"How did I miss that?" Kris walked over to it and smiled, then turned. "I love you but hate you."

"How does that work?" Claire quipped.

Kris didn't reply but instead opened up the case. It contained more than just a reversible drill. It was a handyperson's dream possession. "How about I put the batteries on charge and we go for a walk on the beach. Do you know how to catch shrimp?"

Claire frowned. "Is there a *catch* in there someplace? Haven't a clue, to be honest."

Kris took the battery charger and attached it to the outlet. "Okay, maybe I'll show you. Although you are still in the doghouse for keeping these tools from me."

Claire chuckled. "Doghouse I can live with. Dogs are faithful friends."

"You are incorrigible, Claire. Let's go."

Chapter Fourteen

The beach between the cottage and Seasons was about a quarter of a mile long and generally considered private. The next property was a mile away. A rocky outcrop separated the two properties' beaches. Claire flicked the hair away from her face, watching Kris virtually skip along on the sand as they walked toward the surf. The tide was out.

Kris appeared to be relaxed at Seasons. Claire had thought that at the cottage, but on the beach, her face glowed and a smile was permanently etched on her lips. Like a kid given the run of a candy shop.

"Slowpoke, catch up, there's a rock pool…they are awesome. Come look, Claire."

Claire chuckled. Her feet padded on the soft sand as her Havaianas Espadrille sneakers ebbed and flowed with the fluid grains.

"I'm not a slowpoke. You must be a child of the sea and sand," Claire chided her with a wink.

"My dad used to say that." Kris shrugged as she pointed to the three-foot rock pool in front of them.

Claire heard the sad wistfulness in her tone wondering about Kris's parents. *Hell, they can't be worse than mine are.*

"Then your dad was right. Okay, so what's so awesome about a rock pool? Is this where the shrimp live?"

Kris giggled and Claire bit her lip.

"Okay, give?"

"Sorry, Claire, there aren't any shrimp here to fish. It's just something I'd like to do one day so I can actually say I caught my own food. I was naïve the first day I was here and I tried fishing with a hand net in a couple of the rock pools. Do you know some are deeper than a swimming pool?"

"No, no, I never knew that. You are such a mine of useful information about sea stuff for a city girl. When you are in the city, do you have useful titbits there too?" Claire grinned as she peered into the clear water of the rock pool.

Kris shifted and knelt to inspect the pool closer. "Maybe some would call it useless. See there, Claire, a cushion star. Do you know the difference between her and her cousins?"

Claire gazed at the pale crustacean. "Well, first, I don't know the difference, and second, how do you know it's a she? Can't quite make that anatomy part out. Are you a marine biologist in the disguise of a meek, brilliant handyperson, by any chance?" Claire laughed and a fish shot by. "What's that?"

Kris grinned up into Claire's face. "A blennie. See, its eyes are at the top of its head. They can see predators easier that way. Don't we all wish for that at least once or twice in our lives?" Kris laughed, continuing to gaze at the pool.

"Yeah, we all do," Claire quietly answered. "The cushion fish, you never said?"

Kris chuckled and stood. "They have shorter arms, and as for the she part…well let's face it. When it comes to harsh conditions, and a rock pool is harsher than the sea, women are adaptable survivors. It's just the order of nature."

Claire stared at Kris, a bemused expression on her face as she shook her head at the simple explanation. "Let's go paddle. I love the surf tickling my toes. Don't you, Sea Girl?"

Kris held her arms up and laughed. "Me, a sea girl? What does that make you? My sea urchin?"

"Probably." Clair grasped her hand, and then they ran as fast as the malleable sand allowed to the surf.

Kris swished her hair and it flew around her face. She giggled as the surf washed over her feet. "Take your shoes off…too late," she squealed.

Claire looked at her clover-green Espadrilles being soaked by the sea. Then she looked at Kris's face—simply pure enjoyment. *Who cares about a pair of shoes? I can buy more.* She laughed.

"Are you game, Sea Girl, for a deeper paddle?" Without releasing Kris's hand, Claire dragged her deeper into the surf.

"Claire!"

†

Kris threw Claire a towel she'd retrieved from the bathroom of the cottage.

Claire attempted but failed to catch it.

Kris was mortified, and her cheeks heated up. "I'm sorry, Claire, I didn't think—" She began to walk over to pick up the object.

Claire raised her good arm and smiled. "That's what I like about you, Kris. You don't think...as in you treat me like a normal human being and not an invalid."

"Why would I do such a thing? You've done brilliantly. There's no reason for me to think of you as anything other than...." Kris frowned. *Other than what?*

Claire stared hard at her and waited.

"Other than a rich socialite who needed to find out what real work is." Kris grinned.

Claire shook her head and rolled her eyes. Kris knew that look meant Claire was okay with the teasing.

"A rich socialite, huh? How do you think my repatriation to normality is working?" Claire said in a drawl, emphasizing *rich socialite* and *normality*.

Kris drew her fingers through her damp hair and knew she must look like a scarecrow. "Hey, I can't say anything about normality. Who the heck knows what that is, anyway?"

Claire bent, picked up the towel, and begin drying her hair.

Their impromptu splashing around had left them three quarters wet but not enough to change totally. Besides, they were working on the porch in the hot sun, so their clothes would dry quickly.

"So very true. Then I guess the question is, am I coming up to scratch?"

Kris chuckled. "Absolutely. Your grandmother is going to be proud of you."

"Grams is always proud of me. It's the rest of the family that need convincing I'm not totally useless."

Although the towel over Claire's head muffled the words, the frustration in her voice was clear.

Kris dragged out a kitchen chair and motioned for Claire to sit. Surprisingly she did without any comment. Kris sat in the chair next to her. "My dad thinks I'm a waste of space. My mom is ambivalent on that."

Claire raised her eyebrows. "Ambivalent?"

"When Dad is around I'm a waste of space. When he isn't, I'm her only daughter who might eventually come around." Kris linked her fingers and grimaced. "I can't change my sexual orientation, and I don't want to. Mom tends to have her head buried in the sand on the issue. Dad is totally hateful. He said I'll never be anything in this world. How can anyone say that to their child?"

Claire reached across the worn wooden table and touched Kris's hand.

"So you see, Claire, you are not the only one who has family that doesn't accept who you are. I guess we have something in common."

Claire shrugged. "More than you think."

The quiet reply made Kris stare harder at her. "You sound obscure like Shirley. I've never told anyone about my parents before. That must mean something." The warm hand that enclosed hers felt perfect. Tears she had held in for years threatened to fall but no way was she going to threaten the fragile connection she had to Claire by being oversensitive.

"Obscure, sure, I can do that. Shirley certainly is a strange duck, I have to say."

"A strange duck?"

They looked at each other, and Claire furrowed her brow several times. "Sorry, the best I could do. The sea and all." She stood and wriggled her ass.

"It's more likely a seagull than a duck, Claire." Kris stood and laughed so hard at Claire's wriggling she nearly peed her pants. "Come on, Sea Urchin, we have work to do." Claire winked.

"Thank you, Claire, for being...you."

"Don't know how to be anyone else, Kris."

Kris smiled. "Let's go, we have sandpaper duties."

†

"Pizza, wow, I love pizza. Who thought of this and where did you get it from?" Kris munched on a delicious pepperoni-filled slice.

Claire jabbed her chest. "Me, it's all me." She smiled at Shirley. "Oh okay, Shirley wanted the seafood. How is it?"

Shirley, her hands poised to cut up her pizza with a knife and fork, stopped and nodded. "Looks delicious."

"Oh no, not cutlery, Shirley, it's a free-for-all. Tonight, if it's okay with Shirley, we are going to celebrate Calvin with pizza. Would he approve?" Claire stared at Shirley.

Seconds later Shirley gave a tight smile. "Yes, he definitely would. I recall he could devour a whole pizza in the time I ate one slice."

"Then tonight we celebrate the life of Calvin and all the lives he touched and the special memories created." Claire raised her slice.

Kris with a small smile did the same. "For Calvin."

Shirley tentatively picked up her pizza slice. "For Calvin." She frowned as she bit into it.

Claire looked at Kris and winked as they both sank their teeth into the pizza.

†

Kris sat opposite Claire in the conservatory, who was nestled in an oversized wicker all-weather sofa in a deep charcoal with bright red cushions. Her feet were stretched out and she looked totally relaxed. The flicker of the candlelight on the matching coffee table accentuated her high cheekbones and latte complexion; the sun agreed with her.

Having looked in the mirror prior to coming down to dinner, Kris saw that her own skin, normally a pale, waxy color, was now mottled with brown spots, which couldn't even be called partway to having a tan. It just looked unattractive. Thank goodness Jess was blind. Mentally she chastised herself for the thought.

She continued her observation of Claire. Today she'd again turned out to be completely different from what Kris had expected. She'd seen a mischievous side to the socialite that obviously didn't appear that often in her other world. *Other world* was the right expression. Here at Seasons and especially at the cottage, life appeared to have stopped or at least moved so slowly you never thought the day would end. In fact, her time with Claire seemed like an endless string.

The more she thought about an endless string and Claire, the more foolish she felt.

"I'm going to ask, so be prepared."

Kris blinked rapidly. "I'm sorry, did I miss something?"

"Nope," Claire chuckled. "In fact, it's more the other way around. I know I like strong coffee and Shirley made it that way, but it isn't that bad, is it?"

Kris frowned. She sat up in her chair with difficulty since the round cushions were so soft that she sank into their depths. "What's strong coffee got to do with missing something?"

"Nothing. Well, that's not strictly correct. For the last few minutes, your expression has gone from reasonably happy to downright pensive. Figured it was the coffee, or should I say, I hoped, because otherwise it's me."

"No, no, of course it isn't you." Kris laughed. "It isn't the coffee either. I was lost in silly thoughts. Sorry."

"Don't need to say sorry to me, Kris. Anyway, in twenty-four hours you will be enjoying a wonderful date. So much better than sitting with a reclusive housekeeper and a has-been party girl."

"Has-been? I don't understand." Kris pulled at her lip. Where had that come from? Claire had been so upbeat most of the day. This was the lurking depressive side Melissa warned her about before she came here. It had appeared the day before, so she recognized it.

Claire didn't move her body but averted her gaze and stared out over the still-looking sea with the sun about to drop below the horizon.

"You are moving forward with your life, and I applaud that, I really do." She faced Kris. "I was lost, you know, since the accident, probably for a long time before that. Perhaps it's Seasons."

Kris waited for more. It didn't come. "Seasons is a wonderful place. If I had the opportunity, I know where I'd live, and it wouldn't be in New York City. I'd trade my small rented apartment for a tent on the grounds. It's simply magical, Claire."

Claire looked away and threaded her fingers through the tassel of the cushion nearest to her. "Magical, that's right. It's not just the house though, is it?"

Claire speared Kris with an intense gaze that took her by surprise. Flushing, she tried to think how to answer the question. "No. It never is," she softly replied. She reached for the coffeepot and poured another cup. She flashed Claire a look asking if she wanted one. Claire shook her head.

"People."

The word floated in the air between them, and neither seemed to want or have the inclination to say more. Silence descended as they looked out toward the calm sea.

Kris stood, walked the few paces to Claire, and held out her hand.

Claire frowned. Then tentatively took it. The grip was strong like a bond as she helped Claire get off the sofa. They walked hand in hand over to the balustrade of the outdoor area, and Kris, with a smile, pointed to the sun.

"It's almost gone, Claire, but it will be back. If we feel sad about that or afraid, then we have the stars to light our way. We are never truly in darkness. That's what I think, anyway. No matter what there is in life, there must be always light at the end of the tunnel. We worry and lose our way or think we do, but you just need to look toward the sky to see there is always the promise of another day." Kris chuckled. "You probably think I'm a philosophical idiot."

Claire squeezed Kris's hand. "Never."

Kris nodded. "Good, I would be devastated."

"My opinion is never worth someone being devastated, especially someone like you." Claire smiled. The darkness in her expression earlier changed entirely.

"Thank goodness. You might use those power tools on me." Claire begin to tug her hand away, and Kris held on. "Claire, look. What a beautiful sunset." The red hues mingling with the last of the blue and the off-white clouds looked fascinating, at least to her anyway.

Claire stared at the sun setting and then turned to Kris.

"Thank you, Kris."

"For what?"

"Making me see a little of what you do every day."

"My pleasure, anytime." Kris sucked in a silent breath and then blurted, "Why don't you come to the golf club too? Jess won't mind. She's lovely, you will like her. I can call her…."

Claire moved away rapidly and shook her head.

"This is your night, Kris. Enjoy it. You don't want a hanger-on. Trust me, it never works."

Kris balled her hands and didn't know why. "Okay, but the invite is open. I'm going to bed now. If you want a stroll on the beach at seven in the morning, I'm your girl. Otherwise, I'll see you at eight for breakfast. I think Shirley has agreed to finally let us eat in the kitchen rather than the formal dining room." Kris moved away from the railing and walked toward the door to the lounge.

"I think I'll pass on the walk. That is rather early. The other, I wouldn't miss it. See you in the morning. Oh, and all I ask is no bathroom duties."

Kris giggled and left the room.

Chapter Fifteen

Kris preened in the mirror of her room, smoothing over her hips the A-line, cotton, blue summer dress with pink polka dots. It had been an impulse buy two weeks before she lost her job. Not that she had a reason to buy it, but when she saw it on the marked-down rail and it was her size, she had to have it.

Impulsive buying wasn't something she normally indulged, and she could think of only two other occasions. Her cat Knight and an illustrated book on woodworking greats of the twentieth century.

The image she saw before her hadn't really changed since she'd last looked. She still had the same mousy-brown hair in a simple, short cut, nothing remotely fashionable. She touched her nose, always prominent and perhaps her ugliest attribute along with her pale complexion. The makeup she rarely used hadn't helped at all. In fact, she considered that she looked worse. Instead of her skin having a waxy look, it was now dry and powdery. How did people use this stuff twenty-four seven?

She glanced at her nylons. At least they looked good. The denier was the best she could afford. Besides, she felt that her legs were pretty good, and her pedal pushers and shorts never looked bad on her. A dress would be a breeze too.

She looked at the hands of the travel clock on the small bedside table. Five thirty. Drawing in a deep breath, she placed her hands on her belly. She could almost feel the flutters of nervousness as she stood there.

I could call and say I can't make it. Kris ground her teeth. *Can't do that. Jess will be upset.* She bit her lower lip. *Claire will laugh and call me a coward. What's worse, I wonder?* She closed her eyes and then opened them, a determination in them as she stared at her reflection.

This is my time, I know it. Whatever happens.

She fetched a pale gray woolen sweater, picked up her purse from the table, and left the room.

Ten minutes later, she drove out of the gates of Seasons and turned right to head toward Chartres. A mile later, a set of lights indicated road construction was ahead and Kris stopped.

The first and only car to pass her was a bright red, sporty-looking sedan. As a kid she had always looked at the grill of a car to see who the manufacturer was. This one amazed her—Jaguar.

"Wow, didn't know they looked like that now." She chuckled. "How would I? Can't afford one."

Knowing about only three properties were on this road, she set off again and wondered who was in the car. It wasn't someone from Seasons, so maybe one of the other property owners was back. She'd ask Shirley at breakfast.

✝

From her bedroom window, Claire watched Kris drive away in Shirley's car. In fact, she'd been watching the garage area for half an hour. *For what? Yes, what? I like Kris; she's a lovely person. Stupid thing is, I want to protect her. I've never felt like that about someone before.*

Claire remained looking at the empty driveway. About to turn away, she heard a vehicle. *Kris is back!* Her heart somersaulted and she smiled. She turned back and her smile slowly weakened as a familiar car pulled up to the house and a dust cloud enveloped it. When it disappeared, the door opened and a pair of Prada shoes appeared behind it.

"Crap."

†

"What do you think?"

"You look great. Dare I ask, are you actually dressing for an admirer?"

Jess Smith frowned, then laughed quietly. "Yes."

"Why didn't you tell me?" A shriek of shock reverberated around the room.

"Because, sis, you'd react exactly how you have."

Jess shrugged on her jacket and then felt her sister Mary's hands on her shoulders pulling the fabric firmly.

"Jess, if you are taking this much effort, let me at least know her name; if not that, how you met?" Mary released her grip.

Jess felt her move away, but not enough that she couldn't work out exactly where Mary was. She could tell she was still nearby from the smell of her perfume, a cheap but pleasant fragrance.

"Kris and I met a week or so ago at Millie's. She's working at Seasons."

Mary shrieked again. "Really, Seasons and the enigmatic Mrs. Rank. Wow. Is she related to Rank or the family that owns it? I hope it's the latter."

Jess shook her head. "Neither, she's helping out with a renovation project for Melissa Jackson. I don't know the exact details, and I don't care. She's a lovely woman."

"Okay, does it mean she's sticking around for a long time, or just a few weeks?"

"She said she'd be here about a month, and that means only a little over two weeks left. I think she will be good for me. It's early days, but I have hopes she will keep in touch. I look good, right?"

"You look great, but have I ever mentioned that you always do? You make me feel like a frump when I'm next to you. Never change, youngster. You always did exude class."

Mary walked to the door, and Jess heard the click of the doorknob turning. "Always were my greatest admirer, sis. Thank you."

"Anytime. That's what family is for."

"Mary?"

"Yeah?"

"I'm nervous. Only ever felt like that once before." She heard Mary move to her, and her sister dragged her into her arms.

"She wasn't worth it," Mary whispered in Jess's ear.

Jess hugged her. "Yeah, I know."

†

Shirley sipped her coffee as she listened to Kris drive away. *The child hasn't realized yet.* She stood and checked the roast beef. Satisfied it was almost ready, she returned to her chair and took another sip of her coffee.

The sound of a car skidding to a halt in front of the house surprised her. She frowned, then stood and proceeded down the corridor to the front door. *Claire hadn't said she was expecting anyone.* Before she reached the hall, she heard voices. *So, Claire was expecting someone.* She half turned and then walked to the swing door that led to the hall. As she opened it, she saw a tall, beautiful, immaculately dressed woman flinging her arms around Claire.

No! her heart screamed.

Chapter Sixteen

Kris smiled listening to Jess play a fabulous rendition of Billy Joel's "Piano Man." Gazing lazily around the packed restaurant, she saw that most diners were raptly watching her friend. The women looked even more smitten than the men. *I can understand that.*

Jess had the kind of elfin quality that could turn the heads of anyone, no matter their taste in sexual partners. She was no critic, but surely someone in the music business would be interested in Jess. Being stuck in Chartres couldn't be good for a budding music career. Then again, she didn't know Jess well enough to say if her friend wanted to deal with the trappings of the music business. Perhaps this type of venue was all she needed to satisfy her.

Her thoughts strayed to the moment they met outside the club. Kris guessed she had the upper hand because she could have turned around and left. Instead, she tamped down the flutters in her stomach and walked over to Jess, who was standing confidently near the entrance.

"Hey, I'm early."

Jess grinned, and suddenly all the nervous energy that had plagued her disappeared.

"That's okay, so was I. Early is good. To be honest, I was so nervous my sister helped me dress." Jess shrugged.

Kris took a moment to take in Jess's apparel. She wore a black luster cotton jacket, purple linen trousers, and a pristine white silk shirt with the buttons open low at the throat, showing an inch of cleavage—tempting but not overly revealing.

"Your sister has good taste. You look fantastic."

"Do you trust me, Kris?"

Kris frowned and nodded. *Idiot, Jess can't see.* "Yes."

Jess moved closer and began to slowly trail her hands from Kris's shoulders down her arms and then slowly over her body. Kris equated it to a pat down by a TSA officer in an airport, only much more pleasant. At least that was what she had seen on the TV.

"Get a room, Jess," a gruff voice interrupted them.

Kris sharply moved away and Jess began to laugh and turned her head in the direction of the man.

"Sam, you should be so lucky."

Jess turned to her with an apologetic expression. "Sorry. One of the problems with the sight impaired, we can't actually see who might come around the corner. I just wanted to have the impression of what you looked like tonight."

Kris felt relief at the remark. "Sighted can't either, so you are not alone. You mentioned dinner, and I'm starving."

"I did." Jess chuckled, fumbling to take Kris's hand awkwardly. "We have a fine table, and I can recommend the fillet steak, but then again, the pork belly is superb, and then there is the—"

"Stop. I'll check out the menu"—Kris squeezed Jess's hand—"and then take advice from an expert."

Jess laughed as they entered the club. "Not an expert, just tried every meal they have. I've worked here for the last twelve months. How many variations can they give me?"

Kris laughed. "So true. Lead on, oh dilettante."

"Dang, what does that mean?"

Kris laughed. "I'll tell you over dinner."

†

"Claire, I wasn't aware you were expecting a visitor this evening. Do you need me to make up a room?"

Claire glared at Shirley and didn't answer. Instead, she turned her attention to the beautiful woman who had arrived. "Why didn't you call and say you were coming?"

The harsh words sent a shiver down Shirley's back.

The redheaded beauty calmly answered, "You texted me, remember?"

"When have you ever responded in the last eighteen months to any text I've sent?"

Shirley watched their body language. It bristled and not with the right kind of electricity.

"This time you sounded desperate. I still have feelings for you, Claire. We've been through a lot together over the years."

"Yeah, and you conveniently ignore me but keep hold of the engagement farce, for what? Are you afraid no one will take you seriously if you break up with me? You are a joke, Racheal," Claire shouted.

Shirley shrank against the nearest wall and tried to leave, but Claire called her back.

"No, Shirley, don't go. Racheal is an unwanted guest. You can leave now, Racheal, and I promise you I will never contact you again."

"You were always a selfish bitch, Claire. What was that text about if you didn't want me to come see you? I know you still care about me. If the engagement is a farce— as you call it—and so odious to you, why not tell the media?"

Claire paled. "I will when I get back to the city," she ground out.

Shirley moved away from the wall. "Would you like me to make dinner?"

Claire stared at her this time as if she were an interloper, and perhaps she was in this particular conversation.

"No."

"I'll retire to the kitchen, and perhaps you can let me know when you want dinner."

"I don't want dinner here. Racheal, as you came this far, the least I can do is buy you dinner. Come on, you can drive." Claire grabbed Racheal's arm and dragged her out the front door.

Shirley watched in amazement and shook her head after the door shut behind them.

"This is not going to work out well. I just know it in my bones." She retreated to the security of her kitchen and heard the throaty engine of the vehicle as it headed out of the driveway.

†

Kris placed a hand on her stomach and grinned. The pork belly was to die for, and if she did die now she would go out satisfied. She let out a slow sigh and grinned as Jess made her way to the piano to begin another set. So far, it had been a wonderful evening. The meal was superb and the conversation friendly rather than intimate. *Works for me, I think.*

Then she heard a voice she thought she recognized and turned. Sure enough, the woman she'd met on the beach her first day in town sat opposite her. *What was her name, now?*

Then pale brown eyes stared at her, and the infectious smile that had greeted her that day flashed over full lips again. Mortified at being caught staring, Kris looked away but not quick enough to deter the woman she now recalled as Fern Delancy from speaking.

"Hi, are you alone?"

Kris wanted nothing more than the floor to swallow her whole, but instead she managed a tight smile and shook her head.

Fern laughed delicately. Though most would have considered it sexy, Kris didn't. She focused on Fern's dinner guest. The woman, who was definitely younger than Fern by at least ten years if not more, was oblivious to the conversation. Her attention was on the phone in her hand as her fingers dexterously danced over the screen.

"Has your friend gone to the bathroom?" Fern asked insistently.

"No, actually she's working." Kris turned her gaze to the small stage, where Jess was finishing a song. "Jess is my date."

Fern gave her a narrow-eyed look and then nodded. "Really? I didn't think you'd be her type, or you hers."

Embarrassed at the remark, Kris wanted to shoot under the table. Then her inner bravado kicked in. Who gave this woman any right to say such a thing? She might look beautiful, but her manners needed work big-time. "What makes you a judge of who is her type, or mine for that matter? I find your remark offensive." She turned away and focused on Jess.

"Sorry, let me apologize properly. Why don't you join us until Jess finishes her set and have dinner with us? My treat. What do you say?"

Kris shook her head. "We've had dinner."

"Yeah, sure, that would be right. I should have realized. Still, you could have company until she's done. What do you say? I need to make amends for my obnoxious remarks. Champagne works, I find, to lighten the load a little."

"Champagne? I thought you wanted a low-key evening. I'm up for that, darling." The nasal reply from the other woman at the table caught Kris, and she was certain Fern, off guard.

"Yeah, sure, whatever, Rianne. Get back to Candy Crush." Fern pierced Kris with an apologetic look. "Please."

"Okay, but only until Jess is finished."

"Great. Please come sit by me. We can talk."

Kris looked at the woman called Rianne, who barely noticed the new addition with her gaze concentrating on the tiny screen in her hand.

"Ah, Candy Crush."

Fern laughed this time, and it appeared genuine.

"Yeah, one of those silly, addictive games that has millions in its clutches. I bet the developers are zillionaires by now. I wish I had one share in that company. I'd be rich," Fern said.

They both laughed, and Kris felt easier about sitting with Fern. Besides, she'd never had champagne before.

"Ordering champagne means you must be wealthy…at least in my book. What exactly do you do?"

Fern flexed her fingers, looked at the well-manicured nails, and smiled. "I thought I told you that I own Curiosity, a local bar. I know you haven't been there. I'd have known."

Kris frowned, then nodded. "You mentioned you'd been there, not that you owned it. How is business?" Her gaze drifted to the blonde across from her, and she wondered why anyone would go to dinner with someone who was ignoring them.

"You need to come by one evening. Bring Jess, or better yet, come on your own. I can for certain say you will have a good time."

Kris frowned. Then Fern waved over a waiter and ordered the best champagne in the house cellar.

"Champagne is champagne, right?" Kris asked.

Fern shook her head. "My dear, absolutely not. There are so many derivations of champagne. Some are genuine, some not. Don't be blinded by the price either. That's a whole other story."

Kris laughed. "I should really dislike you, shouldn't I?"

Fern winked. "Yes, but I'm always hopeful that people will give me a second chance. Have I got that second chance from you?"

"Maybe." Kris glanced at the stage and Jess, who was looking in the direction of their now-empty table with a smile, and she felt terrible.

"I need to return to my table. Jess—"

Fern placed a hand on her arm, preventing her from leaving. "Hey, Jess will be cool, trust me. Besides, you're not the only one in the room who isn't looking at her. Stay, please."

Kris sucked in her lower lip. *You are obviously not very observant.* "Okay, but only until Jess finishes this set."

"Excellent, and right on the mark, our champagne has arrived."

✝

"Stop here," Claire stated.

Wheels screeched to a halt at the curbside.

"A bar? I thought we were going out to dinner," Racheal demanded.

"We are. This, according to the local paper, is a great place to eat and be discreet. Let's go." Claire flung her door open and climbed out.

A minute later, Racheal stood next to her. "Why do we need discreet?"

"You might not, but I do. Have you looked at me lately? I'm not exactly the poster child for any establishment. I'll find us a table and you can order our drinks. I'll have a bourbon," Claire snarled and then entered the bar.

Five minutes later, Racheal set the drinks down and sat. "I said we wanted to eat, and they will send over a server to take our orders. This place is packed, Claire. Why don't we go somewhere else? We need to talk." She sank into the leather upholstery. "Hmm, at least the seating is comfortable."

"Yeah, yeah, and yeah," Claire muttered and grabbed her drink and drank it down in one gulp.

"Oh, so we are thirsty too. You could have said. I'd have bought you more."

Claire drew back her head and stared at Racheal. "Why are you here, Racheal? Really."

Racheal shuffled the coaster that came with her drink and sighed heavily. "It isn't the same without you. I know you'll think that stupid coming from me, but I actually think I loved you...no, do still love you. As well as I can. There isn't anyone that can replace you."

Claire digested the information and the server appeared with the dinner menu. They ordered more drinks and Claire told the server to keep them coming when they were empty. "It's been almost two years, Racheal, and you say this now. Look at me. I haven't had the surgery. I'm as useless and ugly as you once called me. What benefit are you going to gain from me being on your arm in our old haunts?"

Racheal sipped on her water and then clasped her glass. "We were going to be married. You made the mistake of taking that drug whore to bed. It isn't my fault you are the way you are...it's hers and yours. We could make it work, Claire. You just have to see that. Is living in your apartment or here alone what you want for the rest of your life? Don't you remember the good times we had together?"

Claire drew in a huge breath that was so big she almost choked on it. "If I could change that night, I would, Racheal, in more ways than you will ever know. Except I can't. What's done is done, and I will pay for it the rest of my life. You have spent two years avoiding me and what happened. I understand that, but...."

"But?"

Claire shrugged and took Racheal's hand. "Coming here now and asking us to go back to how things were can never happen. Seriously, look at me. I know in a few weeks you'll go back to what you thought before—the abhorrence of it all."

"Well actually, do you remember Binky and his brother?"

"Binky, the bouncer at the club? Sure." Claire frowned. "His brother? I never met him that I recall."

"Yeah, I guess you wouldn't. Well, he's a plastic surgeon and he can help. He really can, Claire."

Claire dropped her gaze and sucked in a huge breath. "Racheal, I chose to remain this way. My parents are annoyed as hell. They had the best plastic surgeon in New York set to work on me, and I refused. Other than having me committed as insane and taking over my rights, they couldn't do anything about that."

Racheal's eyes flared. "Why?"

"Altruistically, I realized without something to remind me of the event, I would be that same selfish individual."

Racheal shook her head. "What about the arm? It isn't strong enough to do much; couldn't that be the reminder?"

Claire considered the argument for all of a few seconds. "I want people to know me for me, not my perceived beauty. Does that make sense?" The server arrived. "Let's order dinner." She flicked her finger at the special of the day and then fumbled with the menu as it dropped from her hand.

"I'll take that." The blonde server smiled warmly and took it from Claire's unprotesting fingers.

Maybe I'm making a mistake hiding myself away. Her thoughts drifted to Kris, and she wondered how her evening was going.

Chapter Seventeen

Jess wandered over to the table where she had shared dinner with Kris. She figured the evening had gone well and hopefully it would continue if Kris hadn't become bored. Within ten feet of the table, a hand settled on her arm.

"Jess, my dear, your dinner partner is sipping champagne at my table. I'm sure you could do with a glass or two yourself. You were, as always, wonderful."

Jess recognized Fern's voice and remained still. Kris must have looked fed up, and as always Fern stepped in to save a damsel in distress. Then again, distress or not, Fern would have interfered.

"Thank you for taking care of *my date*." Her lips pursed as she reluctantly allowed Fern to lead her to the table.

"Jess, you were wonderful," Kris gushed.

Jess felt like a lead weight had lifted from her chest. Kris's tone indicated she enjoyed the set. She grasped the seat and sat. "Glad you liked it. I was hoping you weren't bored or lonely."

"Far from it. I could listen to you for hours."

Jess nodded and then felt a tall, stemmed glass pressed into her hand. Her fingers traveled over it. A champagne flute. Fern always had expensive tastes. She mentally shook her memories of Fern away, lifted the glass, and sipped. The bubbles were certainly an acquired taste. One, thankfully, she didn't possess.

"I'm sorry, but you haven't mentioned your guest." She had picked up the clicking sound of fingers next to her.

Fern laughed. "Sorry, Jessie, I forget your affliction at times. You really don't look like you are blind. Silly me to forget about Rianne. Jess, meet my dinner date, Rianne. Rianne, put that damned phone down and be sociable for once."

Fern sounded pissed at her date. *Maybe I like this Rianne even though I don't know her.*

"I'm at level 310 and it's way hard. Damn, I've lost another life. Hi."

Jess pursed her lips to prevent smiling at the petulant child, which the woman sounded like. With Fern's background, she wouldn't be surprised if Rianne were just out of college.

"Hi, Rianne, I'm Jess. You probably didn't notice, but I was the entertainment this evening."

A grunt was the reply, and Jess smiled. "Level 310 wouldn't be Candy Crush by any chance, would it?"

"Why yes it would. Do you play?" Rianne responded immediately.

"Not exactly, but I vicariously play via my eldest niece, who is addicted. When you get to level 325, get ready to be really frustrated. I can give you a great website for cheating on the game if you want."

"Really?"

Jess wanted to laugh. *Wow, the modern way to turn on a woman. Whatever happened to good old-fashioned romance?*

"I'm on level 200. I guess I'd better ask for cheats from both of you." Kris chuckled.

Jess laughed. "Sounds like a plan to me. Kris, do you want to go out for a breath of fresh air?"

"Oh, why don't we all go," Fern said.

Rianne replied, "Let them go, Fern, they are on a date. Go, you two, and I'll hold you to the cheat website addy."

"Sure thing." Jess stood, listening intently for Kris to do the same.

"Thanks for the champagne, Fern, it was lovely." Kris moved to stand next to Jess and took her hand.

"Yeah, thanks, Fern. See you both later."

Jess squeezed Kris's hand, and they headed toward the exit to the garden area.

†

Racheal gazed at Claire, who was shredding the paper napkin that had enclosed the cutlery, her gaze pinned on the bar. She took in her posture, which seemed relaxed except for the finger action that sent erotic memories through her that she tamped down. Claire was right in some ways. Her scars and physical disability had been a problem. In fact, had she come out of the accident relatively injury free, they would probably be married by now. They both had had other lovers and probably would still be having them.

I do love you, Claire, that's the truth, but you need to have the surgery on your face. The other I can live with. Hell, it only takes one hand to take me, not two.

"What's so funny?"

"Sorry, Claire, I was reminiscing about us. We did have fun, didn't we, really?"

Claire shrugged. "Yes, we had fun, but it wasn't love."

Racheal sat back in her chair and stared at Claire. *Not love?* "I don't understand. You always said you loved me. Is it because of the injuries or my reaction to them? I apologize. I do, big-time, Claire. Tell me what you want and I'll do it, I promise."

"From you, nothing. I know what I want now out of life. Coming here with you made me see how simple it was. I'm sorry, Racheal, it's over for good."

"Why do you say that? Have you found someone else?" Racheal scrambled around in her memory for anyone who could make Claire change her mind. *The old housekeeper? Not even Claire is that desperate.*

Claire stared intently at her. "Racheal, I will always love you. We had so many years together. Now I understand what my grandmother was saying when she asked me here. We can be friends, and we should. I'd like that. We have so much history, but lovers, no, not anymore."

Closing her eyes and rubbing the bridge of her nose, Racheal couldn't believe what she was hearing. This should have been a piece of cake. Not many would give Claire the chance she was offering. *What is wrong with her? Did she scramble what little common sense she had in that damn accident along with her memory?* "I don't know what to say." The words echoed hollowly around them, and Claire smiled slowly. It was a gentle smile, almost regretful.

Claire reached her good hand across the table and took Racheal's lifeless one in a firm grip. "Don't say anything. Let's just enjoy dinner together one last time."

That sentence was like a death knell to Racheal and her chance of having Claire back in her life. A part of her was relieved. The prospect of having a disabled partner had never sat well with her from the start. However, the social contacts Claire had and still would if she reached out to old friends were worth putting up with that part. Now their relationship was in shreds and she didn't have a clue what she'd done wrong.

"Yes, let's. I see our meal is about to arrive," she said as steaming pots of mussels were placed on the table.

†

Kris still held Jess's hand, or was it the other way around? Who knew? She only knew Jess was incredibly quiet and that was probably her fault. "Jess, I'm sorry I deserted our table, but Fern was insistent."

Jess stiffened. "Yes, she's always been that. Have you met her before? I noticed she was familiar with you."

Kris bit her bottom lip. She had mentioned meeting Fern before, but then again perhaps she had forgotten to say the actual name.

"I met her on the beach the day I arrived. I thought I told you, but I may have forgotten."

"Forgotten? How could you forget Fern? She wouldn't take kindly to you saying that." Jess lips contorted as she spoke.

"Perhaps because she wasn't important to me." Kris paused and watched Jess's strained features as she grimaced. "Do you have history with her?"

Jess flashed her a grim look. "Why do you ask?"

The electricity in the air was coming from Jess and not any weather front. Obviously, she had, and it must still hurt.

"No reason. When do you have to go back on stage?" Kris asked quietly and moved her gaze to the stars that even with the lights of the buildings around them made a sparkling blanket of the night sky.

"I get a half hour break. What time is it?"

"Almost nine."

Jess squeezed her hand tightly and then turned to place her body in front of Kris. "I'm sorry, Kris, call it a touch of green-eyed envy. Look, I'll be finished at ten. They put on karaoke for the late night revelers. Will you stay and we can spend the rest of the evening together?"

Kris had never experienced this kind of emotional bouncing around before. Her romantic trysts had been rare, and then that was as a teenager. Now in her thirties, she had no reference for what was happening around her. *What would Claire do?*

She smiled, knowing exactly what Claire would say—she was a naïve idiot but a nice one. Her friend had called her that several times over the period they had spent together.

"Jess, I've had a long day. Do you mind if I head home? We can get together next week for coffee. What do you say?"

Jess sighed and dropped her hand. "Sure, give me a call when you are free. You know where I'll always be and at what time."

Kris looked down at her free hand and felt ashamed. Perhaps she was being…. *What?* Even she couldn't put a name on it. *Crazy, I'm crazy.* "I've enjoyed my evening, Jess, truly I have."

"Yeah right, and most of that was with Fern. Look, I need to go or they will come looking." Jess retreated to the entrance and didn't hesitate as she opened the door and entered.

Kris blinked rapidly as Jess left. This had been a confusing evening in one way or another. As she gazed at the glittering canopy above her, she grinned.

"I love being here, even with the puzzling relationships I've managed to forge." She chuckled softly. "Who would have thought it that plain old Kris Lake actually has a life outside of her meager apartment?"

The words seemed to float like fairy dust in the air as she turned toward the parking lot, then decided to call a cab. She'd had three glasses of champagne and a glass of wine. Even out here in the boonies, the cops might be on patrol. Shirley would never forgive her for driving her car inebriated.

She headed back inside to the reception area to call a cab.

†

Shirley focused on her book, an old faithful, *Jane Eyre* by Charlotte Brontë. It might have been written in the mid-1800s, but it still had that innocent appeal of romance trumping the system. Life threw curveballs, and indeed in this novel, several. Yet strangely, modern romances mirrored at least in part the phenomenon of love traversing the human condition of not being perfect.

"My Ricky saw just that," she muttered. She began to read about Mr. Rochester riding over the moors and encountering Jane for the first time.

The sound of a vehicle churning up the drive startled her, and she threw down her Kindle on the coverlet. She flicked the curtain aside and looked down at the driveway.

Eventually she saw Kris alight from the taxi. A few minutes later, she heard the young woman take the staircase and uncharacteristically slam the door of her bedroom.

"Oh, well, I warned her." Sighing, she nodded. "My dear, you will be okay. I'm certain of it. I wonder what's happened to my car. Hmm." Shirley settled back into bed. "Let's see how long it will be before she arrives."

As the Kindle slipped from her fingers and sleep crooked its finger, beckoning her to the abyss that allowed the body to rest, Shirley thought of a specific quote from her beloved book. *"There is no happiness like that of being loved by your fellow creatures, and feeling that your presence is an addition to their comfort."*

About to succumb to the darkness, she heard a vehicle slowly crunch the gravel. Blinking rapidly to starve off sleep for a few minutes, she heard the front door open and the vehicle speed away. There were no rapid steps up the staircase as with the previous entrant; no, in fact, silence abounded.

"You made the right choice, Claire," Shirley mumbled and allowed sleep to finally take her.

Chapter Eighteen

Shirley moved the bacon around on the griddle and added a couple of eggs. Kris loved eggs. Claire had snarled the first time she had offered them to her, and Shirley smiled at the memory.

"Wow, you must have had a good night. All smiles and it's only eight thirty," Claire flippantly remarked as she sat down heavily on one of the kitchen chairs.

Shirley switched her gaze from the sizzling food to the woman. "From your expression, you didn't have the same."

"Hmm, it was and wasn't. Don't you think it's weird to tell someone the truth but at the same time feel terrible for doing so?"

Shirley waved her spatula. "Life, Claire, is never easy. What you believe is the truth can be someone else's lie and they can settle for maintaining that and making everyone else feel guilty about it."

"No, no, Racheal isn't like that. She wanted to start again." Claire dropped her head into her hands. "I have a headache from all that bourbon."

Shirley gazed at the broken woman, a far cry from the spoiled teenager who had refused her eggs at seventeen. No, she had grown up to be a woman who at this time in life was worth saving. "I didn't mean any disrespect. You didn't want to go back, presumably."

"Back, how the hell can I go back? I'm a wreck of a woman compared to what I was then. I need to move on." Claire dragged her fingers through her hair. "I need to find my place in this life. I think I might—"

"Good grief, am I late?"

Shirley drew in a breath of fresh air; *fresh air* were the right words to describe Kris. She was exactly what she said she was. Some would say she was average, nothing extraordinary. *Yet isn't everyone extraordinary in their own way?*

"I'm late. Sorry. My watch has stopped and I need a new battery. Plus, I walked into town to fetch your car. Sorry, I had a couple of drinks and decided it was safer to come home by cab last night." Kris quickly took her seat opposite Claire at the table.

"Excellent call, and, no, you are not late. Look, we haven't eaten. Did you have a good night?" Shirley turned her attention back to the food she was cooking. *Darn, some of that bacon is scorched.*

"Well, it was and wasn't."

"It wasn't? Sounds like my evening," Claire said.

"Yeah sure, what did you and Shirley do, watch reruns of *Xena* or *Jane Eyre*? I've seen the DVD collection here." Kris chuckled.

"I'll have you know, young minx, Jane is my heroine." Shirley winked at Kris.

Kris smiled and looked at Claire. "You had to watch the old stuff, right? Once was not enough."

"Jane Eyre might be my heroine too, if I ever read the book or saw the movie," Claire stated blandly.

Shirley switched off the heat and stared at Claire, seeing that Kris's eyes almost popped. "Well bless me, I'm going to have to educate you, young woman. The love interest might not be your cup of tea, but my Jane Eyre and her fortitude…well, no woman worth her salt should ever say she hasn't read this story."

Claire held up her hands. "Okay, okay, it's Sunday, why don't we have a good old-fashioned Sunday afternoon veg in front of the TV and watch this darn movie. Are you both game?"

Kris grinned. "Hmm, sounds interesting to me. Which version do you have, Shirley?"

Shirley switched her attention back to the food and plated it. Before she could take it to the table, Claire arrived at her side and took one of the plates.

"I might not be able to handle two, but I can certainly take one," Claire whispered.

Shirley smiled. "That you can. Thank you for the help."

Claire nodded and placed the plate in front of Kris. "Had to be yours. Two eggs, right?"

"Yes, thank you."

Shirley positioned hers and Claire's on the table and sat. "Enjoy, my dears."

A chorus of thanks and they began to eat.

"So, Shirley, which version?" Kris asked.

Shirley soaked a piece of toast in her egg yolk. "Well, I have a wonderful version from 1943, with Orson Wells and Joan Fontaine, but it's black and white and you modern girls like your color versions. I do have a 1996 version with Willian Hurt and Charlotte Gainsbourg. It's very good. Then of course there are the TV series'. I do so love the BBC versions. Period dramas are their specialty."

Claire chuckled. "I have to say I never knew this book was so popular. Just how many versions are there?"

Kris grinned, waving a piece of toast in the air. "Way too many to mention, I suspect. A great question for a quiz. Oh, did you know they do a quiz at the local bar, Curiosity, on Tuesday evenings? Do you both like quizzes?"

"Not me, my dear. I'm not a bar or quiz person, never have been." Shirley shrugged and watched Claire stare at Kris.

"Never been to one. Does that mean I might actually get a first here?" Claire asked.

"You have had many firsts here in the past," Shirley retorted.

Claire faintly blushed. "Yeah right. Well, I was here at puberty, so that would work."

"You've been coming here since you were a baby, and there were lots of firsts."

"Thank you, Shirley. Does that mean you will be getting out the baby pics later?" Claire sarcastically replied.

Kris frowned. "I don't think she was being facetious."

Shirley waved away Kris's words. "I can if you want. However, that will only happen when you bring home the person you will be spending the rest of your life with. Eat, or breakfast will be cold."

✝

Kris flipped a stone into the sea. It tanked as the memory of her dad attempting to teach her how to skim a stone on water came to mind. He had been so patient. She'd made only one good shot that she recalled.

They had had a late summer vacation at Long Beach. At least they'd stayed near the area but spent the days on the beach. She had been ten. The innocent age when her dad loved her for who she was, not what she was. She wiped away a tear. "I miss you, Dad."

Kris skimmed another stone and watched in amazement as it went the farthest any ever had. "You would be proud of me for this, yet not the woman I became. How crazy is that." She turned and looked toward the house and moved seventy degrees to see the tip of the cottage. "If only life was fair to everyone."

She picked up another stone and this time laughed as it barely reached the water.

✝

Claire leafed through the DVD collection next to the TV and was amazed at what she found.

"Jesus, *Dawson's Creek*. Wow, I loved Andie McPhee. She is a very hot woman. I wonder what she does now?" She flicked through a few that didn't register with her. They must be Shirley's." Then she clutched a case and dragged it to her chest. She slowly turned it to face her and gazed at it, entranced.

"I love you, Sarah Connor. Hell, you are my heroine. This Jane Eyre better be a badass." She placed *Terminator 2* to one side. Her cell vibrated, and she pulled it out of her pocket and looked at the caller ID. Racheal.

She waited until the tone ended. Then heard another ding indicating that she had a voice mail. She looked long and hard at the screen. *Shall I delete or listen? Dilemma after dilemma.* She pressed Delete.

✝

Claire bent forward on the sofa and shook her head. "I love the premise, and yes, Jane Eyre is pretty darn tough. She's almost on a par with one of my other movie heroines but not quite…no guns."

Kris laughed. "May enquiring minds ask who that might be, or do we need to guess?"

Claire turned to look at Kris seated in the recliner to her left. *She looks like she always does, except she's beautiful. Crazy, I'm crazy.*

"I suppose you will make us guess." Shirley smiled as she struggled out of the high-backed, tartan-upholstered chair "I'm going to make dinner. I'll leave the guessing games to the both of you."

"Do you need help?" Kris jumped out of her chair.

"No, please. I enjoy my kitchen and cooking, especially for more than one." Shirley moved to stand beside the door. "Your grandmother called. She said to expect her to inspect your work in a couple of weeks. I'll call you when it's ready." She left the room.

"Cripes, your grandmother might think we are slacking. Maybe we should have worked today instead of vegging out." Kris bit her lip.

Claire shook her head before settling back in the sofa. "We've done great...no, let me rephrase that, *you* have. Although I have done as much as I can."

"Oh, Claire, you've done lots. It's a team effort, right?" Kris smiled.

Kris's smile traveled across her face to her eyes. *She really is quite beautiful. How on earth did I ever think that she's plain?* Then she recalled a part of the movie they had watched, and somehow it was pertinent. *"I am strangely glad to get back again to you: and wherever you are is my home— my only home."*

"Team effort, right?" The tentative words pierced her.

"Yeah, sorry, team effort." Claire concentrated on Kris and the burning question in her mind for the last twenty-four hours. "How was your date?"

Kris frowned, averting her profile.

"That bad. I'm sorry."

"No." Kris turned back immediately, her face flushed. "Jess was upset because I met someone from the beach and we were drinking champagne, and oh, well, it was innocent, but...."

Claire's stomach double flipped. *Where did she meet someone else? I thought it was only this Jess person in town.* "I see. Well, I guess she might be upset at that...I think."

Kris retrieved the disc from the player. "I have a feeling Jess has a history with Fern, and as absurd as this sounds, is jealous."

"Why absurd?" Claire softly asked, her eyes riveted to Kris moving in front of the blank TV screen.

"Look at me. I'm hardly the type anyone would fight over. Besides, have you seen the two of them? They are gorgeous. They can have anyone. Ah right, sorry, you haven't met them." The quietly spoken words had an edge.

"No, no, I haven't. Maybe I should and put them right." Claire drew in a shallow breath. *What the hell am I doing? This is just like me, or the me I was.*

"Don't be silly, Claire, it's nothing. Jess and I weren't really on a date. It was friends having dinner. I bet you do that all the time."

Claire settled back in the sofa. "Not anymore, and even back then friends were few and far between. Racheal and I met at Columbia University, and I suppose it was a comfortable relationship. No surprises, if you know what I mean."

Kris turned and sat on the floor and gazed at her. "I wish I did. I never went to a university or a college, as I mentioned. Finances were always tight, and when my family found out about me being a lesbian, the money pot leaked and voilà, no money for my further education."

Claire moved off the sofa, sat in front of Kris, and touched a pale cheek. "Parents don't know everything. They think they do, but they don't. I'm sorry, Kris."

For a few moments, they stayed connected until Kris moved her face away. "Yeah, thanks. Still, at least you have had those moments, and that's good."

"Kris, you deserve the same. More so," Claire adamantly replied.

Silence invaded the room for a few moments more than there should have been, and then Kris said, "Don't patronize me, Claire. Look, I need to check on the paintwork at the cottage before dinner." She stood in one lithe movement and strode to the door.

"I didn't mean to sound patronizing, Kris. I believe in you, and I think you were poorly treated last night." Claire struggled to get up. For some reason her body refused to act when she told it too.

136

"I was treated as well as a person like me can expect to be treated. I'll see you at dinner."

Claire watched Kris leave the room and wiped a hand across her mouth in disdain. *How the hell can you expect her to understand compassion from you when you are worse than Jess and Fern? Now why does that name seem familiar? Damn, I hate this memory loss.*

Chapter Nineteen

Early autumn skies over the ocean were stupendous, filled with long, white, wispy clouds bursting into deep blue or orange splashes as the sun set. Tonight the clouds were blue. Glorious brightness just before darkness fell over the cottage.

In a subtle way, it mirrored Kris's life at this moment. Her cell phone rang and she immediately answered. "Hi."

"Kris, it's me, Jess. Any chance we can catch up tonight?"

"I'm sorry, Jess, not tonight. I'm busy."

There was a brief pause. "I'm sorry about last night, I figured you'd be upset."

"Yes, I know you're sorry, and I'm not upset. Look, how about we meet up at Curiosity on Tuesday evening and take in the quiz you mentioned? I think Claire will come too. I want you to meet her. Is that okay?"

"Sure, I'd like to meet your friend Claire."

"Great, see you at seven outside. Take care, Jess."

Kris sighed as she placed her phone in her pocket and then looked toward Seasons where a few lights burned. *Two weeks and I go home...home. Hmm. The only thing I miss about New York is Knight.*

"I miss you, Knight, big-time." She turned and trudged back to the main house.

✝

Claire sat in her usual spot after dinner—the wicker sofa in the conservatory. Under normal circumstances Kris and Shirley joined her, at least for a short while. Tonight she wasn't so sure Kris would since she'd been reticent during dinner.

Her hand touched her most prominent scar. It meandered down her right cheek like a river. The protrusion of skin where the stiches had held that part of her face together, though not as angry after two years, still informed her that the event had happened.

She smiled and felt the skin on the right side of her face, which didn't move. She thought it made her smile lopsided. Once she'd recovered enough to see people, she had arrogantly thought no one would care about her appearance. They had.

How could she forget the debacle of Racheal's reaction to going for a simple walk in the park together? It was on par with the train wreck.

Claire snorted at the irony of her thoughts. "Train wreck is right. What's the saying? 'A train wreck waiting to happen.' Darn, I beat that one and I've worn the T-shirt on my face ever since." Focusing on the tranquil backdrop of a sky filled with stars should have eased her churning thoughts of the trauma of the accident. It didn't. "Go figure."

The door to the conservatory opened, and Shirley walked in with a tray. It only had two mugs and a side plate of cookies. Her favorite chocolate chip, probably. Kris always refused them.

"Hi, Shirley. It's a beautiful evening. The sky is full of stars."

Shirley placed the tray on the table and smiled. "It most certainly is. Kris will be here in a second. She had some laundry to put in the machine."

The words threw Claire, but she recovered quickly. "You're not joining us?"

"Not tonight, my dear. It's the anniversary of when I met my husband. I'm going to celebrate that alone. Might sound strange to you young folks, but it's my tradition." She smiled and turned to leave.

"When and where did you meet him?" Claire was fascinated.

Shirley's eyes glazed over, and then she shook her head. "Here actually. I was merely the assistant to the cook at the time, and he was employed in the vegetable garden. A bit of a rogue they said, and the girls loved him. I never thought he'd ever look at me."

Claire felt her pulse race. Odd really, because they were talking about a heterosexual relationship, yet it resonated. She sat there silently, neither inside the room nor out, as Shirley continued.

"He was very handsome, my Ricky, and let's face it, I'm hardly a picture postcard. It was raining on the day we met, and I fell in love." Shirley's cheeks grew red. "I was walking by the cottage. There used to be a decent herb garden there back then. My, it must be oh, almost forty years now."

"What happened next?" Claire asked.

Shirley laughed. "He gallantly offered me his coat. You see, an unexpected shower. After that, the magic of the cottage encased us both. Now, enough of this." She turned and smiled at Kris as she entered. "Seasons cottage is a very special place. Take advantage if you can."

Claire was speechless but watched as Shirley left and Kris ventured farther into the room and sat in her usual chair. Eventually finding her voice, she said, "What do you make of that? I want to know more. It's like that Jane Eyre movie."

Kris grinned. "You don't need to whisper, Shirley has left. For the record, I think it's romantic, like it used to be in the good old days. Darn, did I really say that?"

"Yes, you did, and for the record, I agree—well, as much as I know of the good old days." Claire chuckled. Then reached over and picked up a mug of hot chocolate. "Better drink this before it gets cold."

Kris picked it up and took a sip.

"Look, today I was out of line. Your affairs have nothing to do with me. I'm sorry, Kris."

After a few moments of silence, Kris replaced the mug on the table.

"You are right, they aren't."

Claire's heart sank to a new low.

"Except for some unknown reason, I think it does matter…what you think, that is. I've arranged to meet Jess on Tuesday for the quiz."

Claire sucked in her left cheek and then balled her hands. "Okay, that sounds good."

Kris beamed. "Actually, I said you were coming too. Sorry if I spoke out of turn."

"No, I will come. Hey, as I said before, another first. Tuesday it is."

Claire sipped her cooling drink and grimaced.

Kris chuckled and stood. "How about I make us another."

Claire grinned and stood as well. "Why don't we both do that."

They left the room.

Chapter Twenty

Buddy, the Baltimore oriole, languished on the bottom branch of the tree outside the cottage. He was preening his orange chest, and several feathers glided slowly to the ground, where they landed on a mess of russet fallen leaves. He hopped to another part of the branch and glanced around, then continued his grooming. His beak was making a fine comb. Then his head became still, and seconds later a similar bird with paler markings landed on the branch. His chirp of welcome must have impressed the other bird, as it hopped closer and within seconds began tugging at Buddy's head. To the untrained eye, it looked aggressive, but Buddy seemed to like it.

A commotion of moving foliage indicated that more intruders had arrived, and Buddy along with his friend flew to the top of the tree to safety.

Out of the relatively sparse undergrowth, Kris and Claire arrived for their daily toil at the cottage. Both women were upbeat and smiling.

"What's next on my docket, boss?" Claire asked as she looked up at the tree before them.

Kris pursed her lips and then grinned. "We should start on the shutters now, I think. I fixed the last one on Saturday and sanded them down."

"You sanded them down? When? I don't remember." Claire's face registered her surprise.

"That's because I did them, well most of them, when you left me to my own devices the other day. I can assure you that I have three more for you to tackle, and I want them done by lunch. No dallying." Kris winked.

"Hmm, I'm going to have take care not to leave you on your own, or Grandmother will think I've been no help while I've been here." She rummaged in her pocket.

"Never a time waster, Claire. Right, I'll leave you to it." Kris mounted the steps to the deck.

"What? What do you mean? I thought you said you wanted me to—"

Kris laughed, and then pointed to the tree. "I think your friend will be waiting for his treat."

Claire's eyes widened, and she looked at the now-crumbled oat cookie in her hand. She shrugged, holding out her palm. "He has a name: Buddy. How did you know about him?"

Kris turned. "You are a very special person, Claire. I just knew. Don't forget you have work to do," she said gently as she unlocked the door and entered the cottage.

"I'm a special person." Claire frowned as she neared the trunk of the tree. Kris was perplexing, maddening even, but…. Buddy's irritated chirrup drew her out of her reflections.

"Buddy, sorry I didn't come yesterday, but occasionally I get a day off. Here you go." She threw the crumbles to the ground, and the bird immediately flew down and began vacuuming up the feast.

Then as she was about to turn away, he squawked loudly. That wasn't normal. Frowning, she looked at Buddy, who was standing there defiant. He reminded her of her dad when he disapproved of something with that crossed-arm, negative look.

"Okay, yeah, I know. I'm sorry about yesterday. You can't be starving though, right? You live by the darned sea. Plenty of fish in the sea, pardon the euphemism." As she spoke, she noticed a flicker of movement about three feet above her.

"Now I know why you are mad. Okay, Buddy, damn." She reached inside her pocket but found nothing. "Crap." A few moments later, she entered the cottage and smiled as she saw Kris pouring over color palettes.

"Kris, did you by any chance snatch a spare oat cookie at breakfast?"

Startled, Kris swung around and frowned. "No, I don't like them."

"Me either." Claire frowned.

Kris gazed at her for a few moments. "However, I do have—" She walked over to one of the newly renovated kitchen cupboards and withdrew what seemed to be a ball-shaped object. "Here you go. I think they will like this. It's a wild bird feeder ball. Saw it the other day and thought of…doesn't matter. Take it and hang it from the tree."

Claire, having had the seed ball thrust into her hand, just looked at it. "How? Oh forget it, you know everything." She grinned and headed out the door. Moments later, the ball was hanging from a branch that was too high up for most predators.

"There you go, Buddy, and you can thank…my friend for this. Share with your lady friend and enjoy." Claire, with a satisfied expression, reentered the cottage. Sneaking a quick glance over her shoulder, she was delighted to see Buddy swinging from the ball.

†

The sage-green shutters totally made the renovation of the outside. They'd whitewashed the outer boards, at least the ones on the lower half of the building. They mutually agreed a contractor would be best for doing the upper area. They cleaned the interior from floor to ceiling and varnished and repaired the kitchen cabinets—those that could be. Only two would require replacing.

All in all, in three weeks they had the place looking good. They only needed to complete the interior paintwork in neutral colors and stain the deck. With that, they'd restored the place's homey atmosphere.

"What do you think?"

The hairs on the back of Claire's neck stood up as Kris's tentative question broke her out of her musings on the work they'd done. "Love the color. It's a perfect match. Was that your idea or…?" She turned and burst out laughing.

Kris's eyes flared. "What? What?"

Claire crooked her finger, and Kris moved closer, so close they could touch. She gently traced a finger over several splatters of pastel green paint of Kris's face.

"That color suits you too."

Kris chuckled. "Darn, and I thought I'd gotten off scot-free. Fortunately, it's water based and will easily wash off."

146

"Excellent, because I'd hate to see your pretty face with red blotches where you'd scrubbed hard to remove the evidence." Claire winked.

Kris moved away with a jerk and pressed her body against the deck rail, her cheeks glowing.

Oops.

"Did you choose the color or did Grams?"

"Hmm, well, I did. Do you think I should have consulted with Melissa?" Kris's body went rigid.

"No, Grams will love this. It's her favorite color. Well, green anyway, and shades of it must be a plus. Right? You did great. They look wonderful." Claire stepped over to the rail and stood next to Kris.

"Thank you. I toyed with sand as they were originally, but I thought a fresh start needed a fresh outlook."

"No. It's perfect, like I said."

Soft footfalls came up the stairs and they both turned to see Shirley arrive with the picnic basket.

Claire watched Shirley's facial expression change from neutral to entranced. Her smile softly curved, and her eyes took on a glow. As she neared them, Claire stepped forward. "What do you think, Shirley? The color works, doesn't it?"

Shirley hugged the basket closer to her body and she beamed. "It's exactly how I always wanted it. Ricky and I talked of changing the color to this." Tears welled in her eyes.

Claire felt helpless at the show of emotion. *What the hell? It's only a color change.*

"I'm glad you like it. I noticed you loved greens, and you said this place had many happy memories," Kris stated and stepped down and took the picnic basket from Shirley.

Claire bit her inner lip. *How does Kris know all these things?*

Shirley blinked back tears and nodded. "Ricky and I disagreed about many things in the beginning but found agreement in the color green. As strange as it sounds, it was the start of our relationship, that and the rain."

Kris smiled, and Claire watched the two women, comparing them as best she could. "Okay, I'm famished. Are you joining us, Shirley?"

Shirley shook her head. "No, I have…I need to do something. It's important." She turned away and gave Kris a teary smile before disappearing into the foliage.

"I think I upset her."

The anguish in Kris's voice galvanized Claire. "Hey, she loved it. You brought back memories for her, Kris. I think that should make you feel good."

"It doesn't. It really doesn't. She was crying. How can that be happy for her? Damn, I wish I'd chosen blue instead."

Claire sped down the steps to where Kris stood clutching the picnic basket and took it from her. Then she tilted Kris's chin up. "You know, from the first moment I met you, you have tried to be everything to everyone." Claire shook her head. "Don't you dare think that's a bad thing. It isn't. I wish there were more caring people out there. Maybe there are, but I have never met any. Granted, I lived a life that probably excluded that privilege."

"I'm just ordinary."

The whispered reply had Claire's heart racing. She wanted to drag Kris into a hug but wasn't sure she would take that well. "Hey, how about we have our lunch on the beach and enjoy the sea, surf, and the company?"

Kris grinned at the suggestion.

I was right. She is beautiful; she just doesn't believe it.

✝

The sea gently ebbed and flowed ten feet from where they had placed a blanket and the picnic basket. They had expected the beach to be deserted, and it was, save for the odd dark figure that appeared in the distance, either walking or running, sometimes with a tiny companion, obviously a dog. Right now, the scene couldn't get any more tranquil.

Kris opened the basket and removed the plates and glasses. Then she spied the mineral water and poured two glasses. She passed one to Claire, who smiled gratefully. Kris removed the sandwiches, salad bowl, and fruit, placing them on the blanket. Then she noticed two other items and giggled.

"What's so funny?"

"Claire, Shirley has left you a treat, or should I say one for your best buddy."

Claire frowned, and Kris held up the oatmeal cookie and they both burst out laughing.

"Does she have second sight too?"

"No"—Kris shrugged—"and I don't have second sight."

Claire didn't reply immediately, instead gazing around her at nature. "How beautiful it is sitting here on the sand and watching the sea that makes up seventy percent of the earth's surface. Don't you wish you were a mermaid and could swim in it all?"

Kris handed Claire her favorite sandwich and settled back on her haunches with her own. "Not me, a mermaid at least. I'm not much of a swimmer. You know, if I could do anything at all, I'd love to live in the cottage with Knight, my cat, and enjoy both realms."

"You wouldn't consider more company?" Claire pressed a finger to her own chest.

Kris grinned. "Maybe, though they would have to be like-minded. Are you?"

"Sure."

"How do I know this for sure?"

Claire leaned in and gazed into Kris's eyes, and Kris's body tensed with anticipation. Then she felt a finger tenderly run down her nose, followed by a gentle chuckle, and Claire moved away to prop herself up on the blanket.

"You'll have to test me, I guess."

Kris's heart beat double-time as she pondered that prospect. "I don't think you'd enjoy spending the rest of your life here quietly by the sea. You're a city girl."

Claire munched on her sandwich and waved it around, only speaking once she'd swallowed. "You know, if you'd said that to me two years ago, I'd have agreed. But now, having been here and getting to know people properly, it changes your perspective."

"Got to agree on that. It does change things. I'd love to live here, but realistically I don't have the means and I doubt there are many jobs in town that would match up with my skill set." Kris sat upright, selected a shiny, red apple, and heard the delightful crunch as her teeth sank into the flesh. Juices overflowed.

Claire grinned and then threw her a napkin. "Kinda juicy, huh?"

Kris laughed as she mopped away the juice. "Yep, kinda."

Several gulls must have detected they were eating and made a pack about three yards from their position, squawking madly.

"Not having my lunch, fellas, and I'm not giving you Buddy's either." Claire jutted out her chin defiantly as she stared at the birds.

The gulls didn't seem to be intimidated, as one or two moved closer, obviously on a fact-finding mission.

"Gulls are notoriously greedy and can be quite nasty too. I fed one twice a day at my apartment, and then one day it nearly took my finger off. Needless to say, I never got that close again." Kris peered down at the finger in question. "Must have looked like a delectable morsel." She wriggled it.

Claire laughed, then her face took on a serious look. Kris had seen it before—it meant she was concentrating.

"Which skillset?"

Kris frowned. "I'm sorry, what?"

"You mentioned the town probably didn't want your skillset. Which one?"

"I…well, I only have one. I'm a clerk at an insurance company, or was." Kris drank from her glass and then replaced it on top of the basket.

"That was in the past. There must be insurance companies here. I was thinking of the renovations you've carried out. Don't you think you could have opportunities to do that? I do," Claire declared.

The squawk of a gull close to her left ear had Kris turning to swat it away.

Claire leaned back and nestled on her side. "You could be the only female renovator in the area. What do you think of that?"

"Claire, don't be silly. I don't have qualifications. When people spend good money, they expect the best."

"You think because you don't have a diploma you won't give it your best. Never going to happen."

Kris was lost for words. Why did Claire have so much faith in her? They hadn't known each other long enough for her to make those kinds of judgments. *Then again, how long does it take to know someone? A day, a week, a year?*

Claire shredded the sandwich she hated but which Shirley had religiously made for her and tossed some of it to the gulls. Unfortunately, with her weak arm it landed in Kris's lap.

The commotion the gulls made along with her own noisy response, as two of them virtually landed on her lap to take the food, was something to see.

She turned to Claire, who was looking remarkably innocent. *Hmm.* "Well, one thing I know for sure, your aim definitely needs work. Give it to me."

Seconds later, the shredded remainder of the sandwich was in Kris's hand. She shook her head, then turned back to the gulls and tossed the morsels into the pack. The scuffles and pandemonium that broke out were loud but entertaining.

Ten minutes later, they collected the debris and picked up the blanket. "This was a good idea, Claire. Thank you."

"You're welcome, and it was rather nice, even if our unwanted friends need to tone down their conversations."

Both women laughed.

"Come on, let's go and finish the final shutters. We'll have them done by suppertime."

"Slave driver," Claire muttered.

Kris nodded. "Absolutely, Rich Girl. Can't have you slacking."

The Promise

They amicably trudged their way back to the cottage.

Chapter Twenty-one

Curiosity Bar had the perfect location in Chartres. It was to the left of the entrance of the walkway to the largest wharf and within fifty yards of the main street. The building itself resembled the timber houses all around it, although it didn't look as old—maybe late nineteenth century. Curiosity was a good name for it as lobster pots adorned one wall that faced the boat sheds, and nets and fishing paraphernalia hung on the main frontage. Identifying everything could take hours. The wall facing the wharf had a mural of a fishing boat struggling against lashing waves. The blurry image of a sea creature, the details of which the artist left to the viewer's imagination, chased the boat. The painting was cleverly done with vibrant colors on a whitewashed wall.

The lights inside the building were warm and incandescent. Rain greeted them when they parked the car.

"You'd better text your friend to say we'll meet her inside," Claire said as they walked as fast as possible to the back entrance of the building. She gallantly held the door for

Kris, and a warm feeling washed over her at Kris's grateful smile.

"I'll call her. We are half an hour early." Kris pulled out her phone.

Claire moved away as Kris talked to her friend. Glancing around, she noted they were in a small corridor leading to the toilet facilities as the signage indicated. Another door indicated *Staff Only*, and another led to the kitchen.

Several giggling young women jostled past them, heading for the ladies' room, their clothes showing off far more than perhaps they should.

Oh crap. When did I become my mother? Claire watched them enter the bathroom. *In another lifetime.* Then she glanced at Kris, who was placing her phone back in her pocket. *In this lifetime.*

"Hey, everything okay? You look miles away."

"Sorry, I'm good. What do you want to drink?" Claire moved ahead and began to open the door in front of them.

Kris chuckled. "Have you been here before? You seem to know your way around."

Claire glanced at Kris, who gave her a quizzical look. *Do I lie about my previous visit, and why haven't I mentioned before now that I was here with Racheal? Damn the complications of omission. I'll explain later.* Claire pointed to the Main Bar sign on the door.

Kris rolled her eyes. "Silly me."

Claire grinned as they headed inside. The bar wasn't as busy as it was last Saturday; in fact it was pleasant. Sure, there were people milling around, but the room wasn't stifling. In the far corner of the bar, a small stage was set up.

I don't remember that from the last time. Must be for the quiz.

"Tonic water for me, please." Kris said.

Claire frowned. *Oh right, she's driving.* "Absolutely. Shall we find a table?" Claire turned to find out why she didn't reply. Kris's jaw had dropped and her eyes were like saucers. "Hey, are you catching flies? What gives?"

"Claire, look, isn't it wonderful?"

Claire glanced around and looked the bar over. *Well thought out, I accept that, but what is Kris so enamored by?* She chuckled. "At what? It's a bar."

"It's all copper and sofas, and look at that center table. It even has its own heating source," Kris whispered.

Claire looked in the direction she pointed. An oversized, round table with six comfortable-looking chairs. A copper funnel vent above the table obviously to take away the fumes of the coals in the triple-ring metal casing in the middle of the table.

"Can we sit there?"

Claire felt sure that someone must have reserved the area, but Kris's plea didn't fall on deaf ears. *Damn, this is going to be a first for me, actually not hiding in the shadows since the accident.* A hand settled on hers, and all of her nervous worries dissipated.

"That would be selfish. We only have three on our team. There's a table near the door that seats four," Kris said.

Claire was relieved, but as she looked at the next destination, she mentally shook her head.

"Not going to happen."

"What?"

Claire smacked a hand to her forehead. "Sorry, Kris, I'm more inclined to sit with the fire, not next to the entrance where it will be freezing. How does that booth look?"

Kris grinned as Claire indicated with a finger. "Great, want me to order?"

Before Claire could say anything, the blonde server from Saturday sidled up to her.

"Hey, I can help you with the order. Where are you sitting?"

Kris smiled at the woman and gave her their order, and Claire forthrightly said, "The booth over there." She pointed to the closest vacant one.

The server grinned. "Great. Are you eating tonight?"

For a split second, Claire thought she was referring to last Saturday evening. "Not at this time. We are waiting for a friend, then we might have a snack or something."

The server grinned. "Join the quiz tonight and the snacks are on the house." She sashayed away.

"Well that makes it all worthwhile, right? Free food." Kris chuckled.

Claire nodded as they took a seat. She idly picked up the plastic holder that displayed a list of snacks on one side and wine choices on the other. Then she discreetly glanced at Kris and smiled. Her brown hair hung like a curtain against her face and reached her shoulders. Most of the time she didn't notice the length, as Kris tied it up when they worked. It wasn't thick, quite the opposite, and didn't hold the luster Racheal's always did. Of course, Racheal spent a fortune on hair products and hairdressers.

I know Kris can't and probably doesn't have the inclination. In the semidarkness the booth afforded them, Kris's nose didn't look as sharp. In fact, it fitted her face perfectly.

Kris's phone pinged, and she took it out and looked at the screen. She frowned before pressing a button on the phone and dragging it to her ear. Claire continued to stare for a few seconds as Kris answered the call. It was her new friend, Jess.

Hmm, Jess. What will I make of you, I wonder? Shortly I'm going to find out.

Kris began to stand, disconnected the call, and glanced at Claire.

"Is she here?"

"Yes, I'll just go outside and bring her to the table."

"She can't do that on her own? It's not exactly busy in here yet."

Kris's eyebrows furrowed, and Claire threw up her hands. "Go, I'm looking forward to meeting her."

Kris looked like she was about to speak before shaking her head and leaving.

Well, that was interesting. It was a perfectly reasonable question. Gone are the days women looked odd arriving at a bar on their own. The door swung open and Kris left just as the server from Saturday night arrived with their drinks.

"Here you go, enjoy."

Claire looked up into the smiling face. "Do you have a name?"

The woman laughed and pointed to the badge positioned over her right breast.

"Well, Summer, it's a beautiful name and suits you. I guess my eyesight needs checking, because I didn't notice it on Saturday either."

Summer chuckled and leaned against the side of the booth with the tray nestled against her belly. "It's the ambiance the owner went for… 'subtle dark,' she calls it."

"What do you call it?" Claire grinned.

"'Too damn dark.' You never see a customer's face properly, and I like to know who I'm serving. I've found

over the years in this job that you learn a lot by expressions."
Summer stared at Claire, her eyes unflinching.

Claire shifted in her seat and gave Summer an intense
stare right back. "You can certainly see why I like this type
of light."

"Sure can, darling, but I've seen a lot worse. Not sure
what happened to you, but some of the folks around here
have had harpoon injuries where it tore off most of their face.
Trust me, you don't look out of place to the regulars here,
only to the tourists."

Summer looked at the entrance as the door opened.
"Got to go, customers."

For a few seconds, Claire didn't register that the
newcomers were Kris and her friend.

"Whoa, Jess is here. I simply love that woman. If
only…," Summer drifted off.

Claire was semi-euphoric over Summer's words
about her not being out of place and barely heard the woman
speak. Then Kris arrived with her friend.

"Jess, this is Claire," she said.

Claire twisted her lips into a half smile as Jess's hand
thrust forward and almost punched her nose.

What the hell!

She grabbed the hand and shook it. "Good to meet
you, Jess. I've heard…some things about you."

Jess softly chuckled. "I've heard about you too, but
not from Kris. Your family is well known here."

Claire was distracted when she noticed Kris was
holding Jess's arm. Her stomach did a giant flip. "Yeah,
family. You can't change that, but thankfully you can change
friends." *Stupid comment. What the hell are you saying?*

Kris's expression was definitely not jovial.

"I heard good things about your family, particularly Melissa. She's a lovely woman."

"Yeah, Grams is a nice woman. Are you sitting, or loitering with intent?"

Kris frowned at her again. "Jess, this is a booth; there is a step—" Kris looked at the step up they had taken to get into the booth "—about six inches high."

"Got it, Kris. Thank you." Jess smiled, and with Kris still holding on they mounted the elevated platform and settled onto the seat.

Claire felt that she was a third wheel, then all the pieces came together as she saw a cane. Jess was blind. *Why the hell didn't Kris say something? Damn, I feel terrible now.* "Kris tells me you are a wonderful crooner. I'll have to make a point of seeing one of your sessions."

Jess turned her head to face Claire, and Claire swore the woman saw right through her, and she shuffled in her seat. "Everyone who pays the toll is welcome. I'm average or I'd have been snapped right up."

Claire heard an edge to the words that she couldn't fathom as Kris slowly shook her head. *Okay, this is definitely going to be an interesting evening.*

"Jess has a great voice. You'll love it, Claire."

Claire smiled slowly at Kris. Her enthusiasm was hard to combat, and Claire simply didn't want to. "Before we leave for the city we must do that."

"Yes, we must." Kris smiled.

Summer arrived at the table. "What can I get you, Jess?"

"Summer, my favorite server. If you don't know Summer, and you probably don't, she's my number one fan. A great buddy too."

Claire watched Jess as she spoke, giving Summer a genuine "happy to see you" look. It wasn't as gushing as Summer's expression was, and that made her wonder if a sexual history existed between them.

"I'll have a low-carb beer, thanks."

"Put it on the tab," Claire said, and Summer winked at her as she left.

Then silence descended, and Claire wasn't sure why. She hated not sitting next to Kris. Now Blind Girl had the privilege. *Damn, that was harsh, but true.*

"So tell me, Claire, when you go back to New York, what will you do?"

Claire blinked several times at the question, the upmost answer screaming at her, *"I don't want to return to New York, I want to stay here."* "Oh this and that, rich parents and all."

This time, Kris gave her a look that would have withered even the strongest. "Don't be flippant, Claire. You are better than that."

Claire sucked in a deep breath and then looked around. "When do the snacks arrive?"

†

"Last question tonight. When was the Metropolitan Opera House opened?"

A general groan escaped from the vast majority of the five teams at the quiz.

"Piece of cake, we have a native in the house." Jess giggled.

"Claire, what's the answer? Do you know it?"

"How the heck would I know that? Opera isn't my scene. Let me think." Claire scratched the back of her hand.

161

"I figure it has to be mid-1890s," Jess confidently responded.

Claire frowned. "I think it might be earlier. Not sure though, sorry."

"For a bonus point, what was its nickname?" the quiz mistress asked.

"The Old Met." Kris smirked.

"How do you know that?" Claire and Jess asked in unison.

"Hey, I know some things, just not much. I might be wrong too." Kris giggled.

Claire raised an eyebrow and slowly shook her head. Kris was having a great time; she knew that because she was so relaxed. When they had first met, she was all formal. *But once you get through to her, wow what a change.* Jess was nice too. *Damn, it would have been so much better if she had been a heel.*

"So, Claire, what shall we put down? Eighteen ninety or 1895, what do you think?"

Claire sighed. "Hmm, do you mind if I say 1880?"

Summer arrived at the booth. "Any more drinks, ladies?"

Jess answered, "Sweet Summer, we need help. We have three options but can't make up our minds. Eighteen eighty, 1890, or 1895. Please, as devil's advocate, just choose."

Summer grinned. "Only if you will play one song for us tonight before you go."

Claire watched the interchange, sure Summer wanted more than a song from Jess.

"Got it." Jess clutched Kris's arm, and Claire's heart contracted.

"Yeah! Go for 1880 plus three. I want to hear 'Always on My Mind.'" Summer then moved to the booth three tables down.

✝

Kris laughed as they entered the parking lot.

"Can you believe it, Claire? We won. Jess said she's never been on a winning team, and it was only by two points. She was so excited, and to be honest, so am I."

"I think Summer's answer and yours on the last question were the killer blows." Claire chuckled.

"Oh and don't forget you helped. You said it was 1880. Pretty darn close if you ask me. All in all, a team effort, and Jess had to sing. Jess can use the prize though, as we won't be here."

"Yeah, fifty bucks of free beer. Probably keep her in drinks for a year. She didn't appear to drink much. And you were right."

Kris pressed the key fob, and the headlights on Shirley's car winked a couple of times as she turned to Claire. "About what?"

"She has a great voice. In fact, she's a great girl. Her story makes me feel terrible. At least her disability didn't come from stupidity." Claire walked toward the passenger door and jerked it open.

Kris watched before she entered the car. After placing the key in the ignition, she didn't immediately start the engine.

"We're not going home?"

Kris gripped the steering wheel and sighed. "Why do you constantly put yourself down, Claire? You were in an accident, and yes, according to you, it was your fault, but you

163

have to get over that and forgive yourself. You can't have a fulfilling life if you don't."

Claire's lips thinned. "When did you become a shrink? I had enough of them at home, including my parents' constant nagging."

The harshness of her tone sounded doubly loud in the confines of the car. Kris turned on the ignition and began to pull away from the parking spot. "I'm not. I was talking to you as a friend. I think we are friends now, and no matter how you take what I said, it's still true." She turned onto the main street and headed in the direction leading out of town.

Claire remained silent the rest of the journey, her eyes fixed on the windshield. When they arrived at Seasons, she didn't even say good night. Instead, she grunted something unintelligible and got out of the car.

Kris didn't move as she watched Claire enter the house.

"Wow, how do you communicate with someone like that? Claire is just unfathomable at times. I wish she'd let me in properly and not just on the surface. Darn these rich people who spoil their kids." She climbed out of the vehicle, locked it, and headed to the door. Her phone pinged. Smiling, she read that Jess had arrived home safe.

"I should be grateful Jess isn't so volatile, and she has more reason. How on earth does life become so twisted?"

The front door swung open, and Claire stood there, her face a blank mask.

Tentatively Kris smiled. "Hey, I thought you'd gone to bed."

"I was going to say sorry for my attitude during the drive back."

"Oh, there was no need. We were having a friendly conversation and silence is good too between friends. Right?"

Claire's expression didn't soften. "Perhaps. I'll see you at breakfast tomorrow." She turned away, then swung back. "Thanks for this evening. I enjoyed it."

"So did I." Kris walked up the steps, but Claire had gone. She shook her head and locked the door behind her before heading to bed. Yes, *frustrating* was the best word for Claire.

Chapter Twenty-two

She had smudges everywhere. The paint roller had decided to be a law unto itself and sprayed her with as much paint as she'd applied to the kitchen wall. Going at it one-handed had been tough, but she hadn't given in. It was slow work, sure, but she wasn't a quitter. Especially as Kris had painted three quarters of the area and it looked perfect. What couldn't her friend do when it came to this renovation business? Kris had been about to start the final wall when Claire had volunteered.

In hindsight it was a stupid offer. Most probably the wall will need another coat. She glanced at the patches and even some parts that had no paint at all. Hand on hip, she compared her workmanship with Kris's. There was no contest. "Damn she's good."

Claire walked over to Kris's pride and joy, the range. Admittedly, it looked great all polished up, but Kris needed to get a life if she thought this stove was the best thing in the world. Her left hand traced over the black switches that controlled the burners.

"She said it worked. Maybe I should try it out and see if this is something I can do." Several minutes later, dragging a hand through her hair for the fifth time, she gave up.

"How the hell does it ignite?" Her instinct was to kick the brute, but instead she turned away and looked at the clock they'd placed on the kitchen table. An ornate wall clock still resided on the wall. Kris had painstakingly cleaned it, but it hadn't worked. *No simply changing batteries for that monster.* It was made of metal with the signs of the zodiac decorating the border. In itself, it was nothing particularly exciting, but the signs were very intricate. Kris loved it, as she seemed to do most things here.

"Damn, I wish I could do something that would help her stay. She deserves this."

The door opened, and the person on her mind slipped through it.

"Hey, Claire, that looks great. I think your grandmother is going to be delighted by the change in this place. I got Stanley Masters, the owner of Chartres Painting Company, to agree to paint the top part of the exterior early next week and at a great price." Kris was grinning widely as she placed a small box on the kitchen table.

"All that sounds good, but what's in the box?"

Kris laughed. "The mystery gets you every time. I must remember that."

Claire smiled. *Yeah, you must. Damn, what am I saying? In ten days, we will go our separate ways.* "Predictable, right?"

"Never." Kris smiled and opened the box. "I couldn't come back without your favorite, could I?"

"I love you and it's just what I needed. That painting really took it out of me." Claire didn't realize what she'd said until she saw Kris's troubled expression. "Well, I know you

167

don't take me loving anyone seriously, right? You read the tabloids."

"Why?"

Claire frowned as she neared the prize of the wonderful dessert in front of her. "Why what? I just told you."

Kris moved to within inches of her and shook her head. "I'm so sorry. If only you said...." Tears trailed down her cheeks.

Claire stared at her in confusion. *What the hell is going on?* "Said what?"

Kris scrunched up her face and turned away.

Claire caught her arm and they faced each other. "What?"

"I'm so sorry, Claire, I didn't realize this would hurt you. Can you forgive me?"

Claire didn't know what was going on. "You never hurt me, Kris. How could you? You are my friend...right?"

"I need some space." Kris rushed out of the cottage.

Standing in the empty room awash with the smell of fresh paint and covered furniture, Claire didn't know what just happened. Whatever it was, Kris was upset. Frowning, she followed in the direction Kris had gone or at least she hoped she had. Her friend Buddy hadn't been any help, for he'd just sidled up to his new girl and ignored her request for assistance.

The path to the house maybe, or, *Yeah, the beach.* She suspected Kris would go there. Less chance anyone would see her if she were upset.

The path down to the beach was relatively steep but safe enough she'd traversed it several times in the last three weeks. *Damn, I feel like I've been here for years.* She passed a cursory hand through her hair and felt a couple of areas where paint had congealed.

Then she saw Kris standing at the edge of the incoming tide. *She must run fast to have gotten here already.* Negotiating a couple of branches that had twisted together on the shore, she walked slowly up to Kris, whose body appeared stiff as she stared out to sea. A few moments later, Claire stood next to her and looked out to the horizon. They remained that way for a couple of minutes.

"You know, this must be one of the most peaceful pastimes in the world. Don't you think?"

Kris sniffled and nodded, her arms folded tightly across her chest.

"Have you ever thrown pebbles into the sea? I think it's called skimming? I haven't done it for years. In fact, I can say it's about the only time my father spent with me when I was a kid. He must have liked to do it or we wouldn't have done it. My father was all about him." The instant memory gave Claire a warm glow, even if it was about her father.

Kris half turned and gave her a weak smile, her face red and blotchy from tears. "My dad too, when I was a kid."

"Yeah." Claire grinned. "We have something else in common. Want to try to beat me? I was pretty darn good at it back then. At least I think I was." She bent and selected a couple of inch-long, gray stones that populated this area of the beach, then held one out for Kris.

This time, Kris gave her a full-on smile and took the stone. "Thank you."

"Do we toss a coin for who goes first? For the record I don't have any coinage, but we can improvise." Claire looked around for something suitable. A hand on her injured arm had her glance at it. The touch was so gentle and it made her feel wonderful. *I've taken in too many paint fumes.*

"I'll let you go first. I have to say my success rate wasn't exactly Olympic medal proportions."

Claire laughed. "I never realized they had added this as an event. Hell, I might have been a champion." She winked and tossed the stone into the air and caught it. "Okay, let's see if I still have the magic."

She flicked the stone, and it traveled in the air for ten feet, then simply plopped into the sea. "Oh come on!" Claire held out her hands.

Kris chuckled. "Have you been taking lessons from me? That happens to me every time."

Claire's eyes crinkled as she grinned. "Right, Olympic Girl, your turn."

Kris looked at the flat stone in her palm, then rolled it over twice and suddenly threw it. It skimmed the water for all of a foot, and then disappeared. "Yeah," she shrieked, her grin almost bursting her face apart.

Claire watched the happiness erupt, and her heart raced at the reaction. How could something so simple change the whole demeanor of a person? And it had, big-time.

"Sorry, I overreacted."

Claire winked. "Guess we both are apt to do that, then. I'm sorry for last night. I was a jerk." She picked up another couple of stones and handed one to Kris. "Will you tell me what upset you, please?"

Kris sighed heavily and then nodded. "On one condition. You do the same about last night."

Claire stroked her, chin contemplating the request. "Sure."

Kris threw her stone, and it sank. "I forget that you are injured, Claire, and that perhaps I haven't taken that into

170

account. Physically I've made too many demands on you."
She stepped back from the shore as the water almost lapped
her shoes.

Claire gripped her stone hard, then threw it. It
skimmed the crest of several waves before it disappeared.

"Wow, your dad must have been proud."

Claire frowned. "Not really. He always had to win."
She turned to Kris and gazed at her. "I've seen five different
shrinks since the accident, not to mention my parents'
amateur attempts. I don't take it well—strangers telling me
what's wrong with me."

Kris stiffened. "Your parents aren't strangers. I'm
sorry I offended you. I didn't mean to." Kris took her hand.

Claire looked down at their hands and squeezed
gently. "Oh yes they are. Don't you think the same about
yours? How long is it since you've seen them?" The hand in
hers stiffened, but she held on.

"Six years. I went to see them for their twenty-fifth
wedding anniversary."

"I hate parties. I had to go to so many it was a ritual.
Celebrations for winning big contracts always took
precedents over birthdays and anniversaries as far as my
parents were concerned. They took second and even third
place in my father's eyes to a golf tournament. Sorry, how
did it go?"

Kris's lips pulled into a tight line. Right now, Claire
really hated Kris's parents even more than she did her own,
and that was a hard feat to accomplish.

"They thanked me for the gift. Told me the party was
for old friends and it wouldn't suit me. I still can't get over
that. How can you do that to someone you love? Unless they
never loved you."

Claire dragged Kris into her arms and hugged her close. "They loved you, Kris. They did, and probably still do. Sometimes our sexuality doesn't always make sense to people. We keep trying, and look at the strides we've made. We can get married—well, in lots of countries and here in the States. Maybe by today they have educated themselves better." Claire leaned her chin against the top of Kris's head and felt a shudder go through Kris.

Kris pulled away from the embrace and looked into her eyes. "Thank you."

Claire smiled slowly. "Anytime. For the record, you are no stranger to me. You can say what you want, and I'll probably listen."

Her eyes captured Kris's, and Kris moved closer and captured her lips in a kiss.

She kissed me.

Oh no, what have I done?

Chapter Twenty-three

Shirley sang out of tune to the Taylor Swift song "Shake It Off," her body moving with the rhythm as she flipped a cheese omelet.

"Well, Shirley, I never suspected you were a Taylor fan." Claire laughed as she took her seat at the kitchen table.

Shirley swung around with a faint smile. "I listen to the radio. I'm not dead yet." She glanced at the finished omelet. "We are having omelets with a side of bacon and homemade bread tonight. I'm sorry it's not sophisticated, but the range has acted up recently. I'm waiting for the company to send someone out."

"No problem with me. You spoil me with the dishes you've prepared since I've been here. I'm going to have to go to the gym when I get back to the city."

"Oh don't be silly. You could always eat a horse and never put an inch of fat on as a girl." Shirley put the completed dish onto a warming plate. "Kris is late. Was there a problem at the cottage?"

"Not that I know of."

Claire's words had an edge, and Shirley glanced at Claire who looked…embarrassed. "Hmm…."

The door opened and Kris entered. She gave Shirley a tight smile and avoided looking at Claire. *Interesting.*

"Oh, I thought you'd decided to skip dinner. It's an omelet. Will you help me with the plates?"

"Of course." Kris walked over, took the first plate, and placed it on the table.

"Smells great," Claire said. Kris froze and then seconds later carried on with her tasks.

Eventually they all sat at the table.

"Where is your omelet?"

"Claire, have you forgotten I'm allergic to eggs?" Shirley took a hunk of fresh bread and smothered it in butter.

"So why are we having omelets?" Claire asked.

Shirley looked at Kris, who was staring at a blank wall. *Something has happened.*

"Thank you, Shirley. I love omelets, especially the cheese ones."

"You are welcome, Kris. You both make it easy for me to cook for you. Any plans for the rest of the evening?"

"No," they replied in unison.

They both looked at each other before turning away just as suddenly. Kris's cheeks were stained red. "Enjoy the night. I'm going to meet my nephew and his wife tonight, so I'm afraid it's just the two of you. I'd recommend watching *An Affair to Remember*, but it's up to you."

Claire shuffled her omelet around the plate and sighed.

Kris picked up her water and drank it as if she were in a desert.

"It's really very good, you know. In color, not a black-and-white oldie. I have to admit Cary Grant was very handsome and Deborah Kerr an understated beauty." Shirley popped a forkful of bacon in her mouth. "Of course there is always *Pride and Prejudice*. My, that's a wonderful tale. I have the original with Greer Garson." Shirley laughed when the two groaned. "However, I also have the TV series. It's only six episodes, and you can watch it over two nights, I suspect. Colin Firth was such a handsome Mr. Darcy, and that fountain scene…my, he sent my temperature soaring."

Claire cleared her throat. "Thanks, but I think I'll have an early night. We worked hard today."

"Yes, yes, we did. That's a good idea," Kris jumped in enthusiastically.

Shirley glanced from one to the other and shook her head. "Hmm. Oh well, if you change your minds, they would be my recommendations."

The meal was relatively silent, and Shirley eventually gave up trying to make small talk. After the dishes were disposed of, Claire wished them both a good night and left the kitchen rapidly.

Shirley turned to Kris. "Anything going on that I might need to know about? You were both quiet at dinner."

Kris, appearing focused on the kitchen door, didn't reply.

"I don't think she's coming back." Shirley wiped her hands and then touched Kris's shoulder. "Is there anything I can help you with? I'm a good listener."

Kris frowned and shook her head slowly. "No, it's something we need to work out, and we will. We are friends. Friends always work things out," she muttered. Then with a shrug, she wished Shirley good night and said she hoped she enjoyed her evening.

"Yes they do, my dear. Sleep well."

Kris tentatively smiled and then left the room.

Shirley stood for a moment, musing over what could have happened and then decided that was fruitless. She would find out when the right time was for her to do so…if there ever was one.

†

Claire rummaged in the DVD cabinet and then held aloft what she was looking for. "Yes." Moving away from the furniture, she opened up the case, selected DVD one, and slipped it into the player.

Then she scrambled up and settled on the sofa, her legs stretched out. Pressing Play on the remote, she heard the snick of the door opening and looked across the room. Kris stood in the doorway.

"I'm sorry, I didn't know you were here."

Claire struggled to sit upright. "No, no, it's fine. Look, did you want the TV or…?" She didn't know what else to say.

Kris seemed unsure how to answer as she shuffled from one foot to the other.

"Or I was about to watch a movie if you want to join me?" Claire pressed the Pause button. "So far only the trailer for the next blockbuster is playing."

"I don't really want to disturb you." Kris entered the room and the door gently swung shut behind her.

Claire bit her lip, wanting to laugh or at least smile. Kris's action was contradictory to the words. "It's not an oldie, if you wondered."

Kris gave a small smile. "Thank goodness, although *Jane Eyre* was a good movie. Wasn't it?"

"Yes, surprised me, really. I guess you decided like I did that it was too early to retire."

"Yep, my brain refuses to stop working, so I thought maybe an hour or so of TV or a movie would help." Kris walked toward the chair she always used and sat down.

The nervousness that had been part of Claire's reason for taking refuge in the media room dissipated. "Me too."

"Well, if you don't mind my company, then yes, I'd like to watch a movie."

Claire grinned. "I can't think of any better company. Though you might regret it when you know what I've chosen."

Kris chuckled, settled back in the chair, and pressed the lever for the recline feature. "Never, what is it?"

"*Toy Story*, the first one." Claire shrugged.

"Oh, Claire, I love that movie. I was ten when it came out. I saw it a zillion times."

Claire smiled and pressed Play, then selected the movie from the menu. "This was the first movie I ever bought with money I actually earned. Grams gave me enough to buy the DVD if I cleaned out the garage. Weird the silly things your memory dredges up, especially mine."

"Guess you must have done a good job. Oh, and you have crackers." Kris's eyes settled on the plate of cheese crackers. "Did you know I'd be coming?" The laughter that followed the statement warmed Claire's heart.

"No, but I always live in hope." She spoke softly and surprised herself when she caught Kris's tender expression. *It is going to work out, whatever that might be. We are friends, and friends work things out.*

Chapter Twenty-four

Anna Tremont stirred her coffee for several seconds. It was her favorite Cubano, and the barista here made a great one. She'd frequented the café for the better part of fifteen years and usually at the same time most days of the working week. For her, when a hot property needed sorting out it could be seven days a week.

Her thoughts were with Claire and her time away from home. What had possessed her mother to send Claire to Seasons of all places? Claire had vowed never to return there as a teenager. Yet she had submitted without any emotion. Perhaps fourteen years had been enough for Claire to forget the trauma at the time, or the accident had made her forget the event. The doctors had said some of her memories were lost and they would only know how many over time.

She glanced around. It was nine o'clock on a Monday night and the weather had turned nasty. Rain slashed the glass of the small picture window looking out onto the street, and the vast majority of the customers had left.

Carl was at his club. When wasn't he? She sighed heavily and sipped the coffee that always settled her emotions. Tonight her melancholy wasn't about her husband, it was about their only child. Claire might not be perfect, but she was theirs, and no matter how Carl wanted at times to forget that fact, it would never change.

The accident should have brought them closer. It hadn't, and they had drifted even further apart, if that were possible. Coming so close to losing a child should have refocused them on being a family again. But as soon as Carl had seen the police report, he had blamed Claire and said it was her own fault and she had to man up to it.

Damn, he didn't even get the gender right! Carl is such an ass. If it weren't for the debts they owed across the state, divorce would have been inevitable now. Except together they were financially stronger, or at least able through the help of her mother, to keep afloat and out of bankruptcy court. Mother would never forgive her taking that path.

Her phone buzzed, and she looked at the text message.

I'm staying at the club tonight.

Anna didn't move her gaze from the words on the screen. *What is this, the fourth time this week? Maybe if I say I'm staying out all night as often, he wouldn't do it so blatantly. Yeah, right.*

A discreet cough behind her had her swing her gaze to Adam the barista. She smiled and he grinned, his boyish expression reminding her he was old enough to be her son— well perhaps not quite. He must be around forty.

"Do you want to close early because of the weather? Sorry I'm keeping you." Anna began to stand, and then she felt a slim, strong hand gently push her back.

"No, please. I was wondering if you'd like to have another coffee." He hesitated, then shrugged. "With me. I've been trying out a couple of new recipes. I need a guinea pig and I know you love great coffee, Anna."

Anna blinked rapidly. Adam was always nice, but he'd never actually engaged her in any significant conversation before.

"Just another coffee, unless you need to be somewhere. I know it's getting late," Adam persisted and then sat opposite her, his lanky frame dwarfing the chair.

Anna looked at the text message again, then pressed the phone off and slipped it into her purse. "I have nowhere to go. Thank you, I'd like to try another coffee…with you."

He grinned back at her and stood. "Great, I'll be back."

He left to go behind the counter. She smiled, genuinely happy for the first time in a long time, and all because of a coffee. *How sad is my life?*

†

"So?"

Kris giggled. "You want me to go into town tomorrow and buy the next two movies. Claire, I might look foolish. Isn't this movie more associated with kids?"

"You have led a sheltered life." Claire winked. "No you wouldn't. Nobody cares what we buy just so long as we do."

Kris shook her head, stood, and indicated the empty plate. "Want more, or will a hot chocolate be enough?"

"Hot chocolate, oh, Kris, you are a marvel. No more food or I definitely won't sleep."

"Hmm, good call. Shall we watch something else for an hour? Maybe that *Pride and Prejudice* series? We can start it, and if we don't like it, at least we haven't invested hours watching it. I hate that, don't you? It's like a really bad book you keep reading in the hope it gets better but never does." Kris chuckled as she headed out the door.

Claire watched the door close and grinned. The movie had been as rewarding as when she had first seen it, and with Kris in the room with her, it had felt even better. The camaraderie they were developing amazed her with how it had taken over without permission or resistance.

She shuffled off the sofa, and by the time Kris returned with steaming mugs of hot chocolate, she had found the DVDs. Kris handed her the drink.

"Why don't you join me? I might need pinching to stay awake. I never was really good with period dramas."

Kris furrowed her brows, then smiled. "Sure." She sat next to Claire, picked up the remote, and pressed Play before retrieving her own drink and sitting back as the program began.

"It is a truth universally acknowledged, that a single man in possession of a good fortune, must be in want of a wife."

Claire laughed and whispered, "A single woman too, my friend."

†

Kris drew back the coverlet and smiled as she clambered into bed. Then she glanced at her Kindle on the bedside table and decided against a reading session. Besides, she had a lot to think about, and that would put her to sleep eventually. She hoped with good dreams.

Her thoughts drifted to the brief kiss she'd shared with Claire and their dual embarrassment afterward. They had both stood apart and apologized. Claire looked more shocked than she had been, if her startled expression was anything to judge by. The afternoon had been edgy, and neither had spoken much. Fortunately, they could be in different areas to work. Dinner hadn't faired any better, but later....

Her lips twisted into a smile as she remembered the closeness of the last hour sitting on the sofa together. Nothing had happened physically, but deep down she knew something dramatic had changed, and it was for the good.

She leaned across the nightstand and switched off the table lamp, sending the room into semidarkness, the full moon bringing a hazy light. She settled back in bed and sighed. *If only we had more time. In another week, I'll be back at my apartment and Claire will be in her luxury home. I doubt we will see each other again. No matter what we say about being friends, money moves in different circles and I don't possess any.*

Kris closed her eyes and allowing herself the fantasy that had Claire in her life forever.

†

Melissa studied her bridge hand, then after prompting by her partner across the table, she laid down the required cards. Her partner grinned and then proceeded to win the hand and the game.

"Excellent play, Melissa. You and I will have to play together again. Are you at the club this weekend?"

Melissa acknowledged the praise with a slight smile. "Perhaps, Angela. However, not this weekend. I'm going to my house at the beach. My granddaughter is expecting me."

"The one who had the accident? How is she doing? I know it was terrible and she's lucky to be alive." Angela stood, as did the others around the table, except for Melissa.

Most wished them a good night and left. Angela remained, resting her arms on the high-backed chair.

"Yes, it was. She's doing reasonably well under the circumstances. I'm trying to engage her in society again. She's helping to renovate the cottage there."

"Really? On her own? I thought she was disabled."

Melissa smarted at the other woman's tone. "Yes, really, and no, not on her own. The work needed requires two able people. There is a rather lovely young woman who is helping too."

"Sorry, didn't mean anything by it. Well, Dan volunteered to buy me champagne if I won tonight. Want to join us?" Angela pushed away from the chair and glanced in the direction of her husband, Dan Rowlands.

"No, thank you. I need to go home early tonight, things to do." Melissa stood and picked up her pocketbook.

"Another time, then. See you next week?"

"Yes, bye, Angela."

Angela disappeared into the throng near the bar. Her peroxide-blonde hair was never out of place, and her immaculate taste in wardrobe was always flattering. She was a nice woman but loved being the center of attention. Right now, a mass of people enveloped her as Dan shouted, "Champagne for my wife."

Melissa turned and headed for the cloakroom to collect her fawn cashmere three-quarter coat. She headed out of the building into the coolness of the night air. A taxi stopped outside, and she climbed in and told the driver her destination. He sped off before she had time to clip in her seat belt.

Fifteen minutes later, she was outside her apartment building, and the doorman greeted her with a wide smile.

"Lovely evening, Mrs. Jackson." He tipped his hat and opened the door for her.

"Certainly is, James." She entered the building and headed for the elevator, her footfalls silent as she crossed the hall on the deep pile woolen carpet.

"Good night, Mrs. Jackson."

"Night, James."

Moments later, she was heading to the penthouse floor and home. The door swished open, leading straight into her hallway.

The light flashing on the phone on the table had her look at the caller ID. *Anna. Hmm, what does she want, I wonder? Not more money, I hope.* She pressed Return Call and waited for an answer.

Chapter Twenty-five

Claire tapped Kris on the shoulder and chuckled when she spun around in mild shock.

"Wow, you scared me. I didn't even know you were here."

"Yeah, I guess I could be considered scary." Claire traced a finger over her scarred cheek.

"No, I didn't mean…." Kris looked aghast, and Claire took pity on her.

"I know you didn't, I was teasing you. So, did you get the DVDs?" Claire glanced at the shopping bag on the kitchen table and then tried to sidle around Kris to get a better look.

Kris placed a hand on her good arm and gently smiled. "Don't go peeking. There might be something there I don't want you to see."

Claire's heart somersaulted at the touch. She twisted slightly, took Kris's hand, and held it gently. Half expecting it to be withdrawn, she was pleased it wasn't. "A surprise? Perhaps for me?"

"You are silly. It could be, but then again, it could be for someone else."

Claire gave her an exaggerated pout.

"I'm not going to tell you…yet. How has the final painting of the window frames gone? Those at the back were the last on the lower floor." Kris chuckled. "Although, I can tell you were having a good time doing it."

"Yeah, and what makes you say that?" Claire furrowed her forehead and stared at Kris.

Kris lifted up a hand and traced a finger over the spots on Claire's face. "I suspect more of the paint is on you than the frames. A bit like yesterday, but I didn't want to say."

Claire laughed and at the same time wanted that moment to last forever. The gentleness and warmth she felt in Kris's touch amazed her. "Well, I guess I need more practice. I've never seen you with as much paint all over you. How do you do that?"

Kris's finger seemed glued to a spot over her left eyebrow. "To be honest, I don't know. I'm just not messy like you."

Claire laughed and reached her good hand up to tweak Kris's hair. As she did, they became very close, their faces almost touching. Closing her eyes, she bent her head and kissed Kris, and this time it wasn't brief. It was a long exploration of full lips.

When they broke for air, neither moved and they stared at each other.

"I'm not going to say I'm sorry this time," Claire brokenly admitted.

"Neither am I." Kris's voice was barely a whisper.

Claire's palm rested on Kris's right cheek, and she gently caressed the smooth skin. Then moved in and kissed her again. This time it was longer still and mouths opened to explore further. Kris's hands moved to the small of her back and began to trace the bottom of her spine. It sent electric impulses all over her body.

Breaking apart finally, they smiled at each other. Claire knew she must look goofy, but that's all she could do.

"I guess we need to do some more work, huh?"

Kris nodded.

Claire smiled. *I wonder what she's thinking.* "Pity lunch is over or we could have gone to the beach."

"Claire."

Claire sucked in a silent breath. *That didn't sound good.* She gazed at Kris, waiting for the shoe to drop.

"Tonight, can we talk after dinner?"

"Yeah, of course we need to talk. I was worried," she blurted out, unsure where this uncertainty was coming from.

"Worried why?" Kris closed the small gap between them and enclosed her in a hug.

"Oh, I thought you might have changed your mind. It's a woman's prerogative. Shall we go out to dinner tonight?"

"Won't Shirley have dinner organized? I don't want to upset her. She's always been so nice." Kris frowned.

"She's the help, we pay her; it won't matter to her one way or the other." Claire wished she'd kept her mouth shut when she saw the silent horror on Kris's face. "I didn't mean it like she's not important, but...." She wiped a hand across her face. "Oh, I'm making a mess of this. What do you say we go out tomorrow and I'll take you to that pretentious golf club? They say it has the best food in town."

Claire sent up a silent prayer that Kris would be happier. For a few seconds she wasn't sure.

"Thank you. But can we go somewhere other than the golf club, please?"

Claire leaned her forehead against Kris's.

"Anywhere you want to go if it makes you happy." Claire stole a quick kiss and then moved away. "Right. Work to do or the forewoman will get all antsy." She chuckled as Kris shook her head.

"Absolutely, Rich Girl." Kris winked, and Claire left the house in search of her painting gear. She was sure her feet had wings as she drifted to the back of Seasons to complete her task.

†

Kris puzzled over what to say to Shirley. Would she guess the dynamic between her and Claire had changed? She was pretty darn astute, yet at times, so cryptic with her explanations. Her hand rested on the door leading into Shirley's domain. She could hear the housekeeper singing off key. It was a bit harsh on the eardrums, but at the same time, cute.

What is it? Oh yeah, "Wildest Dreams." She chuckled. Who would have thought it from the older woman who appeared so prim and proper, even austere? Yet to her and Claire, she was lovely and supportive.

She opened the door and immediately Shirley stopped singing.

"Had a good day, dear?"

"Excellent, what about yourself?" Kris walked over to the counter separating her from the stove and preparation surfaces where Shirley was working.

"Have to say not too bad myself. I've made Claire's favorite dessert tonight, lemon meringue pie. It took me a while; started it this morning. Do you know how to make it?"

Shirley had such pride in her voice that Kris was glad Claire hadn't insisted they go out tonight.

"Do you have a favorite, Kris? One you love above all?"

Racking her brains for a true favorite, Kris shrugged. "I have to admit I have a sweet tooth, so I pretty much like everything."

Shirley shook her head and wiped her hands on her apron. "Nonsense, there is always one above the rest, and that goes for everything in life."

"I once went to a posh restaurant with my old boss for his fortieth anniversary, with his wife and the others in the company too, of course," Kris quickly explained. "They brought out something with a French name that I'm not sure I can remember. I know it started with an *M*." Shirley's eyes sparkled as she grinned. *Odd, I've never noticed that before.*

"Tell me what it looked and tasted like."

"*Divine* comes to mind."

"Yes, I'm sure." Shirley chuckled.

"Lots of puff pastry layers filled with cream. Oh just talking about it makes me crave another."

"Oh, that's a Napoleon, or its French name *mille-feuille*. Millie's does a great one, but for you I will attempt to make that on your last night." Shirley turned away.

Kris's heart dropped like a stone at the reminder of her imminent departure. Engrossed in her miserable thoughts, she didn't realize someone had entered the room until another voice joined the conversation.

"Hi, Shirley, smells great. In fact, I swear I can detect a subtle aroma of lemon."

Shirley giggled like a teenager as Claire went around the counter and pulled her into a slight hug. "Made my favorite, right?"

"Oh, I never could keep it from you."

Kris lifted her head slightly. A wave of satisfaction flowed through her that they had remained here for dinner tonight. It was made even more poignant as Claire winked at her and mouthed, "Thank you."

"Hey, what's for dinner really, other than lemon?"

Shirley shook her head as Claire released her. "Tonight we are having chicken schnitzel with green beans and roasted mixed capsicum. The lemon is for—"

"My fav lemon meringue pie. You'll love it, Kris."

Kris looked at the two women, and a feeling of peace and rightness settled over her. *This is where I'm supposed to be, with the right people at the right time. No one can take this from me. No, from us.* "Absolutely."

"Oh, Shirley, Kris and I are going out tomorrow for dinner. We have a date."

Kris was relieved, shocked, and amazed at the same time at Claire's words.

"About time. Though I'd have to admit that you beat me and Ricky by a week. Still, it was slow considering you have been together for three weeks at the cottage. Right, I need to finish dinner. Off with you. Claire, collect the glasses. Tonight in celebration, I'll have as my drink of choice a Chardonnay. It's a white wine."

Claire's mouth fell open at Shirley's reply and she had to sit down.

"But-but you don't drink." Claire held up her hands in surprise.

Shirley didn't turn around and continued to prepare the food. "Now who told you that, the tooth fairy?"

190

Kris laughed. "Well in that case you can replace my water with Chardonnay too. I hate to see a woman drink alone."

Claire's surprised expression made her laugh even more.

"I guess it's wine all around." Claire, shaking her head, left the room.

"You love her, don't you?" Kris quietly said.

Shirley's back stiffened but she didn't turn around. "She was born on the very day my Ricky was killed—ten years later, of course. I sometimes wonder if he had lived, what the family we might have had would have looked like."

Kris heard the tears in that statement. It was heart wrenching. "She loves you too."

"In her own way, yes, I'm sure she does. But then, her own way is selfish. You need to understand that."

Kris closed her eyes and balled her fists. "Do you think she can change?"

"Yes, always, for the right one."

The words were out of her mouth before she could prevent it. "Am I the right one?" Her heart almost stopped in anticipation.

"That's for you to decide."

Claire reentered the room.

"Hey, were you two talking about me? It went all quiet when I came in."

Kris smiled, walked the few yards that separated them, and whispered, "Yes, and it was all good." She dropped a kiss on Claire's cheek as they drew apart.

"Excellent. I love being the center of attention. Want a glass before we eat, girls?"

Kris laughed. "Absolutely. Shirley?"

Shirley turned briefly and grinned. "Of course. Tomorrow is now my day off."

✝

Claire opened the second bottle of wine, glanced at the label, and nodded approvingly. Washington State had superb wines. She smiled as Kris and Shirley discussed some French pastry that was damn hard to pronounce. "Milly fluff" or something along those lines. Carefully she refilled their glasses and settled back in her chair as she simply listened to the two women. Reflecting that she had never felt this content in her life, she knew the feeling was all down to Kris and Shirley. Thank God Kris had mentioned that Shirley would have dinner along with her favorite desert. The older woman would have been devastated.

Damn I'm selfish.

Her parents had brought her up to be, insisted that she was, particularly her mother. It hadn't felt odd to her until this moment. Now, as she gazed at the two women who weren't selfish at all, she wondered what type of person she would have been if things had been different. Briefly, she closed her eyes, and the image of her dad came to mind.

He's the most selfish son of a bitch I've ever encountered, and that includes me. His genes would have dictated she'd be like him for sure. How did you outrun family traits like that?

Kris looked in her direction and winked before raising her glass and smiling. She then took a sip and set it down on the table.

Dinner had been delicious. Then of course the best of all, for her at least, the lemon meringue pie. She liked it so much that she'd had two helpings. Her stomach protested, but every mouthful was a wonderful pleasure on her taste buds.

They'd toasted just about everything possible during dinner. The one that made the most impact on her had been Shirley's toast. *"May we always accept that there is a risk worth taking, and it will fulfil us for the rest of our lives."*

Hell of a statement. Maybe I'll check Google and see if it's a famous quote. She allowed her gaze to drift to Shirley. She wasn't very attractive, and from Shirley's own admission had never been.

Claire ran a hand through her hair and tried again to recall the name of the lover she'd had here who hadn't worked out. It could have been her unused sex drive that had made her imagine such a thing. Yet it seemed real. Dare she ask Shirley, who would know for sure?

"Are you going to speak to us or just sit there with a faraway look on your face?" Shirley said.

Claire quickly diverted her attention to the women at the table.

"Now with two lovely looking ladies in front of me, why do you think I'm not interested in you both?" Claire winked at Kris, who shook her head with an amused smile lingering on her lips.

"Lovely be damned. Around this table we all need help in that department. That's why I have my hair done every month. Works for me," Shirley declared.

Claire stared at Shirley in shock and was glad when she saw a similar expression on Kris's face. "Shirley, you must have had too much to drink. You never cuss. I'm amazed."

Shirley looked confused for a moment, and then she giggled and giggled. "I don't cuss."

Raising her eyebrow slightly, Claire nodded. "Okay. Now what I want to know is—" she glanced at Kris, who gave her an expectant look—"you said you met Ricky in the rain and at the cottage. Just how did that happen?"

"Oh, I've told you, surely."

"Nope. Kris?"

"Me either," Kris replied.

Shirley drew her shoulders up, and this time she was the one who had the so-called faraway look. "I told you I was a cook's assistant, right?"

"Yes," they replied in unison.

"Mrs. Shepard was a hard taskmistress and didn't want us young guns to mix with the outsiders. Except her husband, Ben, was the head gardener, so we were bound to mix eventually. I had been working at Seasons for a month before I actually met Ricky and we talked. It wasn't much of a conversation really." Shirley laughed. "I was asking him to bring over some baby carrots for the cook." She stopped talking, seemingly lost in her memories.

"Did you love him at first sight?" Kris asked quietly.

Claire glanced at Kris and took a sip of her wine.

"I was enamored, but love…no, not that first time." The room went quiet, then Shirley chuckled softly.

"The next day was a different story. Cook wanted onions this time and sent me to get them. I wasn't keen since it looked like it was going to pour. I went, and as I approached the cottage, the heavens opened. Ricky saw me and grabbed my hand." Shirley took a drink from her wineglass and settled it in front of her. "He took me under the eaves of the cottage porch. We talked for over an hour until the rain stopped. I took onions back to Seasons and a heart filled with love."

"Did he love you too at that time?" Kris asked the very question Claire wanted to.

"My Ricky was a ladies' man—at least that was what everyone said—but from that moment on he was mine. I was always expecting to hear of an infidelity to two. I'm not the most attractive person out there, as we said earlier. Calvin, Ricky's best friend, was about to go into the Army. He met us at a dance in town. He looked at us and said to Ricky, 'This is it. You'll be sorry if you ignore what's in front of you.' Of course, I felt embarrassed. Ricky shrugged and danced with several other women. Calvin danced with me those times. When it was the end of the night, things changed."

Kris stood, walked over to the faucet, and drew some water.

Claire considered her options. Normally she would have just waited, but not today. "Attraction helps us, but what made you decide Ricky was the one for you? It has to be more than that, and what happened during the last dance?"

Shirley smiled. "Right, girls, I'm going to have an early night. This wine is going to my head. Good night." She stood and wobbled for a moment and headed toward the kitchen door.

"Do we help her?" Kris whispered.

The door opened and closed before Claire could answer.

"I guess if we hear her falling down the stairs, sure."

"Claire!"

"She might not have made the stairs. When have you seen her drink this much?"

Claire frowned. "Never to the best of my recollection, but in anything there is always a first time."

Kris stood and headed for the door. "I'm going to check." She left. A minute later, she was back.

"And?"

Sheepishly Kris shrugged.

"She isn't at the bottom of the stairs, if that's what you mean."

Claire chuckled and motioned Kris to sit by her.

Kris shook her head and walked over to her. "Meeting people that are important to your life is strange, don't you think?"

Claire considered that for a few moments, and then placed her hand in Kris's. "No, I think it's wonderful. So now that she's gone to bed, do you want to kiss me properly?"

Chapter Twenty-six

Claire snuggled into Kris's shoulder and began to nuzzle her neck. The petite giggles in response had her heart doing double takes. How did this woman have so much power over her? Even Racheal, who was a beautiful woman and exuded sex appeal had never made her feel this way. Excited, sure, and the sex had been great, but this was totally different.

I feel the euphoria of having sex just by being with Kris. Damn, I can't wait until we get that far in our relationship. I really want to be that close, yet at the same time it doesn't matter as long as she's here. As long as she's here, yeah, and in a week's time we have to go our separate ways.

"Do you want to talk?" Claire smiled into the delicious neck her lips feasted on gently. When she moved away, Kris pulled back.

"We can talk, but I want you here." Kris's voice was a breathless request.

Claire moved to face her and kissed her soundly. "No place I'd rather be. Sometimes talking can be a distraction."

Kris chuckled and kissed her shyly. "It can also be prudent."

"Prudent, huh? You've been around Shirley way too much." Claire laughed and nestled her head back on Kris's shoulder.

"What do you want to know, Kris, that you haven't actually read in the tabloids?"

The steady beat of Kris's heart close to her ear settled Claire's nerves about the conversation. The tabloids often got it wrong.

"The truth might help. The press isn't always accurate…or are they?"

Claire shook her head slightly. "No, they are not."

"I can see the damage, at least some of it, from the accident. Will you tell me how it happened and how you coped?"

The tentative question hung in the air. In most circumstances, Claire would have ignored it and moved on, but Kris wasn't just someone—she might well be the most important person in Claire's life.

"Bit of a blur, really. I know that sounds like a cop-out, but it really is." She wiped a hand across her mouth and sucked in a deep breath. "I guess you know about the bullshit the papers reported, that I was drunk and it was my fault and I deserved everything that happened to me."

Kris squeezed her hand. "Go on, please. Your version is the only one I'm interested in."

Claire pulled away from her hold and half turned so they faced each other. "You might not like what you hear. In fact, I'm sure you won't, but honesty is the only thing that will work. I know that now." She stroked a finger down

Kris's cheek. "You bring out the good part of me, did you know that?" Kris shook her head. "It's a great thing. Let's see what I can remember. I have problems remembering some things, the whole memory loss and stuff. I was leaving the apartment of a woman I picked up at a club I frequented. Nothing new in that."

Kris softly gasped. Claire didn't have to ask why, yet Kris didn't let go of her hand. *Good sign, I hope.*

"Yes, I know. I was engaged to Racheal, but we had an open relationship. That was the problem, I guess. It was too open. Anyway, the upshot was that I had exactly two drinks that evening. A wine before I went into the club and a shot at this woman's apartment."

Claire paused. The memories of what was real and what wasn't intermingled. She recalled the image of dazzling lights and the sounds of bells.

"I felt woozy when I left the apartment. I should have done the sensible thing and caught a cab, but I drove instead. I had that mentality where I thought I was perfectly okay when I wasn't. I knew I was close to the tracks, and the sound of the bells still haunts my dreams...."

Kris leaned forward and kissed her gently.

Claire smiled weakly. "I didn't put two and two together, and the next thing I saw was harsh lights bearing down on me, yet I still didn't have a clue. The rest, as they say, is history. I woke up a week later in the mess I'm in."

Silence descended on the room.

Claire allowed herself to breathe again as Kris spoke.

"I've lived in New York for ten years now. I'm a country girl, really...from Broome. As I said, my parents didn't understand me. That's the bottom line, really. They didn't look beyond the gender I fall in love with. I was almost twenty-one when I saw an ad for a clerk in an insurance office in New York City. It was in a three-day-old newspaper someone had left on a park bench. I loved going to the park on my break time, enjoying the open air and the birds singing."

Claire heard the regret in Kris's voice—she knew it by heart. Hers often had that tone. "My father said I deserved everything that came to me for my debauched way of life, insinuating the accident was payback."

Kris's eyes widened. "My dad wasn't that vocal, but I'm sure he thought it."

"You're not debauched in any way! He's a prick to say that or think it. Me, on the other hand, I could understand that line of thinking." Claire sighed heavily. "I thought my mother might have been supportive. On reflection, she was for the first six months. She was always there, but I just needed more, I guess. Not that I knew what that would have been. My father, on the other hand, I think I saw him three times during the early stages of my convalescence. He has agreed to me going back to work for them behind a desk where no one can see me. So far, I've declined, but he pays the bills these days. I guess I might have limited choices ahead of me."

Claire straightened her body. Baring her soul grated on her in the therapy sessions, and the frustration at having to talk about her feelings eventually made her angry and self-isolate.

"What about Racheal?"

What about Racheal? Yeah, that's some question. "Ah, yes, you said the press didn't affirm that we were no longer engaged. Truth be told, neither one of us thought to make it official at the time. It was just…yeah right, think, head." At Kris's puzzled look, she shrugged. "Racheal didn't like the way I looked or my disability." She looked down at the motionless limb. "I hate this too." Tears welled and several dropped down her cheeks.

Kris tenderly wiped them away.

"The scars can be fixed if I want them to be, but this"—she eyed the offending limb with venom—"no, this will be a constant reminder."

Gentle fingers took her arm and pulled it forward toward lips that caressed the scars. Claire could barely feel the pressure, but mentally it was a salve on her wounded skin.

"She left you?"

Claire smiled wryly. "Well, I thought so until she turned up last weekend."

"What!"

Claire laughed at the outrage. "You went out on your date with Jess…and we need to talk about that."

Kris's expression turned sober.

"Racheal turned up out of the blue. God knows I didn't expect or want to see her. We went to that bar we had the quiz in for a meal. Bottom line, she wants me back." Claire looked for any reaction from Kris and saw nothing.

"She's rich. That would solve your problems, right? Might be a good move." Kris moved out of arm's reach.

Damn, this truth business is stressful. "For the record, my Grams will bail me out before I have to succumb to Dad's directives. She hates him. Racheal knows it's over, and I told her to finally release the statement to the press. I love her as a good friend and always will. After all, we have a long history. My future, no, that's totally different."

"Why didn't you mention this before?" Kris whispered.

"Wasn't important." Claire shrugged.

"To you, but…. No, you are right, it's your business." Kris's voice dropped to a mere whisper.

Claire knew she had to say something that would manage this debacle of a conversation, but she didn't know how. All she wanted right now was Kris close to her. This distance thing wasn't a good feeling at all. "Do you know what I remember the most out of that dinner with Racheal? I recalled more of what the server said to me than what Racheal said, and she knew it. How would you feel if that was you and Jess?"

Kris dropped back in the sofa, closed her eyes, and sighed. "Horrible. I don't think I'd…I guess I can't say. I've never been in that position. You never know what you might do."

Tentatively Claire touched Kris's fingers and was rewarded when Kris caught her hand and squeezed gently.

"Jess isn't my girlfriend. Our so-called date didn't quite go according to plan. I think she has history, as you call it, with a woman named Fern. Actually, I was surprised we didn't see her at the quiz since she said she's there every night. Anyway, it all went to hell in a basket at the end of the evening, if you could call it that. I arrived home early. I guess I'm not into drama."

Claire laughed loudly. "Darling, drama and lesbians go in hand in glove. The only thing to beat us is gay men and let me tell you—"

Kris pulled her close. "I don't care about that. I just care about what you think about us."

Claire smiled. "I don't think about us." Kris's lips dropped. "I feel about us. I figure that's a million times better." Claire didn't have chance to say more as her lips were captured in an intense kiss that drowned out everything but the woman who placed her arms around her and hugged her close.

Perfect.

Chapter Twenty-seven

"Hey, Buddy, it's snack time. Come on."

Claire craned her neck to look at every visible branch and tried to see those that weren't. No amount of cajoling received a response. She looked at the tree at least ten feet away and saw activity moving over to the next tree as the birds skedaddled.

Hmm, Buddy never does that.

"Come on, Buddy, you've had your fun. I have your favorite here." She crumbled the cookies in her hand and held them out. Five minutes later, she dropped the crumbles on the ground at the usual tree, turned to the cottage, and simply took in the sight.

Gone were the dilapidated windows and the general impression of neglect. Now a glow emanated from the cottage, and it had a lot to do with the hard work that had gone into the property in the last few weeks. However, it was more than that, much more. A positive ambiance surrounded it, as if it had come alive with an ethereal hand held out in welcome.

Crap, that's getting way too deep for me.

She stepped onto the decking and looked at the hard work Kris had done to sand it down for the final finish, which they were going to do today.

Kris. Every time she's in my orbit, I melt away. What does that say? I'm a serial philanderer. How can I feel this way, and yet I do, what does that mean? The question isn't about Kris, it's about me. Can I be the person she deserves?

✝

Kris watched Claire shout for Buddy. Apparently he didn't appear. Not that odd, considering he was courting and the female had probably found a more favorable place to live. It happened. After several attempts, Claire gave up and was now standing on the deck.

She approached the steps to the cottage and Claire didn't move, seemingly lost in thought. Who wouldn't be in a place like this? Tonight, they were going out on a date. As much as this pained her to think so, this might be the only one. She'd read enough over the years to know Claire didn't do commitment. Even her engagement was open-ended. She had even admitted as much the night before.

I can't do that, no matter how much I feel about her. It would eventually kill me. The question is, how do I tell her that without looking like an idiot? I don't think I can live with the fear she is going to cheat on me.

"Is it to your satisfaction? I worked tirelessly over that yesterday." Kris chuckled as Claire started and turned quickly. The look of surprise on her face swiftly changed to a giant smile.

Claire placed her good hand on her hip and nodded. "Sure, but you left a mark or two."

"What!" Kris clambered up the few steps and stared in the direction of Claire's pointed finger. "But...but that's nothing. It's part of the makeup of the wood."

"Even so...." Claire began to laugh, and Kris stared at her.

"You were teasing me."

Claire moved closer. "Absolutely." She kissed her gently, and they lost themselves in it for a short while.

When they broke apart, they both grinned. She guessed they would appear foolish to anyone passing by. Thankfully no one did.

"You have a fabulous smile, do you know that? It's infectious too."

Kris fluttered her eyelids a few times at the compliment. "Actually, no one has ever said that to me but you."

"Then they must all be blind. Ah, sorry, your friend Jess is the exception."

Kris frowned at the mention of Jess's name. *I have to call her and let her know about this change in circumstances. It's only fair.*

Claire moved toward the door and held out her hand for the key. When Kris handed it to her, she rolled the ornate brass object in her palm. She remained doing that for some time.

"Anything wrong, Claire?"

Claire glanced up, and Kris was sure she didn't see her at that moment. She apparently was lost in a world of her own. "Claire?"

"Sorry, everything is just fine. In fact never better." Claire placed the key in the door and went inside.

Now that was odd, even for her.

Following her, Kris breezily said, "Right, you're in charge of the stirring of the decking paint and cleaning the brushes...oh and no stepping on the fresh paint."

Claire stood in front of her and gave a slow smile and then saluted. "Yes, ma'am."

Kris winked. "I think together we can have this done by lunch. Shirley will be amazed, I'm sure."

Claire shook her head and laughed. "So will I. I'm with you one hundred percent and I think the together works for me."

Kris walked up to Claire and kissed her lightly on the lips. "Me too."

†

Shirley placed her hands to her face in a V shape that covered her mouth, clearly overcome by the work completed. Claire smiled at the older woman's reaction. In truth, it was her reaction too. Kris had worked so hard to finish it before Shirley turned up. For some reason only fathomable to Kris, surprising Shirley was important to her.

Claire moved away from the tree she was leaning on and smiled at Shirley.

"What do you think? Has our girl done good or not?"

Shirley moved her hands away from her face and nodded, then indistinctly spoke.

"Sorry, I didn't get that."

Shirley cleared her throat. "Your girl has done mighty fine, and I'm sure you helped."

Claire shrugged and walked to stand next to Shirley as they faced the cottage façade.

At that moment, Kris came from around the back of the building and grinned as she saw them.

"What do you think, Shirley?"

Shirley pulled Kris into a hug and tightly held her.

Tears coursed down the older woman's cheeks, and Kris looked surprised. Then eventually untangled herself from the hold.

"Does it pass muster?"

"Oh yes it does. It reminds me of my time here, although that time was short. Oh yes indeed, the cottage knows the people it wants to live inside it." Shirley moved toward the cottage and ran a hand along the railing of the deck steps. "My Ricky sanded down the rails and painted them before we came to live here. They sparkled just like the deck does now." She turned around quickly and stared at them both. "Do you feel like you've come home when you are here?"

Claire swallowed hard. *It would be so easy....* "Yes, I do. If I had the money, I'd ask to rent it from Grams and live my life out here. Sounds crazy I know, but I love it."

Kris's eyes sparkled as she spoke, and a part of Claire wanted to join in the euphoria, but she held herself back. "It's a nice place."

Shirley shook her head and put the picnic basket on the deck. "One day you will have to take a chance, Claire. I hope you don't miss the important ones. She turned to the path that led her back to Seasons and disappeared behind the bushes.

"You wouldn't like to live here, Claire?"

Claire turned to Kris and tried to understand her expression. She couldn't. "Pipe dreams, Kris. It's only for a summer vacation. Okay, let's go have our lunch by the sea. I've been looking forward to this since I woke up." Claire linked arms with Kris, who picked up the hamper and they set off for the beach.

Chapter Twenty-eight

The Curiosity Bar was definitely twenty times more popular this evening than on quiz night. Well that probably had to do with it being Friday. Fortunately, they had booked a booth near the middle of the bar. *From the seats you could pretty much see all around you if you wanted—though you'd have to switch seats to see the other half.* Kris held back a chuckle at how absurd that thought was. She and Claire could start a new fad changing seats halfway through dinner.

Shirley was in town tonight meeting a friend and had offered them a lift. She'd said she'd be going home around ten if that was okay with them. Claire had jumped at the offer, saying they could both drink that way. Kris didn't care either way, but having a couple of glasses of wine instead of watching others was a change. Besides, drinking together seemed important to Claire.

Tonight was quite warm, so the fire pit in the middle of the room wasn't lit, although the table surrounding it was heavily populated with a group of women laughing and obviously enjoying each other's company.

Kris glanced around and didn't see the server from the previous time they were there. In a way, she was glad. She couldn't work out why, but that didn't matter. What was her name? It had a familiar ring.

"I see Summer isn't working tonight."

Now I know why I'm glad. Give me strength from the pangs of jealousy. "I noticed that too. Pity," She cringed inside at her pathetic response. "I see Fern is here tonight though." Kris pointed at the corner of the bar.

Claire turned and looked for a few seconds, then moved her gazed to rest on Kris. "Does she own the place? She acts like she does. It's in the way she holds her body."

Kris semi-smiled. "She owns the place and said she was here most days, except the quiz night, obviously."

"You think your friend Jess is sweet on her?"

Kris was surprised at the question and frowned. "I just think there's history. It doesn't necessarily mean there's a sexual history, does it?"

"Sure it does. We're lesbians, after all. We love our drama and our history of lovers." Claire eyed her and shrugged. "Okay, maybe not all lesbians. For the record, many of my old friends are happily committed to their partners and it works great for them." Claire picked up her menu.

Kris balled her fists and held her breath. *What the heck do I say now? I'm so out of my league here. Every time we get to an intimate point, I can't seem to get it right. What the heck is wrong with me?* "Doesn't work for you, then. I need the bathroom. Be back soon."

She stood and headed for the door without a backward glance at Claire. Then someone called her name as she held the door to the bathroom.

"Kris, how wonderful. I thought you'd never visit us."

Fern's voice boomed in the room.

"Hi, Fern. Yes, in fact this is my second visit. I was here for the quiz."

"Darn, I had a family event to attend." Fern looked around and then back to her. "With Jess tonight?"

Kris wanted to laugh. Instead she shook her head. "No, another friend."

Fern gave her a hard look, then smiled. "My, you are a friend magnet."

"I need to go. A bathroom break."

"Of course, later." Fern turned away and was as quickly engrossed in conversation with the table next to the door.

Kris escaped through the door. "Damn, this isn't turning out how I expected."

Five minutes later, she headed back to the booth, and Fern must have been watching for her because she waved as Kris passed. Embarrassed, she gave a small wave back and slid into the relative obscurity of her seat.

"You look flushed. Is something wrong?" Claire asked in a quieter voice than usual.

Kris shook her head. "Nope, have you decided what you are having?"

Claire sighed and placed her menu on the table. "Kris, if this was a bad idea, I'm sorry. We can call Shirley and get a taxi home."

Kris pursed her lips and closed her eyes. *I'm so crap at this. What a miracle...me sitting with Claire Tremont and on a date too and all I can do is mess it up.*

"I'm sorry, it's me. All my fault if that's what you think I'm feeling. I want to be here, truly I do." She gently touched Claire's injured hand, which rested on the table motionless. "I guess I'm out of my depth. Who would believe the wonderful Claire Tremont would date me—a nobody." Claire opened her mouth to speak, but Kris waved her attempt away. "I'm afraid, Claire. Afraid that tonight is the only date we will have, and frankly, my mind is all over the place at the thought." She held back the sting of tears.

"Oh, is that all?"

The nonchalant way Claire spoke had Kris's hackles rise. *So, this really was no big deal to her. I'm such an idiot.* "Is that all?" she echoed as her head dipped to gaze at the cutlery on the table and the menu, the words of which her tears blurred.

Then a warm hand covered the one that held Claire's. "Hey, please don't cry. One of the things I like about you, Kris, is you care so much that everything has to be picture-book right. It isn't, as we both know, but in truth, it's me who should be wondering why someone as wonderful as you is sitting with me. You have to agree I'm a cranky, spoiled rich kid who can wallow in self-pity at times. Who'd want to be around such a person?"

Kris lifted her head and gave Claire a watery smile. "I do."

Claire grinned. Kris's blood rushed through her system. It wiped away her doubt.

"I'd kiss you right now, but it's kinda hard in one of these booths unless you want to sit next to me." Claire wriggled her eyebrows, and they both burst out laughing.

"Later, for sure."

"I'm going to have fillet steak with duck-fat-roasted potatoes. If it's half as good as the pork belly, then I want the name of this chef."

Kris shook her head and entangled her fingers in Claire's. "I might be able to provide that. We can ask Fern."

Claire nodded, bent her head, and placed a tender kiss on Kris's palm. "Just so you don't forget about that kiss later."

"Never, and I think I'm going to have the same as you. It sounds delicious."

†

Replete from the sumptuous meal, they ordered triple chocolate cheesecake—something they found out they both always chose when eating out. They agreed that if they asked Shirley, she would have a recipe and make it for them. An empty bottle of Venge 2013 Oakville Estate Vintage Merlot stood in the center of the table. Claire had insisted they order it.

Kris hadn't looked at the wine list, so she didn't know the process. When Claire enthused that she'd never seen this vintage outside the swanky restaurants in the city, she decided it must be expensive. Leaning back in the bench, she patted her stomach. "I think once a year I'm going to take a trip out here to partake in this kind of food and the wine. I've never tasted anything like it. Great choice, Claire, and the price of the meal is reasonable too. Not sure about the wine though."

Claire, leaning back in the seat, her right hand on the waistband of her trousers, waved a finger at Kris. "Once a year might be right. If I lived here, I'd be tempted to eat out all the time, and who knows what would happen to my figure. The wine, by the way, is one I remembered having just before the accident."

Kris shrugged. "Well, my hips expand at the idea of fattening food, so trust me, I'd be worse."

Claire looked directly into her eyes and gave her a soft look that made her smile. "We could counter that darned metabolic problem by running on the beach every morning. So tell me, this Fern person, are you sure she is interested in Jess?"

Kris frowned. Claire had changed the subject rapidly. "Yes, at least I believe they have history…I mean I don't really know. Why do you ask?"

Claire tilted her head slightly, which would give her a view of the bar. "She's been looking in our direction for the last half an hour. In fact, I'd say she's glued to the spot." She grinned. "I know I'm a bit of a draw with the beauty and all." She flicked a hand at her scarred face. "Still, it's odd."

"I don't care about her. We said tonight was about getting to know each other."

"Good call. So, you have told me about your parents and where you lived and worked at in the city, but what you haven't told me is your love affairs."

Kris screwed up her face. "Oh please, do you have to ask that?"

Claire grinned. "Sure I do. I need to know the competition."

"If it was in the past it isn't."

"Trust me, the past catches up to you. Take my tryst with Racheal and how you felt about it. So the more you tell, the less of a shock it is when that person or people turn up."

Kris heard a resigned tinge in Claire's voice. She took a deep gulp of air. "I don't have any old lovers. I'm going to be the world's oldest lesbian virgin. I've been waiting for the right one, old fashioned I guess. That's me."

Kris stared at Claire and saw surprise, and what she expected next—derision—didn't happen. Instead Claire had a look of what she could only say was awe.

"You're waiting for the right one?"

"Yes, guess that makes me weird."

Claire moved forward in the seat and shook her head. "Never weird." She smiled and held out her hand. Kris took it.

"I'm not that pure for you. I'm not ashamed of my past...well, the past I remember...it's after all what makes us who we are. Thank God I'm not a murderer, right? I did meet Racheal last weekend, but she is in my past for *good*."

The emphasis on the word *good* helped Kris, but how could a virgin lesbian and a socialite reprobate—frankly, that was what Claire had been—work? "We are poles apart socially, Claire. You know that, right?"

Claire shrugged. "Yeah, I know that, but I figure if we both want to be together, that's the most important thing."

Kris drew in a deep breath. "To me, yes. I've fallen for you in a big way, but I won't be used. I don't want one of those open relationships, Claire. I'm sorry."

Claire stared at her and was about to speak when another voice intervened.

"So, Kris, introduce me, please." Claire was given an intense stare. "It is you."

Kris almost jumped out of her seat at the ashen expression on Fern's features as she gazed at Claire. The woman looked like she was going to collapse. *Does she know Claire? Surely one of them would have mentioned it.*

"Fern, are you okay? Please sit." Kris motioned for her to sit, and the woman virtually poured herself onto the bench. Her eyes never left Claire. Kris glanced at Claire, who raised her eyebrows and shrugged.

"Fern, this is my friend, Claire, her—"

"I know." The short words were stilted, in total contrast to the upbeat woman Kris had met in the past. Unable to think of something to say, she looked at her watch. It was eight forty-five.

"Hi, Fern. I don't think we've met before."

"Do you want a drink? We were just going to order another bottle." Kris wasn't sure they were, but it was as good a line as any now.

Fern turned to look in her direction, but Kris had the distinct impression she didn't see her. Then she turned her head to stare at Claire again.

"I'm not sure what the problem is, Fern, but frankly, right now you are being a bit weird, and we don't need that." Claire's voice was firm.

"You really don't remember me?" This time her voice was incredulous.

Claire scratched the back of her ear and frowned. "Can't say I do. When did we meet, exactly?"

Kris watched the two women. She was sure from Claire's manner she didn't recognize Fern. Fern on the other hand looked completely disorientated.

"You broke my heart," Fern whispered.

Claire scrunched up her face and didn't say anything.

"When did you meet Claire, Fern?"

"She was in her sophomore year at college and on summer break at Seasons with the family. I was working as a waitress at this place. It was called Rascals back then. You thought I was the most beautiful woman you'd ever met. Do you remember me now?"

The words floated accusingly between the two women. *So this is what Claire meant by how exes could be trouble.*

Claire lifted her hand and traced a line down the scars on her face. "I'm sorry, I really don't know you. As you can see, I'm not the person I was back then. Hell, I don't even remember how old I was in sophomore year." Her lips twisted. "I had an accident two years ago, and I lost some of my memories."

Fern seemed to bring herself partially out of her stupor. "What happened?"

Kris bit her lip, wondering if Claire was prepared to share the details with the woman who to her at least was a stranger.

"I had an altercation with a train on a track. My bad, as they say, and this is part payment. I have memory loss, some recent ones, but many older. I apparently loved my gramps, but I can't recall him at all. I'm sorry if at some time in my life I upset you, Fern, but seriously I can't remember you." Claire sat back in her seat with a heavy sigh.

Kris had the advantage of watching both women, and they looked solemn.

"I think I understand. You might have broken my heart back then, but I bounced back. In fact, it's because of you that I own this place. I'm respectable now. You can tell your father I said hi." Fern stood unsteadily. "I'll send you over another bottle, my compliments. Good night."

Before she or Claire had time to answer, Fern was gone into the ever-increasing throng of Friday evening revelers.

They remained silent until Kris couldn't hold back any longer. "Well that was a bit of a shock. And what was that about your father? That was an odd thing to say, don't you think?"

Claire didn't look at her. Her eyes were glued to her injured arm. Then she looked up suddenly. "Thank God she's sending over another bottle. I need more to drink."

Kris had a feeling this conversation regarding Fern, though far from settled, was over tonight. She understood that to a degree, even if the subject intrigued her.

Kris stood and exited her side of the booth and seconds later sat next to Claire. "Scoot over a bit." Claire duly did so. "I think right now you need a hug. You okay with that?" She didn't wait for the answer. Instead, she took Claire in her arms and held her until she felt the tension Claire had hidden well release and her body sagged against her chest.

"Thank you" was Claire's muffled response as she kissed the top of Claire's head, which was slightly bent toward her breasts.

"You know this could get tricky."

"What could?" Claire tentatively asked.

"Well, this ex business. How are we to know if they are or aren't? Although, I could check the tabloids. We might have to become hermits." Kris chuckled softly.

Claire moved away so they were close but could see each other, and Kris saw tears for the first time in Claire's eyes. She gently touched her eyelids. "I'm sticking around, Claire, until you decide it won't work."

Claire shook her head. "What if it isn't me, but you?"

"I guess it could happen. Except that when I'm around you, I never want to leave. Sounds silly, right?" Kris sucked in her lips, hoping she hadn't said too much. Then again, they didn't have the luxury of time to make decisions like this. Time was the one thing that was speedily running out, even if they did live in the same city. She had the distinct feeling if they parted without having this conversation, there would be no tomorrow for them.

"I feel the same," Claire quietly said. She smiled and kissed Kris, pulling away as the server announced his arrival.

"Oh, girls, don't bother about me, carry on. We love our customers enjoying themselves. That's why I work here. Everyone is welcome. Here you go, our very best Merlot and compliments of the boss. You must be really good friends." He popped the cork and placed the bottle on the table.

"Won't our server be upset that you've brought more wine? Means the tip will be shared," Kris said.

There was a girly laugh. "Oh, Tina knows. I'm the manager, and this was a favor for the boss. Enjoy, ladies." With a flourish of hands, he left.

Kris looked at the bottle, then at Claire, and sighed as she poured them both another drink.

"What was that for?"

"This night was supposed to be about us. We'd have been better off staying home. Next time I'm going to choose where we have dinner." Kris smiled.

Claire picked up her glass and nodded in the direction of Kris's, and Kris took hers.

"To you and me, alone without baggage. We could go to the beach when we leave here and take in a night sky. What do you think?"

Kris knew visiting the beach after ten was a silly thing, really. It would be dark and maybe the tide might be in but…. "Yes, let's do that." She raised her glass to Claire's and they chinked.

Chapter Twenty-nine

The sea was out.

Claire was thankful. They'd said good night to Shirley almost immediately after they arrived home. Shirley had seemed pensive and though communicative on the journey to Seasons, she shut down when they arrived. Neither of them broached the change in the housekeeper; tonight was their night. They needed each other.

Alone.

That crazy woman Fern had made everything tense, although she had provided more wine and they'd brought most of it home. In fact, as she stared out at the sea, with a full moon illuminating the expanse, she was grateful for Kris and her upbeat attitude about tonight's events. It would have been bad enough if an ex she remembered appeared. How much more awkward would a total stranger turning up be if she couldn't remember the woman? Becoming a hermit might be a good option. Kris was right about one thing: that quip about her father was odd. Surely Fern hadn't been having an affair with him at the same time.

"You've gone all quiet. Are you going to sleep on me already?"

Turning to Kris, who was seated next to her on the blanket they'd placed on the beach, Claire smiled. She took Kris's hand and squeezed it gently.

"Not likely. Believe me, you are worth staying awake for. What do you think of the view?"

Kris grinned and rested her head on Claire's shoulder. "Perfect, I have a marvelous view courtesy of Mother Nature and the most important woman in my life at my side." She sighed.

Claire was once more amazed how Kris could say all the right things naturally. She fell more and more under her spell. "Got that right on both counts." Kris sucked in a deep breath and waited, fully expecting Kris to say something more. It didn't happen. Instead, Kris leaned farther into her shoulder and relaxed.

A minor wind that was surprisingly warm tickled her ears. *Can my life get any better than this and what Kris is offering me? I know if I said "Let's go to bed" right now, she would. I know I have to make the ultimate commitment though. Otherwise she becomes like all the rest of the women in my past—disposable. I won't do that to her. She deserves the real thing. Damn, when did I get scruples about taking a woman to bed?*

"What time is Melissa arriving? Do you know?"

The whispered question reinforced her need to do something about where this relationship was going or could potentially go. Except the word *potentially* wasn't right with Kris. It would be all in or nothing.

"Not sure, but knowing Grams it will be in the morning. She's definitely a morning person, up at the crack of dawn most days." Claire placed her arm around Kris's waist and hugged her closer. She could hear her heart beat and would swear theirs beat in unison. *How odd.* "I was thinking."

Kris chuckled and looked up.

Claire dipped her head and kissed the sweet smile that graced Kris's lips. "Yes, I know, dangerous. If you never had to go back to the city, would there be anything there you would regret leaving behind?"

Kris gently pushed herself away from Claire so they faced each other. "I don't understand. You mean stay here or go someplace different?"

"Either. I was thinking about here." Claire waved her free hand across the expanse.

"Knight, of course. I miss him every day, but I can take him with me at least." Kris pursed her lips. "Not sure about here though. Maybe cats wouldn't be welcome. I was thinking about Buddy."

Claire nodded. "He'd be welcome. Buddy seems to have disappeared. I hope nothing has happened to him."

Kris touched Claire's cheek and smiled. "He was courting, Claire. Probably they are getting ready to migrate. I'd say he's going to bring his offspring back here for sure, especially if he thought his best buddy was around with treats."

Claire frowned. "Really? Wow. I never thought of that. Stupid me."

Kris stared at her, and Claire was lost in the serious, brown gaze.

"I guess the cottage has that effect on people, huh? Look at us. Who would have thought it?"

Kris narrowed her eyes, then kissed Claire.

The kiss deepened to the extent that they didn't come up for air for some time. When they did, Claire gasped at the way her body throbbed. She clung to Kris, hoping her world would stop spinning. "If I could make it happen, Kris, would you stay here with me?" Her voice was wafer-thin.

Kris leaned her forehead against Claire's and drew in a slow breath. "Do you mean it and is it even possible?"

"I mean it, and if I talk with Grams…sure, I think it is. Grams always gives me everything I ask for."

Kris gave her a wide-eyed look and simply nodded.

Claire grinned, and her heart, she was damn sure, was floating next to the moon on the sea. Then she made a decision that no matter what happened she would never regret. She moved to kneel beside Kris and puffed out her chest.

"Will you marry me, Kris, and live at Seasons with me?"

Kris opened her mouth, then shut it and stared at her in amazement.

"I know it's unexpected, but I want you to know I'm serious about you marrying me. I'll go one better to ensure you know that I mean this. I will go to Broome and ask your parents for your hand in marriage. I just want to know that if I get their blessing you will say yes."

Claire held her breath, waiting.

Kris traced a finger over Claire's lips and shook her head, but she was smiling.

"You forgot the most important thing. The rest is irrelevant."

Claire frowned and tried hard to think what she could possibly have missed.

"I'm…damn, I'm sorry. What did I miss, Kris?" she pleaded.

Kris smiled. "I love you, Claire."

"Well yeah, I figured if you contemplated this you'd...ah. Oh, how crappy am I. I'm sorry, my love. I love you. I think I have from the first moment I saw you sneaking a peek at me from the window of your room that first day."

"You...you fell in love me then? How is that possible?" Kris breathlessly asked.

Claire chuckled and pulled her close. "You entranced me from a distance. Believe me, attraction is never quite what you expect, and love is ever more volatile. Kris Lake, I do love you. Will you marry me?"

Kris almost fell over as she excitedly replied, "Yes, yes, and oh yes. I love you, Claire. It was breaking my heart to think I might not see you again after Sunday morning."

Claire grinned, tilted Kris's chin back, and winked. "Never going to happen. There is nothing in my life that could possibly do that."

Kris moved forward, and seconds later, they were lying on the blanket, uncaring of the beautiful backdrop, simply engrossed in each other.

Chapter Thirty

The car pulling up the driveway had the three occupants of the house nervous for different reasons.

Shirley waved toward the door. "Go greet your grandmother, Claire. She will like that. Kris and I will wait here."

Claire nodded, then gave Kris a wink as she ambled to the door, opened it, and slowly progressed down the steps to the car and opened the driver's door. "Mother?"

Anna Tremont smiled at her, withdrew long legs from the vehicle, and once standing, enclosed her in a hug.

"Darling, are you pleased to see me?"

The throaty words didn't quite register for a few seconds, and then when they did, Claire drew away. As always, her mother's outfit was perfectly coordinated. She wore pale beige linen trousers, an opaque silk blouse, and a string of pearls that did actually look good with the simplistic outfit. Her dark blonde hair was in a flattering modern mid-length style, along with perfectly applied makeup.

"I'm surprised." Claire glanced to the passenger side and gave Grams a concentrated look. Her grams shrugged and climbed out of the car. "What brings you here? You haven't been to Seasons for years from what Grams said."

Her mother glanced at Grams and then tilted her chin upward. Claire wasn't sure what that was all about, for it looked defiant to her.

"I've left your father."

The four words spun in the air all around them. Claire was sure they became 3-D images about to crash into her.

"What? Why? I'm home on Sunday, couldn't it have waited?" Claire took a step away from her mother.

"No, it couldn't. You can't go home, at least not to the house. It isn't our home any longer." Anna tried to make eye contact with Claire, but she looked away.

"Grams, what the hell is this all about?"

Melissa pursed her lips, walked over to Claire, and wrapped her in a hug. Gram's hugs always worked, but not today. She pulled away angrily.

"I don't get it. You've lived with that womanizer for almost forty years, and now…now it's time to call it quits?"

"Claire, it doesn't matter when your mother finally came to her senses. I think you should applaud her courage."

"No! No, she's been a damn coward for years and *now* she suddenly gets a backbone. I want to know why." Anger flowed through her like a roller coaster. Turning away, she shook her head. *This is so not what I want in my life right now. Complications.* "I'll see you both later. I need some fresh air." She stalked off.

The door to the main house opened, and Kris stood at the entrance. Claire saw her, but this wasn't the time for a nice, friendly chat. Not even with the woman she loved.

226

Kris's heart plummeted at the anguished look on Claire's face as she tore off in the direction of the beach. She was ready to go after her, when Shirley spoke behind her.

"Let her go, dear. Give her a little time. It will all work out, trust me."

Kris turned to the older woman in puzzlement. Then she diverted her attention to a tall, blonde woman accompanying Melissa as they climbed the steps. Her features were familiar.

Claire's mother. She never said...hmm, she obviously didn't know. That might explain Claire's departure a little. Kris drew in a shallow breath. Women like Anna Tremont always frightened her, not that she knew many. Something about their bearing unnerved her. They moved as if they owned every inch of the planet they walked on and ordinary people were of little interest to them.

Anna breezed by her with a haughty look.

Melissa, on the other hand, enclosed her in a hug. "Shirley tells me things are going splendidly with the cottage and Claire. Thank you, my dear. I knew you were the person for the job," she whispered.

Kris gave a half smile. *I wonder if she'd think the same thing if she knew we are in love. Would that change everything?* At this juncture, she wasn't going to add that to the mix.

"Mrs. Rank, you've haven't changed a bit. I'd like my old room made up, then Mother and I will have brunch. We set off early and I'm famished." Anna's eyes seemed to scan the hall for a few seconds, then she spoke again. "You can have your girl take my bag to my room. I'll be in the study making calls."

The heavy *clip, clip* of high heels resonated on the wooden floor as she disappeared to the study.

Yep, people like that are frightening.

"I'm so sorry, Kris. My daughter is spoiled. It is something I have lived to regret over the years. Now please, how have the renovations been going? And Claire, how has she been?" Melissa linked her arm in Kris's and led her away from the door and down the hall. Melissa smiled warmly at Shirley. "Ignore Anna, Shirley. We will eat at lunch at the normal time."

"Oh, I planned to do just that, Mrs. Jackson. I will of course make up the room Miss Anna suggested. I assume you will be going tomorrow with the others?"

Kris felt Melissa stiffen, and then she nodded. "Yes, of course."

†

A minute later, they were in the conservatory, and Melissa sank down on the wicker sofa. A sigh accompanied the action. "It's glorious here on a sunny day. I forget how wonderful it is to live here and enjoy the benefits of nature. The city is marvelous, but it can't beat the raw beauty of natural light and fresh air."

Kris sat down opposite Melissa. "So why not live here more? I would if I could. I love it here." She knew she was gushing, but it was the truth.

"Strangely enough, the reason may be a moot point now Anna has left Carl. She was the main reason I didn't retire here, and Claire of course. Perhaps things will change. It is time for this family to seek the happiness Seasons has always tentatively held for us, had we really reached out and grasped it."

Kris pursed her lips to stop smiling. Melissa sounded like Shirley when she was being cryptic. "Well that's good, right? I know Claire likes it here. She's been a great help with the renovations of the cottage. It's not quite there yet, but I have hired a local painter to finish off the outside of the second story. Shirley has promised to make sure he does what I requested."

Melissa chuckled. "I'm sure that will happen. Shirley is no fool, and not many will cross her in this town."

Kris grinned. "To be honest, I don't understand that comment. She is a wonderful woman and has been so friendly to me."

Melissa laughed and shook her head.

"Yes, a woman of many faces is our Shirley. If she has indeed taken you under her wing, then you are privileged. I was married, Anna was ten, when she began working here as a mere slip of a girl and not attractive at all. From what I heard it was one of the reasons Cook chose her. It was interesting, really, how it all turned out. Tragic too."

Kris nodded. "Shirley told us about her and Ricky. It was a lovely, heartwarming love story and, yes, tragic. I think she sees Claire as the child she never had. I'm probably totally off base, of course, but something in what she said made me think that."

"Really? I didn't know that, or rather think that, but perhaps on reflection it might be true." Melissa looked down at her hands.

"Would you like to see the cottage?" Kris decided the subject had gone as far as it was going and the mood in the room had become solemn.

Melissa smiled. "I most certainly would, but shouldn't we wait for Claire?"

"Claire will be there, talking to Buddy if she can find him. Let's go." Kris stood.

"Buddy, she has another friend? My goodness, what magic has been woven here in so few weeks?"

Kris laughed. "Buddy is a little different."

"Ah, and isn't that the truth of this magical property? Right, I'm looking forward to this immensely. The old place needed reinvigorating."

Kris nodded and opened the door for Melissa, and they set off to the cottage.

†

Claire sat down heavily beside the tree Buddy lived in, or used to according to Kris. "Damn, why did you have to desert me too? I need to talk."

She leaned her head against the bark, its rough texture imprinting into her skull. She didn't care. Her mind was a whirl of whys. Why now? Why did her mother come here? Why did Grams let her? Why did her mother think leaving Father was important to her?

Why can't I just fall in love and have life be happy for once?

Then the whats flooded through her like a tsunami, washing away the whys. *What if Father causes trouble? What if I don't have any money left? What do I do without a home?* The wave came crashing around her. *What will Kris think of me as simply me, without money?*

Kris. Damn, I ignored her and she didn't deserve that. What if she decides we aren't a good fit anymore? Love is fragile and can change with the snap of the fingers. Look what happened with Racheal.

Reality began to surface at the thought of Racheal. *I didn't love her. Not like I do Kris. I'd lay my life down for Kris.* A mischievous thought prevailed regarding Racheal—*I would buy her body armor instead of laying down my life if she were in trouble.*

"Buddy, I hope you and your lady friend are happy, and the in-laws don't step in to cause trouble. One of us should be free of that crap." She sighed.

Glancing down at her weak arm, she used her left hand to trace the scars on her face. "I'm worthless in the beauty department these days, and now it looks like I'm going to be penniless. Father never liked me from the day I was born. I'm pretty sure of that. He will be glad Mother left him. It will mean he can marry some bimbo who will give him the son he wanted. Bastard."

She looked up at the sky. It was light blue with only a few wispy, white clouds. The thought of Kris last night on the beach invaded her. Life took on a lighter tone. "Heaven, yes, heaven."

A chirp above her head distracted her, and she turned to look in the direction. Sure enough Buddy sat on his favorite branch, looking down at her.

She scrambled up, felt in her pocket, and balled her fist. "I'm sorry, Buddy, no cookies today. I thought you'd left me." Claire grinned. Suddenly the appearance of this innocent creature had righted her world, at least in part. Then she remembered the secret package Kris had kept from her a few days ago.

"Wait there, Buddy, I'll be back. Your second-best buddy might just have stashed something away for you. Please wait."

Looking back a couple of times to make sure Buddy was still there, she entered the cottage as quickly as she could after fishing out the key.

"Where did you put them, Kris?" She rushed over to the storage cupboards on the far wall, and the first one was empty. The second had basic kitchen cutlery, plates, and the third—bingo. She opened the first brown package, and *Yes!* It contained treats for Buddy. Clutching the bag, she retreated as speedily as possible out of the room and back to the tree.

"Here you go, Buddy." She ripped open the bag and sprinkled the wild bird food mix on the ground around the tree trunk. She was about to move to a discreet distance so he could feed without fear when he flew down and ate as she stood there.

A lump formed in her throat.

"What's this, Buddy? Saying good-bye and having a feast." The bird switched his head to one side as if he understood what she said. He flapped his wings, ate more, and then flew back to his branch.

Claire looked at him, and she had the distinct feeling that he willed her to stay with him for a while, but then that would be ridiculous. "I'll be back later, Buddy, if you have the time. Just remember if I stay there might be a cat to contend with."

The sound of footsteps crunching the gravel on the path leading to the cottage alerted her to visitors.

†

Accompanied by Melissa, who was a foot behind her, Kris headed to the opening of the path, which showed a full view of the cottage. She heard Claire's voice and stopped, causing Melissa to cannon into her.

"Something wrong?"

With a huge grin, Kris turned to the older woman. "No, absolutely the opposite. I know we shouldn't listen, but...."

Melissa frowned.

"Buddy came back, don't you see?" Kris sucked in a breath. *Thank you, Buddy.*

"Not really, dear. Who exactly is this Buddy?"

Claire left the tree to go inside the cottage.

"Watch this, Melissa. Buddy is a bird, he's very beautiful, and she loves him."

"Really, she always said they were vermin. I'm surprised." Melissa peered over the bush and watched. A few minutes later she gasped. "She really does like the bird. I'm flabbergasted. You have worked wonders, my dear."

Kris didn't know what to make of that comment. "Claire and Buddy had nothing to do with me. I'm a cat person, remember."

Melissa looked like she was about to cry, and Kris smiled.

"I think we're seeing the real Claire here, don't you? She's perhaps someone who got lost over the years but has found her way back."

"Yes, my dear. She was such a helpful and thoughtful child. Thank you."

Kris shook her head. "It wasn't anything to do with me. This is all down to Claire."

"Of course it is. Shall we speak with her and see the cottage?"

"Sure." Kris stamped hard on the ground.

"What are you doing?"

Kris chuckled. "Well, we don't want her to know we've been watching, right? I've done this a few times."

Melissa stared at her and then smiled. "Lead on, my dear."

Kris grinned as they headed out of the foliage.

†

"Hey, you could have scared me," Claire stated, then winked at Grams and gave Kris a smile. "I'm glad you left the other one behind. She would have been a perpetual thorn in the side."

"Claire, don't talk about your mother like that."

Kris walked over to Claire and took her hand instinctively. "Your grandmother is right, Claire."

The softly spoken words and the warmth of Kris's hand calmed her. She could clear up that issue later. "Yes, sorry. Still, Grams, what do you think? Kris has done a wonderful job."

Claire watched Grams closely, and Grams smiled and winked at her, then gazed at the building. With hands on slim hips, she whistled softly.

"My, you are very talented. You did all this without any help?" Melissa turned to Kris.

Kris shook her head. "I don't think Claire is chopped liver. She worked hard too. See the painted ornate part of the railing and the railing itself? Claire did that. She's painted a lot of the interior rooms too."

Claire heard the pride Kris had in her work, and her heart swelled. *Damn, I love this woman.*

"She certainly isn't. It's beautiful work, darling, thank you." Melissa hugged Claire and kissed her on the cheek.

"Well, I had an expert supervisor." Claire chuckled. "Grams, I want to tell you something."

Melissa raised a hand slightly. "You can tell me after you've talked with your mother. As much as it might pain you to do so, she deserves at least a hearing. In fact, I insist. Is that a problem?"

Claire frowned. "No, no, I can do that." She glanced at Kris, who appeared pensive. "Maybe I'll go do that now."

"Absolutely not. You both can show me everything you've done first."

Kris excitedly began telling Grams about the renovation.

Claire held back a moment before joining them on the deck and looked up at the tree. Buddy was gone.

Chapter Thirty-one

Kris scrubbed a carrot for dinner, worried over Claire's meeting with her mother. It wouldn't have been as stressful if Melissa hadn't insisted on sitting in on the conversation. That was an hour ago.

"That carrot must be the cleanest in the world," Shirley gently said.

Kris turned to the housekeeper and shrugged. "My attention was elsewhere."

"I know, and you can't do anything about what's said in that room. It's a family conversation. I found with Ricky it was best to remain out of direct family matters in the early days."

Shirley busied herself with a colander filled with potatoes.

Kris pondered that.

"You know as well as I do it's a hopeless case, don't you? You don't have to save my feelings. I think I knew from the start when I fell in love with her that I was hardly the person she would stay with. Heck, I don't have a job, I live in a small rented apartment in an, at times, dubious neighborhood, and I'm hardly a glamour girl." Kris threw the carrot into the pan and dropped the brush she was using.

Shirley placed the potatoes in the pan and switched on the heat. "My girl, if you think like that, how can you possibly expect the relationship to work? You've pretty much given her up. I didn't give up, and although I didn't have a lot of time with Ricky, I savored every single day. You should do the same. She asked you to marry her. That must mean something." Shirley shook her head and opened the oven to check on the roast beef.

Kris felt deflated at her words. *Shirley is right, but these are different times. Monogamy isn't Claire's strong point. She's already admitted that. How can I think she will change for me? I guess I just have to believe, as hard as that feels right now.* "Yes, you are right. I'm just nervous."

"Tell me about it. The first time I met my mother-in-law...my, she was a dragon but had a warm heart. All she was interested in was if her boy was going to be loved and looked after. I guess I must have won her over." Shirley chuckled.

Kris smiled. "Shirley, if things go well, will you be my family at the wedding?"

Shirley squared her shoulders and Kris was unsure of the outcome. When the older woman turned, her eyes were brimming with tears, and she briefly wiped her apron over her face.

"I would love to, Kris, thank you." Shirley took off the apron and found another, much to Kris's amusement. A few tears wouldn't harm anything.

"Right, let's make those Jackson women a meal that will knock their socks off, and for desert...we have"— Shirley winked—*"mille-feuille."*

"Oh Shirley, you are a darling." Kris walked around the bench and hugged her hard. "Thank you."

Shirley huffed away the emotion. "Right, let's set the table in the main dining room. Tonight we can all eat in style."

†

The light in the dining room was dim as everyone sat around the table. Melissa was at the head, flanked by Anna and Claire. Shirley sat next to Claire, and Kris next to Anna.

Claire frowned at the arrangement but held her tongue. She watched as Kris wrapped her hands in the linen napkin. It looked like a nervous reaction.

Anna turned to Kris. "Did you take my bag to my room?"

There was a wave of silence, and Claire's hackles rose.

"Actually no, Claire did."

Anna's nostrils flared. "You made my daughter a servant? Mother, that's an outrage. Not to mention that she's disabled."

Grams, bless her, held her laughter at the outdated and absurd comment.

"I'm far from disabled, Mother, and Kris isn't a servant. I'm not sure we've had them in the U.S. for decades. Are you living in a different century?"

"Don't be silly, darling. I'm doing nothing of the sort. What is for dinner this evening, Mrs. Rank?"

The lack of respect that money sometimes bestowed on people was evident in how her mother spoke. For years, she hadn't understood it. Now, oh yeah now, she did. Kris was worth a hundred times more than her mother. She would think this even if she hadn't fallen for Kris.

"Beef Wellington, roast potatoes, and seasonal vegetables."

"Well, that's at least decent. I don't want a dessert. I am, however, partial to a decent wine. What do we have with dinner tonight?"

Shirley began to rise from her seat.

"Leave that to me, Shirley." Claire stood and left the room.

"Look, Mother, she's a servant here. Isn't this what we pay these people for? This is your entire fault."

Melissa closed her eyes, shaking her head. "Do you know how outdated you sound, Anna? I brought you up better than that. It's just as well you've left Carl since his archaic views were influencing you so terribly."

Anna glared at Melissa, who simply gave her a sweet smile.

"Ignore my disrespectful daughter. She's going through a hard time, not that it makes what she said right."

"Mrs. Tremont is correct; you do pay me for the work. Claire is being kind." Shirley looked down at her hands, twisting them together. "Perhaps I'll go and check on her."

Kris stood. "I'll do it, Shirley. Excuse me, please."

Melissa smiled warmly and nodded.

Kris left the room.

"Well, that leaves the three of us. What do you think of the cottage, Shirley?"

"Oh, they have done a marvelous job. To be honest, it's just as I remember it when I lived there. My Ricky would have been happy."

Anna sniffed the air and began tapping her fingers on the table.

"You know, if you are bored you can go out to dinner. Take the Chrysler." Melissa shook her head, watching Anna's expression turn from boredom to interest, then a sour look entered the fray.

"I can't have a drink if I drive, and I need one, more than one. Thanks anyway."

The words sounded grudging and Melissa wondered when her only child had become so self-centered. She and Graham had spoiled her, that was normal with an only child, but this petulant disrespect for others wasn't something they had tolerated or taught their child. *Well, she's going to change if she lives with me for any length of time.* Melissa turned back to Shirley. "Have you seen Tony and Samantha recently? How is the baby-making going?"

Shirley smiled. "I saw them last night, actually, and it's good news and bad, from my point of view anyway."

Melissa knitted her eyebrows. "How so?"

"They have been given the opportunity to take part in a fertility program in Alabama, and the prospects are so much better than what they can afford here. They asked me to go with them. Tony can support us for the length of the program. I can't go, of course. I have responsibilities here."

"Oh, Shirley, of course you must go. They are family, and you can always come back if that's what you want." Melissa gave her a sympathetic smile. "Don't worry, I will find a temporary replacement."

Shirley's beaming smile was enough for Melissa to know this was exactly what the woman wanted to hear.

✝

"Damn, damn, damn!"

The words greeted Kris as she opened the door to the cellar and smiled. Obviously Claire wasn't happy about something. She quickly descended the six steps and saw Claire in the farthest corner, one bottle of wine under her arm and one in her hand, as she stared at the largest wine rack in front of her.

"Need any help?"

Claire turned and grinned. "Kris, you are an angel. How did you know I needed you?"

The words were innocuous enough, but Kris warmed all over. "To be honest I didn't. Shirley was going to come and help, but I decided to rob her of that pleasure." The words were out before she realized. "Oh, I didn't mean that the company was bad or anything...." Her cheeks stung with heat.

Claire laughed. "Yes, I know. Even though they're my family, I still volunteered."

Kris rolled her eyes. "How can I help?" She moved to within inches of Claire, who winked at her.

"A kiss right now would be wonderful."

Kris closed the gap and kissed Claire soundly. Their lips were like heat-seeking missiles, and when they made contact it was an explosion of senses. They remained like that for as long as they could support the kiss without coming up for air.

"Wow."

"Wow is right. I nearly dropped the wine. You have a remarkable talent for having me lose all sense of reality when we kiss." Claire's voice was hoarse.

"I hope that's good."

"*Good* isn't the right word. *Perfect* is."

Kris stared at Claire, catching her eyes. *'Perfect,' she said 'perfect.' How can I possibly think we won't work out?*

"I love you," Kris said.

The three words echoed in the cellar, and they both smiled.

"I love you too. Any chance we can skip dinner and take this to a private place?"

Kris shook her head. "Claire, it's your family. I think tonight they need you there. If you don't want to stay for your mother, certainly your grandmother could do with the support." At Claire's downtrodden expression, she said, "There is always after dinner."

Claire pouted. It reminded Kris of Anna's pout, but the twinkle in Claire's eyes made the expression so much less demanding.

"I will hold you to that."

"I certainly hope so. Now, what can I help you with?" Kris moved away. Her instinct was to miss dinner too, but Shirley was right. She had to make the future in-laws like her or at least try.

Claire shrugged, looking down at the wine in her clutches. "As you can see, I have Shirley's favorite Chardonnay under my arm, Grams's favorite Merlot in my hand. My mother will insist on a Cabernet Sauvignon...well a Bordeaux, but I can't find one. The dilemma is, I can't carry a bottle for any length of time with my left hand. Damn it."

Kris tried to think of something to counter the irritation Claire felt with herself. *Ah!* "To be honest, Claire, even if you could, how would you open the doors with three bottles of wine in tow and...?"

Claire frowned.

"You forgot what you like?" Kris winked.

"Damn, I forgot about me and then what about you…oh right you like Chardonnay. To be honest, I can drink any of them, so no problem there. Can you see a Bordeaux in any of the red wine areas?"

Kris looked around and then walked closer to the racks. It was a substantial cellar, considering no one really stayed at Seasons anymore. *It seems wasteful to spend money on something you might never use, but then I've never had the opportunity to squander money. I wonder what that feels like.*

After a couple of minutes, she reached a rack that was covered in dust and selected a bottle. Sure enough, it was Bordeaux. "Got it, Claire. Hard to find, I must say. Looks like this stuff hasn't been drunk in decades with the amount of dust on it. Will it be okay?"

"Red wine has longevity. I suppose we'd better reenter the fray. You know, I feel sorry for Shirley."

Kris frowned as she held the dusty bottle, thinking she'd better clean it up before presenting it to Anna. "Why?"

"She's had to sit with the family on her own for at least ten minutes."

They both laughed.

"Come on, let's go. I'll clean this bottle and bring it in. Oh, I'll open the door for you. That will make your mother think again before she calls you incapacitated."

Claire caught Kris's eyes and smiled slowly. "If I didn't already love you, I would right now."

Kris kissed her and pulled away. "Good to know. Come on, dinner will be getting cold and Shirley will give us a hard time."

Claire laughed and they headed up the stairs.

†

"Where is that girl? What is taking her so long? You're back," Anna said gruffly, looking at Claire. Mother was wrong to bring Claire back here. It had never been a good place for her. Now she was extolling the virtues of the help. *I hope she hasn't gotten into a situation like she did last time she was here. Carl was so annoyed having to bail her out of that debacle with that older woman.*

"Mother, you are the most—"

"Claire. Anna, this isn't your house, it's mine. You will respect the people here. If that's too much effort, go to your rooms. Seasons has always been a place for me to relax and enjoy life. I will not have the bickering or disrespect of others that you both advocate."

"I don't disrespect people, but Mother is out of line."

"Claire, you may not like what your mother says, but she deserves your respect if for nothing more than the fact she gave you life. No one is asking you to be her friend, but she's family and we support family."

"Grams, she doesn't deserve—"

The door opened and Kris walked in.

"Sorry for the delay. I figured this wine needs to look its best."

Anna looked at the wine, then at Kris. "I need a drink. Pour it, please. Wait, let me see that label." Her fingers trailed over the label.

"See? No respect for anyone. She's a loser. I'm not surprised Father didn't care that she left him."

"Claire, that's enough," Melissa growled.

Then everyone in the room seemed to be moving in slow motion as Anna gasped and took the bottle from Kris.

244

"Mother, this is…."

"Yes, the year you were born. Your father and I bought a couple of cases. We had a case at your christening and bought another for your firstborn's christening. As you know, that never happened."

Kris found the corkscrew and held it over the bottle.

"Wait, please don't open it," Anna announced. *All those years she kept it for us. Damn, why did I listen to Carl about not christening Claire here? He didn't care then and cares even less now. He hasn't even contacted me.*

Everyone looked at Anna.

"Claire, you open the wine." Anna gazed at her daughter, who gave that sour expression when she was upset. *This would be fitting for Claire to open the bottle. Daddy would have been proud if he were here to see this. At least Mother is.*

Claire frowned. "Hell, Mother, you've been saying everyone is using me as a servant and now you are doing the same thing. Weird. I have weird parents. That's the only thing I can think. Kris, please give me the bottle."

"It needs a corkscrew, Claire, you won't…."

Claire grinned. "Want to hold the bottle while I open it? Apparently this should have been for my christening and it's long overdue."

"Deal." Kris walked over to stand beside Claire, gave her the corkscrew, and held the bottle as she opened it. The cork popped as one would expect.

"Okay, Mother, duly opened." Claire placed the bottle in front of Anna.

"Thank you, darling." Anna picked up the bottle and poured a generous measure into her glass. "Anyone else want to try this? I do know it was the best of that year." *Yes, for more than just the wine; my baby was born.*

Claire scowled. "Okay, I'm game. The next question is, why didn't you use it for my christening?"

Anna drew in a deep breath.

"Your father decided you didn't need christening at that time."

Melissa shuffled in her seat. "Claire, your father has never shown any affinity to a church. His religion as far as I'm concerned is money."

Anna looked at her with a pained expression. "Mother, we both know he is a lapsed Catholic. He was away on business so much that we just never found the time."

Claire moved back in her chair and stared at her mother.

"Don't give me the spiel that Father would ever resurrect his Catholicism and have bothered. That's like saying the pope is a woman."

"Claire!"

"Okay, Grams, I'm going silent."

"Shall I serve dinner?" Shirley quietly interjected.

"Yes, please, Shirley," Anna said.

"I'll help." Kris stood and left with her.

"See, I told you they know their place." Anna took a sip of her wine and exaggeratingly rolled it around mouth, letting it explode on her taste buds. "This wine is superb, so much better for aging. Tell me, Claire, has this little sojourn of yours been fruitful?"

Claire pursed her lips, then spoke quietly. "Better than I could have imagined. In fact, I want to tell you my news. I should wait for Kris, but under the circumstances, I think it best I do it while she's not here."

"Kris? Why should she be here?" Anna frowned and wondered when Claire was going to see sense and have the surgery to fix her scars and look at least halfway decent. Perhaps Racheal might take her back.

"Mother, Kris and I are engaged."

"Why, Claire, that's wonderful." Melissa smiled.

Anna stared at Claire and then her mother, who appeared pleased by the news. *This is a nobody they are talking about.* "Well, I'm sure this is a dalliance that you think is important at this moment, but of course it's ridiculous. Whatever would your father think?"

Claire stood and glared at her. "I don't give a shit what my father thinks, and I'm surprised you even mentioned him under the circumstances. I love Kris. She loves me. I will marry her!"

Anna placed her wineglass on the table and began drumming her fingers on the surface. The huge diamond engagement ring on her left hand glittered in the half-light.

"What happens between me and your father is our affair. You are his daughter and he'll want to vet this woman, and trust me, she hardly comes up to his idea of a daughter-in-law. Now enough of this nonsense. When we go back to the city tomorrow, I'm arranging an appointment for you to see the best plastic surgeon in the state and we will fix those terrible scars of yours." Anna picked up her glass and drew in a slow breath as she savored the fragrances that assailed her nose. Claire was right, Carl wouldn't care. This would simply give him another reason to cut all ties.

"Anna, Claire has a right to make her own decisions on her future partner and changes to her body. You must respect that she isn't a child anymore, and I for one approve of Kris becoming part of the family."

"Well you would, Mother, you're going senile." Anna flared her nostrils and for once was thankful when the door opened and Shirley pushed in the heated trolley with their meal. "Thank God, the food at last. I'm famished." Anna ignored the glares from her family and gave Mrs. Rank a half smile as she began to place the dishes on the table. "Let's eat."

Claire shook her head and looked at her grandmother. "Sorry, Grams, but I can't sit here with her." She stormed out of the room.

A couple of minutes later, Kris arrived with the gravy boat.

"Where's Claire?"

Anna gave her a harsh stare. "My daughter has refused to eat with us, and it's all your fault," she declared, ignoring the gasp from the younger woman and piling her plate with duchess potatoes.

"Sit, Kris, and eat. Claire will be back." Melissa pointed to her seat, and Kris took it.

✝

Claire sank down on her bed facedown. The sting of tears she'd held back at her mother's horrendous words now poured down her cheeks, soaking the pillow.

"I won't let her dictate how I should live my life. She made a mess of her life, but she isn't going to do the same to mine. I can do that all on my own." The muffled words against the pillow made her realize she'd left Kris alone with her mother.

Am I crazy? Sure I am for thinking someone as gentle and kind as Kris could ever deserve such treatment. She lifted herself off the bed and stared at the red blotches that looked back at her in the mirror.

With a shaking hand, she touched the scars that trailed across her face. It would be so easy to have the surgery and at least look cosmetically normal. In the last twelve months she'd seriously thought about it, but.... *Yeah, that big but.* This was who she was now, and people had to take her this way or not at all. Her mother included.

She walked into the en suite and washed her face, trying to eradicate the tearstains. With renewed vigor, she headed out of her room back to the dining room, but first she'd make a detour.

†

Anna stared at Claire as she reentered the room and sat down silently. "Just as well, or your dinner would be cold."

Claire shrugged and began to help herself to dinner.

Chapter Thirty-two

As she ate Claire had given Kris a few discreet looks and smiled at the pensive expression on her face. When she winked, Kris gave her a tentative smile.

"So, Mother, how long do you intend to sponge?" At the raised eyebrows from her grams, Claire changed her tone. "How long do you intend to stay with Grams?"

"Oh, indefinitely. Mother doesn't mind. I'll have to work the details out with the divorce lawyer, and we all know how long they take."

How the hell would you know if she does or doesn't? Claire gave her Grams a smile. "Grams, is it okay?"

"Of course, darling. She's my daughter. I couldn't see her in trouble and do nothing to help, just as I can't you."

"Am I in trouble?" Claire frowned.

Grams didn't look her straight in the eye at first. "It all depends on how you want to live."

Claire laughed and waved a fork at her grams. "Frugally if Kris has her way. Isn't that right, darling?" She wanted to kiss Kris at the shocked look on her face. *Ah, of course, she wasn't here when I told them.* "Sorry, Kris, I mentioned to Mother and Grams that we got engaged. I hope you don't mind."

Kris didn't say anything. She simply stared.

Hmm, I could be in trouble here.

"I think it's wonderful, Kris. You are exactly what Claire needs."

"What's that, Grams?"

"Someone sensible."

Claire nodded. Kris was all of that, sure. *Except that isn't why I want to marry her and have her by my side for the rest of our lives. Nope.* When her mother spoke, she turned her attention to Anna.

"Well, I don't approve. Sorry, Kay, or whatever you're called, but Claire can do so much better. She has in the past and will in the future. In fact, I'm sure Racheal will have her back in a heartbeat. Once she's had the surgery."

The room went so silent a bomb could have dropped and no one would have made a sound, not even the bomb. The spiteful words shocked everyone except the speaker, who continued to eat.

Claire had never considered her mother a snob. When Anna had been under the thumb of her father, she could have half expected this reaction, but not now. Her eyes tried to catch Kris's, but she averted her profile, and from what Claire could see had squared her jaw. *Oh crap, how do I make this right without a full-scale war?*

"Mrs. Tremont, I may not be what you want for Claire, and I'm sure you believe she can do better. I have told her myself that very thing—"

"Well there you go."

"Shut up, Anna, and let the girl speak. Please continue, Kris."

251

Claire placed a hand across her mouth to stop the laughter as Grams told her mother off and felt pride that at least one member of her family wasn't full of bullshit.

"She doesn't listen. Claire is a strong-minded person and won't be diverted when she wants something. You should see her with Buddy."

Oh I love you even more, Kris. Not that I could ever love you less than I do.

"Who is Buddy?" Shirley asked.

Claire lifted a finger and bit down on her lower lip.

"He loves your oatmeal cookies, Shirley. Claire feeds him crumbles most days." Kris smiled at Shirley.

Claire watched the interaction, and it reinforced why Kris would make her life whole.

Shirley huffed. "Oh well, that's good, just the crumbles. I was thinking she didn't like them."

Claire cringed. "No, of course not. I love your oatmeal cookies. Kris used to snag them for me when we had a coffee break in the morning."

"Well if you had said, I would have—"

"I've heard enough. My daughter is not going to marry you. I don't care what you say or she says. For God's sake, how can you live a decent life? Claire isn't fit for a job and you…what do you do?" Anna tersely interrupted.

Claire couldn't take it any longer. She stood up knowing her face was glowing. She took a deep breath, trying to contain the anger. Then a hand descended on her good arm, and that narcotic called Kris settled her within seconds. She looked into the muddy-brown eyes and wondered what her life would be like without her. One word came to mind: *unhappy.*

"At the end of the day it doesn't matter what jobs we can and can't do. The important thing is we are together. I don't care what you think, Mother. Kris and I are going to get married, and that's the end of the story…according to you."

"What do you mean?" Anna frowned.

"From what you've said, you won't want anything to do with us. So I guess after breakfast tomorrow, that's it." Claire felt deflated at the words. She hated some of the things her mother said, yet at the same time she knew that deep down her mother wasn't this person. Not the woman who had raised her until she was ten, when things had changed and she had never understood why.

"Give me a minute," Claire said. Then with a smile at Kris, she left the room for a few seconds and returned with a magnum of champagne.

"Grams, do you mind? I'll replace it." She held up the bottle.

"I applaud your taste, my darling girl. Unfortunately, even I can't buy another of those, so don't even try."

"Claire, you can't," Kris pleaded.

Claire turned to her. "You are worth it, and Grams knows I'll repay her. Isn't that right, Grams?"

Melissa smiled. "You already have, darling."

"Shirley, when did you and Ricky marry?"

"Christmas Eve."

Claire turned to Kris and raised the bottle. "We'll open this when we get married, on the anniversary of Shirley's marriage. What do you say?"

Kris nodded. Claire saw tears forming and pulled her close.

"I love you."

"I love you more."

There was a shuffle of a chair as Anna left the room.

†

After Anna's departure the evening had slipped by amicably enough for the four of them, and Melissa decided an early night was in order. Shirley had also gone to bed early, leaving the two lovers alone in the dining room.

Claire leaned back in her chair and smiled.

"Great night once Mother left, don't you think?"

Kris looked at her empty wineglass. In in the end she'd decided to stick to water. There'd been enough excitement without alcohol making it worse by loosening tongues. She glanced at the clock. It was nine thirty.

"It was a great night, right? You're not mad at me for telling them our news, are you?"

Claire's anxious tone had Kris shaking her head. "No, no, of course not. It didn't go so well, did it, from your mother's point of view?"

"Does it matter what my mother thinks? Grams was happy and we are, so the parents are irrelevant in the big picture. Are you going to tell yours?"

Kris paused for a moment. In truth, she hadn't thought about it. Everything was going so fast. The proposed wedding date would be in a little over two months, not that she was unhappy about that. She'd marry Claire tomorrow if they could arrange it.

Claire shuffled in her chair, and the tips of her fingers touched Kris's from across the table. "Look, if this marriage thing isn't right for you at the moment, then I'll wait until you are ready."

Kris stared at her and smiled. "I'm not letting you get away from that promise. Christmas Eve works for me. Do you think it might snow? How awesome would that be?"

Kris chuckled and watched as Claire's eyes sparkled and a half smile drew her lips taut.

"Want to retire to the media room? We can watch more of that Pride and Prejudice saga?"

Claire groaned. "You certainly know how to seduce a woman." She grinned. "What about all these dishes?"

Kris frowned. "I'll load up the dishwasher and clean the debris away. Do you want to help?"

"Now that's more romantic." Kris pursed her lips as Claire moved around the table to stand beside her chair.

"Absolutely something we do together." She dropped her head, and Kris was lost in the slow exploration of Claire's lips on hers.

When they came up for air, Kris gasped.

"I have a better idea." She stood and took Claire's hand.

"Where are we going?"

Kris raised Claire's free hand to her lips. "You'll see."

†

Claire lay on the coverlet of her bed, puzzled but ecstatically so. Kris had left for a moment to go to her room but would be back. A faint knock sounded on the door, and it opened. Kris walked in.

She wasn't in the clothes she'd dined in. She was dressed in a deep emerald robe, and her feet were in matching slippers.

"Well, you look comfy. Can I join you?"

Claire knew it wasn't a question as Kris slowly moved forward and stood by the bed. Her fingers entangled in the belt of the robe. "Yes."

Claire was sure she sounded like a mouse. Was this going to be their first time? She'd dreamed of it but had thought with Kris being a virgin she'd have to wait a little more. That hadn't been a problem for Claire.

Kris gave her a shy smile. "I think I'm a little overdressed." Her fingers untied the belt, and she allowed the robe to drop to the floor.

Claire's eyes widened. Kris was naked. Her mouth went dry as she took in the pale skin that was luminous from the light of the moon. Her eyes traveled down the thin neck to the strong shoulders and then the full breasts with the pink aureoles slowly growing as she stood there. Then her gaze moved downward to tuft of hair that covered Kris's mound.

She sucked in a deep breath at the wonder of this woman she loved deeply. The moisture between her legs began to flow. Being this turned-on without touching was a first. "I think I've died and gone to heaven," Claire tenderly said.

Kris let out a slow breath and smiled, her face transforming as she gently moved onto the bed next to Claire. "I...I wasn't sure if you'd like-"

Claire pulled Kris onto her chest and kissed her softly at first until the passion leapt up and she found Kris's tongue. Her hand wanted to feel everything at once, and she silently cursed her weak arm.

Kris spoke hoarsely. "I'd like to see you too, Claire. Please."

Claire didn't need another invitation. "Will you help me?"

Kris, her face flushed, nodded.

As Claire moved to an upright position, her face was within inches of Kris's left breast. She placed her lips on the underside and slowly kissed her way up to the pert nipple, then grasped it in her teeth gently and sucked hard. She was relishing the moans of pleasure Kris exchanged at the contact with her body pressing into her face. With her hand, she trailed fingers over the other breast and tugged at the neglected nipple.

"Oh God, Claire, this feels wonderful."

Unable to speak, as her mouth was full, Claire eventually released the nipple and moved upward to travel along the sleek neck, and then recaptured parted lips.

Her hand moved down to the triangle of hair, and she laced her fingers through the curls, her heart racing as she encountered a moist center. Her target was Kris's clit. Once she touched the sensitive point, Kris virtually jumped out of her arms.

"Are you okay?"

Kris looked at Claire, her eyes wild and animated. "Don't stop," she finally breathed out.

Claire grinned, then kissed her again as her hand continued its exploration. She was about to place her fingers inside when she pulled away from Kris and smiled at her gently.

"Do you want to do this, Kris? It might hurt and I really don't want—"

Kris decisively took Claire's hand and replaced it in the position it had been in. "I love you."

Claire didn't need anything more as she rhythmically moved inside Kris. Her virgin lover began to writhe as Kris moaned and throaty, indecipherable words erupted.

As Kris came to a climax, Claire gently released her, kissing her slowly until she tasted salt tears. Her eyes flew open and she stared at Kris.

"I'm sorry, Kris, did I hurt you?"

Kris shook her head as she rested it against Claire's shoulder.

"I've never experienced such a wonderful thing in my life before. Thank you, Claire."

Claire's heart swelled. She slowly shook her head.

"I should be thanking you, my love. That was tremendous."

If she died now, having given pleasure to the woman she loved would be enough for her. *Now I really do know what love is.*

Kris slowly moved up to Claire and came face-to-face with her.

"You do know that you are overdressed still. We didn't quite manage to strip you of your clothes." Kris chuckled as she slipped her arms between them and began to unbutton Claire's blue linen blouse. "Now it's my turn."

Claire let out a squeal of pleasure, and hands deftly removed her blouse and with a dexterity she never thought any woman possessed, removed her lacy bra, and soft lips descended on her small breasts.

I have died and gone to heaven.

Chapter Thirty-three

Threading her fingers through her hair, Claire couldn't prevent the smile that widened her lips and pulled the scars on her face tighter. Kris hadn't wanted to stay the night for propriety's sake, of course. She'd laughed at the old-fashioned attitude but at the same time was proud too. It had been around three when Kris reluctantly left. Now Claire was chomping at the bit to see her again, drawing in the sweet smell of lovemaking as the delicate floral scent Kris always smelled of permeated the room. It was six in the morning, and though there was a good chance Shirley would be up, Kris probably wasn't but just might be.

At least my mother won't be. Thank God for that. I'm done with her supercilious preaching. The disparaging words in her head rolled around as she headed out of her bedroom and tripped lightly down the stairs.

The hall was so silent you could hear a pin drop as she headed for the kitchen entrance.

"I was hoping you would get up early."

The hairs on the back of her neck stood up as she turned at the voice.

"Mother?"

Anna stepped out of the study doorway. "You sound surprised."

"Well, yeah. When have you ever been up at the crack of dawn, unless there was a sale to be had?"

Her mother approach Claire, and she placed her hand in her pocket and clenched it into a fist.

"I always loved the sunrises here. They are still as beautiful as I remember. Do you mind if we have a few words?"

Claire moved her head to one side, considering what her mother wanted other than to break her and Kris apart.

"If it's about Kris, forget it."

Anna frowned and shook her head. "No, it's about you and I."

Claire was surprised. "Okay, but I'm helping out at breakfast this morning, so I can't stay long."

"I understand." Anna stepped back into the study, and Claire followed.

Once inside, her mother sat in the leather, high-backed chair that dominated the room.

As always, wanting to be in charge. This was a bad idea. "Out with it, Mother. Time is precious."

They traded stares for a few seconds and Anna cleared her throat. "Leaving your father wasn't easy for me, Claire. In fact, I'm not sure I will be strong enough to go through with it alone."

Claire frowned and leaned against the nearest bookcase. *What is this bullshit?* "Mother, you are one of the strongest women, barring Grams, that I know. You are better off without him. Before you say it, I know he's my father.

Like they say, you can't choose your family, but you can choose your friends. I think the divorce is a good thing, and you have Grams."

Her mother sighed heavily. Anna actually looked worried. The lines on her forehead were pronounced, and she placed a hand to her temple as if she were suffering from a headache.

"Mother has been supportive throughout my life with your father. That, of course, does not mean she approved. To be frank, she has never liked Carl or accepted him as a husband. I need your support too, darling."

Claire straightened. "Exactly what kind of support?"

Her mother looked down at her manicured nails and then shot her a direct glance. "You and I can take over the business. It's the ideal solution. Carl won't want the financial mess. It's heavily in debt, mainly to Mother, and he'll take other equity to be out of our lives. He has a mistress. He's never been without one since the day we married…probably even when we were engaged. The Jackson-Tremont girls can take the city realty business by storm."

The impassioned words were the most energetic Claire had ever heard from her mother, other than when she was talking to a possible customer. *I'm not a customer.* "What does Grams say about this?"

"Why would my mother have an opinion?"

The words were typical of her mother. Selfish to the core. "It sounds like Grams owns the business with the debt. Sorry, Mother, but the realty business isn't what I want to do with my life. At least not the business you and Father have."

Anna stood and glared at Claire. "Do you know how selfish you sound? What do you know of the sacrifices I made once I knew you were on the way? I put up with Carl and his infidelity because I didn't want you to grow up without a father figure."

"Yeah, and what a father figure he was. I can't stand the man."

"Claire! When I approached him for a divorce when you were ten, he threatened violence, not on me but you. I had nothing but his word against mine to go to the authorities. When you came out, he wanted to disown you. It was at the time the business was floundering. After all I'd put up with, I wasn't going to lose everything and have my daughter ostracized in public. I had Mother reinvest in the business to stop it going under and Carl became compliant."

Claire knew her mouth looked like a guppy's. "Did Grams know all this?"

"No." Her mother held her head upright. "Do you tell your parents everything?"

Claire bit her lip and shook her head.

"I told Mother when I left Carl. To be honest, I was ashamed of what I'd become. I still am, but you can help me, Claire. I'd like to try again in the mother-and-daughter department if you will allow me. I know I can do better. I used to be a better person, honestly."

The words seemed to bounce like a rubber ball on a pathway.

"I need to speak with Grams, Mother. I'll see you at breakfast."

Claire turned to head out of the door, her mind swimming with information she wasn't sure was true.

"After you have breakfast, I'd like to view the cottage and see your handiwork if that's okay?"

"You're not joining us?"

"I have a terrible headache. Perhaps I'll have coffee and a roll."

"Okay, and sure, I'd like to show you that I can be of benefit to society, contrary to other people's ideas."

Claire left the room and closed the door behind her, and when it shut, she leaned against it and took a deep breath. *Surely she didn't stay with that slime ball for me. It can't be true. No one does that these days. That must explain why she changed overnight back then.*

†

Claire looked at her watch. It was a quarter after six. *Hell, it doesn't take long to drop a bombshell. I wonder if Grams is awake.*

She galloped up the stairs and stopped outside Grams's bedroom. Down the hall at the end was Kris's room. She moved away from Grams's door, walked to the far door, and tentatively knocked.

There wasn't an answer.

Damn.

She tried again and put her ear to the door to see if she could make out any noise inside.

She placed her forehead on the door and sighed.

Then she jumped guiltily as a voice from down the corridor spoke.

"Claire? I didn't think you'd be up yet."

Claire sheepishly looked at her grandmother, who was peering out of her door.

"How can anyone sleep late in this house? There is always someone moving around. I decided that as everyone else seemed to have risen, I'd at least catch up on my emails before breakfast. I believe Kris left her room about ten minutes ago. Even your mother is up and around, not that I'm surprised."

Claire walked to Grams and gave her a kiss on the cheek.

"Grams, we need to talk. It's about Mother."

Grams rolled her eyes and Claire shrugged.

"Come inside. It's been a long time since you sat on my bed and we've had a girly talk."

Claire grinned and sank onto the end of the bed as her Grams settled under the coverlet.

"Okay, spill it, although I suspect I know. It's about Kris, I suppose?"

Claire frowned. "Not directly."

"Really? Well, go for it."

Claire related her mother's conversation, and when she finished she stared at Grams, who looked surprised.

"Is it true?"

Grams took a deep breath and motioned for Claire to come closer. When she did, Grams placed an arm around her, hugging her tight.

"Yes, probably. Carl was never…shall we say, good enough for Anna. Ah, before you call me a snob, he wasn't good enough for anyone's daughter. He showed his true colors the day he married Anna and announced to his friends that he'd bedded Anna's best friend Diana the night before. They all thought it funny. Unfortunately for him, your grandfather heard the conversation and told me. We didn't know what to do. Anna looked so happy. I confronted Diana and she denied it. She did finally admit it to me six months into the marriage. By then, of course, you were on the way. I chose to ignore it. Graham never forgave Carl. If they were invited to the house, he was always away."

Claire couldn't believe her Grams would ignore such a thing. Shimmering tears brimmed in her grandmother's eyes. That hurt. "Mother said he threatened her, or rather me when I was ten and she asked for a divorce. Did she ever tell you?"

"Not then, my darling. If she had, you both would have been taken away from him, even if Carl caused a scene." Grams's face became thoughtful. "Your mother never confided in me after she met Carl. I missed that. But she was young and in love. You can't keep your children tied to your apron strings. They have to find their own way in life."

Claire closed her eyes and sighed.

"Grams I…will she change if I go back to live and work with her?"

Grams kissed the top of her head. "She used to be so sweet-natured as a child and very loving. I think your father killed that over the years and she became a shell of a woman. As to if you can bring her back? I really cannot say. If she thinks so, perhaps there is a chance."

Claire felt her world begin to rotate at a speed that wouldn't allow her to make sense of what she should do. "The house is worth at least three million and that's the only equity they have, so what the hell does that mean the business debt is?" Drained emotionally, she still needed to ask, because this was an important practical issue and practical was better right now than the emotional baggage.

"Oh, darling, don't worry about such a thing. The house won't be going to your father. Besides, you own the freehold. I have the title as collateral for the debt in your name. When you had the accident it was my stipulation that I keep hold of the deed for you."

"So I can sink him, right?" Claire gave a half smile.

"Well yes, I guess you can."

"Good to know. I know we didn't get a chance to talk after dinner last night, but Grams, I want you to know Kris and I are in love. I love her so much it hurts to think of my life if she wasn't in it anymore."

Grams chuckled and Claire frowned.

"My darling, that was one of the reasons I wanted you here. I knew from the first moment I met Kris that she would be good for you, and I was right. In fact, it's more than I could ever have expected. Besides, Shirley has been keeping me apprised of your progress."

Claire opened her mouth. "Grams, that's like…like spying. How could you?"

"When Shirley called me a week into you being here and said, 'This was the time,' I knew I was right too."

Claire rolled her eyes and shook her head. "Grams, you sound like Shirley. She says odd things like that. Exactly what does it mean? *The time.*"

Grams moved away and held her at arm's length. "It means the enchantment of the cottage has worked its magic. Now go and see if our breakfast is almost ready. I will meet you downstairs in half an hour."

Claire kissed her grams again and slipped off the bed.

"I love you, Grams. Thank you."

Grams softly chuckled, blew her a kiss, and waved her away. "I love you too. Now away with you, scamp. You need to speak with Kris about this. Don't leave her out of the loop."

Claire sagely nodded and left the room.

Damn, but I don't want her tarnished by my family problems.

Chapter Thirty-four

Kris was excited yet at the same time frightened to see Claire. So many what-ifs. Her head had been spinning with them since she left Claire. Sleep had been impossible.

What if Claire has what she wanted?

What if Claire decides I'm not a good enough lover?

What if Claire decides she doesn't love me after all?

No matter how many times she tried to eradicate the words spinning in her head, they persisted. Even though the heady reminiscence of their lovemaking tried very hard to erase them.

Shirley had been her usual self. The reticence of last evening had disappeared, and she smiled a warm welcome when Kris entered the kitchen.

"Breakfast will be early today, I believe."

Kris furrowed her brow.

"Oh, I figured Melissa and Anna might need a sleep-in as they had a long journey yesterday." Shirley shook her head and wiped her hands on her apron. "Anna is up. In fact, she almost beat me. Claire is up. I needed something from my coat pocket in the hall and saw her as she and her mother were entering the study."

"Okay, but what about Melissa?"

Shirley chuckled. "Mrs. Jackson is a light sleeper. All that activity of doors opening and shutting will wake her and she will be up too."

Kris laughed. "I guess. Anything I can help you with?"

"Today Miss Anna can 'slum it' with the rest of us. We will eat in the kitchen. Will you set out the cutlery and plates?"

Kris nodded and smiled at Shirley.

"I think this is a wonderful place to eat. She should be grateful." Kris headed for the cutlery drawer and began removing the items for the meal.

"Kris, Miss Anna was a nicer person at one time. Right now, she's in a state of flux. I can't ask you to give her a second chance, because you will make up your mind when you know all the facts."

The door opened and Claire walked in.

Kris's heart rate tripled.

"Hey, anything I can do? Grams will be up for breakfast in half an hour, and Mother is in the study."

Claire didn't immediately look at her. Kris felt her worries had been right, but which one? Or was it all of them?

Shirley pointed to sink. "I'd appreciate your refilling the orange juice pitcher."

"On it."

Kris watched as Claire busied herself with the chore.

When she finished, Kris stared directly at Claire and gave a tentative smile.

She felt that Claire returned it reluctantly.

Her stomach hit rock bottom and bile soared in her throat, threatening to embarrass her. "Good morning?"

Claire seemed to hesitate to reply but eventually muttered, "Morning."

Tears stung as she turned away. "Life sucks," she brokenly said, then took the back entrance out of the house.

✝

Shirley refrained from speaking while the two were in the room, but when Kris left hurriedly, she felt the time was right.

"I don't know what the problem is, Claire, but if you don't nip it in the bud, then you will most definitely lose her."

Claire gave her a glower, then bent her head. "Pretty shabby behavior, huh? It was, I know it. Kris deserves so much more than my baggage and me. How can I ask her to take on my mother? She deserves happiness, not acrimony."

"Let her be the judge of that. She's seen your mother, experienced her bad vibes, and yet I suspect she never once doubted your affection for her. Give the woman credit. Lots of them would have run." Shirley tutted. "I guess we will have one less for breakfast, and I was going to make her that Spanish omelet she said she'd love to have but has never tried."

Claire vividly recalled their lovemaking and kicked herself for being such an idiot. Who else in the world would treat her with such gentleness and respect for her disfigurements, then put up with the terrible jibes from her mother? Still, Kris had given herself to Claire, tenderly making love, even ignoring the horror of the numerous scars that traversed her body.

Melissa entered the kitchen. "I'm a little earlier than expected. When is breakfast and do we really have to go formal, Shirley?"

Shirley smiled. "This morning I make the rules, and we are having breakfast here. Kris is upset, and I was thinking of delaying for a little while."

Melissa frowned and looked at Claire, who was bending her head. "Let me see if I can fix that. What direction did she go?"

Claire looked up and frowned. "Grams, I'll go."

"You will not. I want a word with Kris, and this is as good a time as any. We shall both be back shortly."

Shirley grinned. "She went out the back door, and if I know Kris, she will head for the cottage."

"Lovely. I need a little bit of exercise before your marvelous breakfast, Shirley."

Melissa left the room.

"You know it should be me. It was all my fault."

Shirley shook her head. "Yes, it was. Hopefully you will be given a second chance to redeem yourself. Now get on with the chores, and when your grandmother is heading back, you can have the privilege of telling your mother where breakfast will be served."

Claire raised her eyebrows. "Wow, that's harsh, but under the circumstances a totally great call, although Mother only wants a coffee and roll."

Shirley turned away and smiled.

†

Melissa traced a path toward the cottage and then spied Kris sitting on the top step of the porch. She seemed so

270

engrossed in her own thoughts she didn't hear Melissa's approach and jumped when she was almost in front of her.

"Melissa, is anything wrong?" Kris stood.

Melissa smiled. Something inordinately welcoming reverberated around this young woman. In many people's eyes she was an average person getting on with her life. Yet from the moment their lives joined, she had simply interwoven with not just Melissa but with Claire too. That was the most momentous thing to happen.

"No, my dear, I'm the messenger. Breakfast is almost ready."

Kris shook her head. "I'm not hungry, thanks. I'll skip it."

Of course you would say that. So would I, especially if someone I loved hurt me deeply. I've been there and understand completely.

"I have a proposition for you, and I'm hoping you might consider it."

Kris frowned. "What would that be?"

Melissa smiled at the innocent defiance. *You go, girl.* "Shirley needs to leave Seasons. It could be for a few months, but then it could be forever. I need another housekeeper to take over. With what you have done with the cottage, I know you are the perfect choice."

Melisa watched a look of surprise, then excitement flash over Kris's face.

"Can I bring Knight, my cat, with me?"

"My dear, you can bring your whole family. Kris, this is where you were meant to be. I don't want to pressure you though, because I can advertise the position."

"No, I'll take it." Kris rapidly ran down the few steps and hugged Melissa. "Thank you."

Melissa returned the hug. "Don't give up on my granddaughter. She needs you," she whispered in Kris's ear.

Kris turned to her with a pained expression. "She has to find her way, and right now she's being pulled in other directions. I'm hoping it's me she chooses in the end."

Melissa caught her close. "I hope so too. Now, let's go and see what Shirley has conjured for us."

†

When Grams and Kris returned, Claire wanted to look in any direction but at her lover. Words sunk in her brain, and a delicious rivulet of excitement at the memory of their lovemaking the night before washed over her. She couldn't help but feel good. Her eyes caught Kris's, and she slowly nodded and gave her a smile. Kris reciprocated tightly. *I deserve that. I deserve worse than that.* She was about to engage Kris in conversation when Shirley reminded her about her mother.

"I'm just going to fetch Mother. I'll be back."

The swing door almost revolved with the speed at which she left the room.

Claire walked as fast as she could to the study. Her core purpose now was to speak with Kris and find out what the woman she loved would do in her circumstances. Surely, between them, they could brainstorm a solution and everyone would be happy.

She knocked on the study door and entered.

There was no sound from her mother, who sat in the big leather chair. It was currently facing the window looking out onto the grassy area leading to the swimming pool.

"Mother, breakfast is ready and we are all eating in the kitchen."

Fully expecting her mother to protest, she was amazed when nothing happened. Her mother was there; she could see a small portion of her shoulder. Walking closer, she frowned.

"Mother, breakfast. Are you going to give it the cold shoulder because it's not being served in the dining room?"

No answer. Worse than that, no movement.

Bile backfilled her throat and a sensation of dread hit the pit of her stomach. She moved to the chair and walked around it.

"Mother." This time she spoke tentatively as she saw the closed lids and her contorted mouth. She rapidly felt for a pulse. It was there.

"I'll fetch help, Mom, I promise." Claire rushed out of the room and fled to the kitchen.

✝

When Claire entered the kitchen, her face was deathly white and she incoherently said her mother had collapsed and was unconscious.

Melissa tried to stand and then sank back, her face drawn as she gasped for air and held a hand to her heart.

Shirley called the ambulance.

After administering to Melissa, who needed her asthma medicine, Kris decided it was up to her to take over.

"I'll go sit with Anna until the ambulance arrives. Shirley, I think strong tea might help them."

Shirley nodded and gave her a half smile of what she figured was approval.

"I should go," Claire finally said with tears streaming down her cheeks.

Kris went over to Claire and placed a gentle hand on her shoulder. "I promise to take care of your mom, Claire. Have the tea and then come sit with us until the paramedics arrive. Do you trust me to take care of her?"

"Always. I'm sorry for earlier. I love you," Claire whispered.

"I know. I love you too." Kris gently kissed her cheek.

Within ten minutes the ambulance came. Anna, Melissa, and Claire left Seasons.

Kris finally sat down, and the smell of the breakfast made her stomach growl, but she couldn't eat anything. The paramedics who arrived said Anna had had a seizure, possibly a stroke, but her pulse was strong, and they'd found her early enough. They also checked over Melissa, who was still having breathing difficulties, and decided it best she went with them for a checkup. Claire, her darling Claire, looked devastated. She sat in the back of the ambulance, her face ashen as the doors closed and the siren blasted out as they headed away from the house.

Shirley walked back in the kitchen and gave her a shake of the head, tears slowly tracking down her cheeks.

"I was certainly not expecting that. Thank you, Kris, for being strong. We all needed it. Now, I must call my nephew. This changes everything."

Kris reached for Shirley's arm. "It doesn't."

Shirley gave her a long look. "Melissa told you that I needed to leave for a while?"

"Yes, and she offered me the position. I took it...but only until you get back, of course." Kris smiled.

Shirley began to cry. "You are a very special woman, Kris Lake, thank you." The older woman wrapped her in a hug so tight Kris could barely breathe.

Eventually released, she smiled. "Out of the sorrows of life, there is a kernel of hope that eventually grows to happiness. I believe that wholeheartedly, don't you?"

Shirley gave her a strange look, then nodded as she wiped away tears.

"You really do belong here, Kris. Now let me make you something for breakfast. What we had is spoiled."

"I'm not really hungry."

"Nonsense, you have a lot to do still. Claire will need your guidance, and I know she would love you to be by her side right now. A quick omelet and then take my car to the hospital."

Scratching the side of her face, Kris frowned.

"Okay, but I might need help with the hospital part. Melissa could do with a friendly face too."

"Thank you. I am worried about Mrs. Jackson."

"Anytime." Her mind flooded with the events of that last hour. She refused to think about them and how the future would affect Claire and their lives. Now the most important thing was to ensure Claire and her family got well. *What else is important when you love someone?*

†

Kris asked at reception for information on Anna Tremont and was met with the standard "are you family?" routine.

She was about to say she wasn't when Shirley interjected, "She's the daughter's fiancée. I think that qualifies."

When Kris saw the stern way Shirley looked at the receptionist, she now knew why people said some of the things they did about her.

"Of course. She's in ICU. There is a family room adjacent to the ward."

Kris turned to Shirley and gave her a look of gratitude. "Can you tell me where Melissa Jackson is, please? She's family," Shirley asked.

The receptionist told her the ward.

"I'll see to Melissa, and you go find your Claire." Shirley turned in the direction of the ward where she'd locate Melissa.

A ten-floor elevator ride later, Kris arrived at the floor for the ICU and looked around for the room described by the receptionist.

Twenty paces down a white-walled corridor, she saw the room marked *family*. She tentatively opened the door. At first, she thought there was no one present, then from the shadow of a pillar, there was movement.

"Claire?"

Claire appeared. Her face was gaunt as she stared at Kris before it miraculously changed. Seconds later, Claire was in her arms.

"Thank you for being here. You are a godsend."

Kris held her trembling body close. "I love you. Where else would I be?"

"Mother's had a stroke. They won't know how bad until…if…she recovers consciousness."

Kris held her closer and kissed the top of her head. "Then we will wait it out together. If your mom is as strong as you are, she'll be out of here in no time."

"Is Grams okay? Damn, I can't lose her too. I just can't think."

Kris looked directly into Claire's eyes.

"Melissa is doing great, and Shirley is with her. Once she stabilizes, she will be with you too. And you are not going to lose anyone, trust me." Crossing her fingers, she hoped she had made the right call since it could bite her back later.

Claire sank into Kris's shoulder and began to sob. "I don't want my mom to die."

Kris simply held her until she could cry no more.

Chapter Thirty-five

Kris looked over the drive, giving a half smile. A part of her was soul-sad because Claire wasn't with her, but another part of her relished living in this beautiful place. Her caretaker duties helped her cope with Claire returning with her family to New York. Two months passed, and in that time, she and Knight, who now wrapped his tail around her leg purring incessantly, had settled into a routine. She bent and picked him up, and he pushed his head against her cheek.

"Yeah, I love you too, Knight. I don't need to ask you how you like being here, do I?" Kris chuckled. Since she rescued—that was the right word for it—Knight from the cattery, he'd been beside her like a lapdog. Even the change of surroundings had been perfectly fine as long as she was in sight.

It helped the loneliness of being in such a grand house alone.

Claire's mother's stroke severed Kris and Claire's physical interaction, but they still talked most days on Skype.

Last night Claire had discussed her mother in more detail than normal.

"Mother's doing well, thank goodness. I miss being with you." Claire had laughed, and Kris smiled and wanted to reach into the screen and hold her close. "Of course the therapist said she could be doing better. I guess they always say that. She remembers my twenty-first birthday party now. Her memory is in little snippets, a bit like me."

Kris heard the sadness in her lover's voice. "That's good, right?"

"Yes, yes, it is. She doesn't remember leaving Father and has asked why he doesn't come home. Not that she can recall his name." They both laughed. "Doctors say her memory is something that might never fully recover. I guess Mother and I have something in common now."

"She will. Who wouldn't with support from you and Melissa? It must be great in your house at the moment, having all those girly chats helping your mom remember things from the past."

Claire rolled her eyes at Kris. They smiled, and she touched the screen as Claire did the same.

"I miss you."

Kris bit the inside of her lip and tears welled up as she forced a smile. "I miss you too, but right now you are exactly where you should be, love. Hey, did I tell you that the furry devil Knight caught a mouse in the pantry? Well, three actually. I daren't tell Shirley when she calls me tomorrow."

They both laughed and it eased the tension.

"I just want to hold you and make love to you. It's so damn frustrating. Every time I've planned a visit for the weekend, Mother takes a turn for the worse. I swear she does it on purpose." Claire sighed.

"Oh don't say that, Claire. Maybe she's just frightened. I've been reading about strokes. It says that for someone like your mom, she must feel like she no longer controls her life."

Claire sighed. "Yes, I'm sure you're right. You always are. I still miss just being in a room with you."

Kris grinned. "You're alone and so am I. Have you ever played show and tell?"

Claire gasped. "I can't believe you said that."

Kris chuckled. "What do you think? That I don't want the same as you now that I've experienced the Claire Tremont loving?"

Claire laughed and began to unbutton her blouse. "Never."

Kris crossed her legs at the memory of their first Skype sex session. To take her mind off her erotic thoughts, she turned to Knight. "Well, Knight, time for you to check out the cottage. Maybe you can find a mouse or two there, but no birds, remember?" She gently tapped his head.

†

As she made the finishing touches to the snacks for the evening, the excessive crunch of gravel caught Kris's attention. Frowning, she peered out the window and saw a car she didn't recognize. It was a sporty-looking model for sure. Watching for the driver or passenger if there was one to exit the vehicle, she was surprised when no one did.

Nervousness assailed her. The gate was foreboding, but anyone could open it. Instinctively she reached inside her pocket for her phone. If it was anyone she thought the least unsavory, she was calling the police. Her finger poised to call 9-1-1.

"Fern? Oh, and there's Jess."

She replaced the phone in her pocket and went to the door.

Once she opened it, Kris watched the two women negotiate the few steps, Jess using her cane to check out the distances between each one.

"Kris, how's things? I haven't seen you at the quiz recently."

Fern's voice held mild interest as she twisted the car keys in her hands.

"Blame Jess, she's been busy. Isn't that right, Jess?" Kris smiled as her friend reached the top step.

"Yes, all my fault. Darned if I forget how many steps there are to get to the front door. By the way, if you wondered why she is here, Fern volunteered to bring me over for our weekly get-together since Mary had to work."

Kris laughed. "I almost called the cops. I haven't seen this car before."

Fern huffed, looking back at the drive and the vehicle. "It's a Dodge Viper GTS. Don't you just love the blazing red color?"

Kris smiled. "Certainly. It suits you. It looks great though, and I bet it's fast."

"'Fast' isn't the word for it. I thought I was taking part in a rally race. You really need to slow down, especially around corners," Jess said. "Let's go inside or Knight might decide to venture out. I do not want to be tapping my cane all night in search of my feline buddy."

"I won't come in. You two enjoy your evening. When you are ready to come home, call me, Jess, but please give me at least half an hour warning. Enjoy, ladies." Fern smiled and began to take the steps back to the drive.

Jess caught her arm, and Kris was fascinated how she homed in so accurately. "Thanks, and if Mary has finished her shift, I'll call her."

"Why, are you chicken?" Kris could hear the strain in Fern's voice.

Jess chuckled. "No, well maybe a little, but I don't want to bother you. Thanks again."

Fern nodded and left. Jess gave a frown and then smiled at Kris.

"What's for supper?"

Kris took her friend's arm and pulled her inside gently as she chuckled. Jess was easy to please in the catering area. "I made your favorite."

"My favorite? When you cook, everything is my favorite."

"Mini meatball pizzas with aioli dip."

Jess hugged her arm closer. "You are a goddess."

Kris laughed and they headed for the media room.

†

Claire gazed at her mother sleeping peacefully. She thought her life had finally taken on a new meaning when she fell in love with Kris, and in love she definitely was. Kris's features and gentle manner invaded her mind and created the need to be with her every day. Yet right now, the dream of being with Kris in the short term was fading as her mother became even more demanding of her time.

Am I destined never to spend the rest of my life with my love? Right now, I believe so. Tears formed and she wiped them away. *I'm being selfish. Mother could have died and here I am thinking about me.*

The door to the bedroom opened, and Grams entered. "How has she been today?"

Claire smiled at Grams. At least she wasn't alone in this. Grams sat on the edge of the bed, gazing at her daughter.

"Not too bad this morning. She was quite lucid, and then her speech problems must have frustrated her and she had a major meltdown this afternoon."

The quiet words settled around the room.

"It's early days, Claire. The doctors said it would be a while before she can cope with not articulating as she had before. We have the best speech therapist in the state booked for next week. I think things will change."

The words sounded positive, yet the tone didn't.

"Grams, if it doesn't work out, I won't abandon her. From what she said at Seasons before the event, she was there for me."

Grams gave her a serious look and shook her head. "My darling, she wouldn't want you to spend the rest of your life as a nursemaid. Anna had so many dreams for you when you were a baby, and though many haven't come to fruition, one has, and she'd want you to pursue that."

Claire knitted her brows and pulled at her lip. "Which one?"

A tinkle of laughter followed.

"Grams?"

"Love, my darling, love."

Claire snorted. "And she approved like hell." The words echoed off the walls.

"Let's go and get a drink. I for sure could use one after spending the day in front of lawyers and your father." Grams looked at Anna. "We have a baby monitor if she needs us."

They both looked at the object plugged into the wall.

"I could do with a drink, but just one. Mother might need me."

Grams stood and held out her arm. "Darling, I will take the nightshift. You need to relax and get some sleep, so have a whole damn bottle of wine. You deserve it. Besides, Anna is my child, and no matter what, a mother will always, and I mean always, be there for her children."

Claire shrugged. "Thanks, Grams, I love you." She took the offered arm and levered herself out of the chair and felt a weight lift.

†

Jess grinned and gave Kris a wide-eyed look. "I loved the food combo." She dropped her head. "I just wish I could convince you that there are other people out there who might be made for you too."

"Sorry, Jess, we've been through that wish. I love Claire. I always will until the day I die. There will never be anyone else. I know that sounds clichéd, but it's true."

Jess clutched her hand and Kris squeezed it.

"When is she coming back?"

Kris sucked in a breath. "Not sure. It could be tomorrow, a month, a year, or never."

"That's a rather pragmatic way of looking at love. Love should be all about emotion and not practical."

Kris dragged a hand through her hair and considered what Jess had said. *Is she right?* "Want a coffee?"

Jess sighed. "Sure."

Ten minutes later, she sucked in a deep breath as she opened the door to the media room and entered with the tray. Practicing the maneuver numerous times when she was on her own meant this was a piece of cake. She'd taken longer than normal getting the coffee and the Hershey cookies Jess adored. That was primarily because once out of Jess's hearing, which was acute, and behind the closed door of the kitchen she'd burst into tears.

Practical and Claire did not go together. Not at all. She had to remain positive even though a part of her suspected Claire was lost to her. Anna needed her more at this time, and how could she possibly compete with the circumstances? Another woman maybe, but that was debatable if it was Racheal. She still wasn't totally convinced Claire's ex wasn't in the background somewhere, and Racheal had wanted her back. What better time than when Claire was vulnerable?

"Hey, I thought you'd gotten lost," Jess amiably said as Kris placed the tray on the table.

"The percolator had a hissy fit and I had to do it over. I have your fav cookies." A look of happiness crossed Jess's face, and Kris wondered not for the first time why life had made her choose Claire instead of Jess. Jess would have been less complicated. *Hmm, maybe not.*

"Hershey's, oh I love you, but you know that, right?" Jess reached forward and felt for the plate that held the cookies.

"You have radar, I swear." Kris laughed as she sat and poured their coffee. "Here, take this."

Jess grinned, took the mug of coffee, and placed it in a position where she knew exactly where it was. Then she went back to unwrapping her cookie.

"Jess?"

"Yeah?" Jess sank her teeth into the cookie, and her face was a picture of supreme joy.

"I know we touched on it once and I won't pry, but have you ever been in love?"

The joyous expression changed. Only for a few seconds, but it did change. Jess ate her mouthful of cookie. "Once. It didn't work out, and I can honestly say I'm not like you and will wait forever. She's a user, and one day it will bite her in the butt."

The charged way Jess had spoken had Kris speculating.

"How did she use you?" Kris picked up her coffee and sipped it as Jess took her time replying. She didn't push the matter. The point was obviously neither of them had a good track record when it came to falling in love.

"You know you should, in the big picture, have chosen me." Jess sighed heavily. "Except you knew, didn't you, when we had dinner at the golf club that I hadn't let go."

Kris nodded, forgetting for moment Jess's disability and she couldn't see. "I knew something was amiss. I wasn't sure what, but does it have something to do with Fern?"

Jess gave a strangled laughed. "Fern, sure it's Fern. That woman is the worst womanizer on the planet, and she takes anyone to bed. The younger, the better. She was with that Candy Crush kid when we saw her."

The bitter words exploded into the quiet room, and Kris leaned back, unsure if it was the potency or just that Jess had admitted it.

Kris picked up a cookie, unwrapped it, and placed it in Jess's hand.

"I heard chocolate is a great comforter, and what the heck, we both need it, right?"

Jess placed the cookie in her mouth, then like a snake wrapped her hand around Kris's wrist.

"I signed up because of her. I guess she feels guilty and gives me rides occasionally. Not that I want or need her charity."

Once again, the hostile tone ricocheted around the room.

"Jess, from today you and I will forget and forgive and move forward. Is that a deal?"

She watched the sightless gaze look to the window as if Jess could see the stars outside that often comforted Kris in the lonely evenings. "I want to do that, Kris, I really do, but can we? Can we forget all the hurt and just move on?"

"No, no, we don't forget it. We learn from it."

"What have you learned? You say you will wait until you die. Is that good?"

Kris didn't hesitate. "For me, yes. Claire is the love of my life. I can't explain it really. I just know it goes soul-deep. I guess they will be calling me a kooky kind of person when I'm old and gray."

"You mean like Mrs. Rank? I have to say that until I met her and talked to her with you, she frightened the jebezzers out of me. Well she does with most folk around here, I can tell you."

Kris chuckled. "All a ruse to keep the men away."

Jess frowned. "I heard she wasn't that attractive, in fact, quite ugly. The rumor was that her husband was quite the womanizer in his day and very handsome. Everyone was shocked when he married her and didn't have to, if you know what I mean."

"Where do you get all this information from?" Kris laughed and sipped her coffee.

"Oh, a little bird or two. Gossip in a small town like this is rampant. Want to know what they say about you?"

Hugging the coffee closer to her chest, ignoring the heat, Kris contemplated also ignoring the question. *Why would anyone bother gossiping about me? I'm a nobody.* "Sure."

Jess smiled, and that gave Kris comfort. "That they hope that you don't end up like Mrs. Rank, alone and living in a house that is barely used. Some of them say it is cursed. There are a lot of stories of love and loss at Seasons." She held up a hand. "Not that I know of them, but maybe we can research them. What do you think?"

Kris was relieved that the gossip, as Jess called it, was general. "Great idea. Now come on, the rest of the cookies must be calling your name."

Jess picked up her coffee and raised it. "You are right there, but I want to make a toast. To love, wherever the path leads us."

Kris smiled. "I'll drink to that."

†

Claire poised a finger over the instant message name and hesitated. Then the bottle of wine she had consumed talking to her grams kicked in. False bravado was kickass when you were floundering, and she was. This was dangerous territory. She drew a deep breath and touched the name. It rang for several seconds. *Thank God, she's not there.*

"Claire?"

Racheal's voice resonated in the room. It was familiar, and in a strange kind of way soothing after her conversation with Grams.

"Hi, wasn't sure the green light meant you were online properly or if it's just a permanent feature."

There was a tinkle of laughter, and she could hear other voices in the background.

"I don't answer just anyone when I'm on a date, but you know you are different."

Claire felt humbled by Racheal's words. She could so easily have blown her off, but this was compassionate she felt sure. "Thanks, but it can wait. I'll call you tomorrow."

"Oh no way, because we both know you won't. Give me a min."

In the background, she heard Racheal make apologies for the call and saying she would be back shortly.

"Okay, what's on your mind? Don't give me the bullshit 'there's nothing.' You and I these days don't do social calls, do we?"

The bland perfection of the words made Claire smile. The old Racheal would have prevaricated, but this new Racheal was right to the point. *I like it.* "I have a vague recollection and it is vague, so if I'm wrong don't hesitate to tell me."

"Recollection of what, Claire?"

"Yeah, right. Sorry. Grams wants me to go back to Seasons and said she will take care of Mother. I vaguely recall that you had a similar problem, but it could be a phantom memory."

The silence that prevailed had Claire on the back foot, then Racheal spoke.

"Yeah, about five years ago my mother had a major stroke. We were given a fifty-fifty chance she would survive. As you know she's still here."

"Yes, yes, she came to see me several times after the accident. I'm sorry I didn't recall that your mother had the stroke. You used someone, right? To take care of her." Claire was clutching at straws.

"You know we did. Ah, right, your memory stuff. It cost a fortune, but Dad said money wasn't any object, and frankly, he was right. For the record, I forgot after your accident what people mean to each other. I'll live with the regret for the rest of my life."

"Yeah, I know. This place or person, where or who is it?"

Voices resonated closer, shouting at Racheal to join them.

"Please, Racheal."

"Right sure. It's called the Calleston Foundation. That's all I remember. I can ask Dad to call you if it would help?"

"Thanks, I think I have this. I owe you, Racheal." Claire nodded as she clutched the phone tighter.

"Okay, coming from you I might redeem it one day. Claire, I'll always love you, and I hope you find what you are looking for."

Claire didn't have the chance to reply as the connection severed. "I already have," she said to the empty room.

Chapter Thirty-six

Kris snuggled up to Knight curled up next to her on the sofa. It was barely seven o'clock, but she was shattered. It didn't help that Claire hadn't made any contact in almost a week. How hard could it be to text or email if she hadn't the time to Skype? Claire hadn't indicated in their last conversation that she was going to have a problem communicating. Maybe the Skype sex had been too much for her. She raised a hand to her forehead and rubbed hard enough to cause pain.

It can't be that, I would know. Claire was on fire when they made love virtually. They both were. What if something had happened to Claire?

Her heart raced at the thought. Then she realized Melissa would have contacted her.

Yawning, she closed her eyes and pondered whether Claire had finally given up on their relationship. After all, it had been almost two months since they had physically seen each other. Time enough for her to reacquaint herself with old friends. "Especially Racheal."

The pangs of jealousy were triggered, and she opened her eyes and they rested on Knight, who was a contortionist for sure. His body was in such a convoluted shape she wondered how he could do that. His paws were reaching out, and he snored like a trooper. It made her smile. "At least you love me, Knight, no matter what."

The phone in the hall began to ring, and puzzled she stood. It only ever rang for Shirley's weekly call, and that wasn't due until tomorrow. Knight protested the movement and then turned into a furry ball and shut his eyes.

Kris smiled and left the room, shooting across the hallway to pick up the phone.

"Hello?"

"Hello, Kris."

Kris grinned. "Shirley, how wonderful." She pulled out the chair next to the hall table.

"I'm going to be a great aunt at last. The in vitro has worked."

"That's so special, how wonderful." Kris smiled. "I bet the proud parents to be are over the moon.

"Ecstatic. It's such a marvelous thing."

"Does this mean you are staying longer?"

""For a little while longer. Is that a problem?"

"No, you know I miss you, but it's more important to be with family."

Kris listened intently as Shirley spoke about her time in Mobile, Alabama. It was the most conversation she'd ever had one-on-one with Shirley in all the time she'd known her.

"How are you?"

"Me? Oh, you know. I love living at Seasons, and Knight loves it here. He hasn't even wanted to escape, though I think he prefers the cottage for some reason. He whines when I take him back to the main house."

Knight certainly does love the cottage. How odd is that? They must be in tune. I wish Claire had met him.

"What about your other friends, Jess in particular?"

Her attention went back to the conversation.

"Jess comes over here every other week, and we go to the quiz on alternate weeks. Yes, a convoluted way of saying Jess and I see each other every week." Kris laughed. "She's in New York this weekend. An agent wants to represent her. Says she's perfect and they can play on the returned-injured-soldier card." Kris listened. "Yes, I don't think she's into that. Very prideful is our Jess, but she deserves more people to hear her, don't you think?"

"Sorry, only ever heard her at a funeral."

Kris cradled the phone to her ear and laughed. "Really, at a funeral? Well when you come home and if she's still working at the golf club, then I'm taking you for a treat."

"What about Claire?"

Her face went serious at the next question. She struggled to answer it without breaking down. "Claire has her mother to think about. We agreed it was important that she be there for her. I talk to her all the time. We Skype every other day." *Lies, lies, why? Shirley would understand.*

"Got to go. Pizza has arrived."

"Oh okay, that sounds delicious. I might go into Chartres and have a pizza tomorrow. By the way, I never did say thank you for leaving your car for me to use. Yes, go, go or it will get cold. Talk to you next week. Stay safe."

"You are welcome."

Kris was about to put the receiver down on the cradle when Shirley spoke again and then disconnected.

"Time, my dear, and faith. Never give up."

Kris's eyes widened. "How did she know?"

She walked slowly back to the media room. Her hand was poised to open the door when the sound of tires on gravel had her head spinning around. She cautiously headed back to the hall as the vehicle came to a halt. She tried to see clearly from the side window near the front door. Squinting in the dark at the unfamiliar car stopping mere inches from the steps, she couldn't make out who it was. If it had been any closer, the vehicle would have mounted the steps.

The outside sentry lights had failed the day before, and she was waiting for an electrician from town to fix the problem. She pulled away from the window and was puzzling over what to do when the doorbell rang.

"Now what do I do?" Kris sucked in a deep breath and considered her options.

The bell rang again, she drew up her shoulders as she opened the door, and her mouth gaped open.

"Wow, am I that much of a surprise?"

Kris gasped, unable to do more than throw her arms around Claire, hugging her close.

"I thought you'd forgotten me."

Claire whispered in her ear, "Never. You are in my blood and part of me. How could I ever?"

Kris did cry then and sobbed against Claire's shoulder.

Claire stroked her hair and whispered softly into her ear, not that Kris knew what she said, for she was far too emotional. Except for three words…. *I love you.*

"You haven't called me!"

Claire pulled away and stared at her. Kris thought for a brief moment that Claire looked guilty, but Claire smiled and Kris was lost.

"I'm sorry, love, but the last week has been hectic. If I told you what I was doing, I wasn't sure you'd approve."

Kris's eyes flared. "What have you done?"

Claire shrugged, then winked, and that melted any doubt she had.

"Mother now has a full-time caregiver, and she likes him, but I had to be sure. I've been almost a twenty-four-hour watcher, shall we say, to check that this guy does what we need. Grams offered, but that wouldn't have been fair. I'm sorry for not telling you, but, love, I did it for us. Will you forgive me?"

Kris stared at the beloved face and knew no matter what Claire did she would forgive her. It left her at an insurmountable disadvantage, but didn't love do that? And she loved Claire beyond life itself. The rest of the world held so many more possibilities with Claire in it than without.

"I love you. That goes without saying."

Claire drew her close and kissed her. At that moment, she knew this was what everyone should experience in life.

Her body floated with the sensation of having her soulmate close again. Then she looked around Claire. "Who brought you?"

Claire chuckled and threw back her shoulders. "I did. Grams bought me a new car, complete with disabled features. I had the review test a week ago and passed with flying colors. I was sick of this separation business."

"I think we should retire, don't you?" Kris reached out to draw her in for another kiss and was surprised when Claire wagged a finger and grinned.

"Give me a minute." Then she rushed down the steps to the car.

A couple of minutes later she arrived with a box. A pet box.

"I figured Knight, not that I've met him personally yet, anyway I figured he would like this."

"Always good to have Knight happy.."

"Don't you dare laugh." Claire thrust the box into her arms.

Skeptically she eyed the item, and then there was a noise. "You didn't?"

Claire grinned. "I thought it was only right."

Kris opened the box and out popped a ginger kitten, so cute you couldn't do anything but love it. It jumped out of the box and clung to her neck.

"Claire." Kris grinned. "As much as I want you and I to be alone, you've made it a tad difficult. Come on, I want to introduce you to Knight." Claire frowned, and with a ginger cat clinging to her, Kris kissed Claire's lips. "It's all good, trust me."

Claire gave a weak smile. "I do. I always have from the moment I saw you in the window and you scampered away when I arrived."

Kris gasped. "How could you feel that? We hadn't even met."

"Sometimes it's just right. Although I didn't know it at the time. I'm sorry I messed up again this week. I promise I will do better."

"You made me a promise, Claire, that you would be back, and you made good. Darn, Shirley was right."

"What?"

"She told me all my dreams would come true, and Claire Tremont, you are every one of my dreams. Come on, let's see if Ginger makes friends easily, not to mention Knight." Kris took Claire's hand and dragged her to the media room.

†

"That was exhausting, and I thought my family interaction was hard." Claire chuckled.

Kris nestled into Claire's shoulder as they watched the two felines snuggled together in Knight's padded bed.

"Why did you buy another cat? You might not have liked them."

Claire's shoulder moved, but she remained as close as possible.

"Hadn't met my feline son yet, but I figured I was going to monopolize his mother, so the least I could do was provide a sibling. As to liking them, hell, if you do, I will." Claire bent her head and kissed Kris slowly.

"I love you," Kris declared as they separated.

Claire smiled and took Kris's left hand and stroked her fingers.

"I have another present."

Kris's eyes flared. "Darling, you are the only present I will ever need."

Claire half smiled, then placed her weak right hand in her pocket. She straightened and looked directly into Kris's eyes.

"I love you, Kris Lake. No, in fact, I adore you. I have baggage that has and probably will always cause us consternation." She cleared her throat. "I asked you to marry me a while ago, and you said yes. We even set a date. Damn this is too long-winded. Kris, will you marry me on Christmas Eve?"

Claire held her breath.

Kris didn't move. In fact, Claire thought she might have dropped off. Frowning, she looked at the clock on the wall. Nine thirty. *Was Jess right when she visited me a few days ago? Could I have left it too late?*

Then Kris turned to face her with a beautiful smile wreathing her features. "I love you. I will never love anyone like I do you. You are perplexing, frustrating, and...."

"And?" Claire held her breath. Had she really left it too late?

"My life belongs with yours. Now take me to bed."

"I have something else." Claire withdrew her right hand and thrust the velvet box forward.

With her eyes wide, Kris took it and opened it. Then tears flowed. "Claire, it's beautiful."

"Of course it is. I have to match the most beautiful woman I have ever met in my life." She removed the single diamond solitaire ring from the box and placed it on Kris's finger.

With tears flowing, Kris threw her arms around Claire. "I love you so much."

Claire's heart soared at the words as she took Kris in her arms. "I love you too, and I'm going to make your life as happy as it can be while I have breath left in my body."

She took Kris's hand, and they left the sleeping feline kids to ascend the stairs to Kris's room.

"One last thing, Claire."

"Yes?"

"I'm not wearing the dress."

They laughed entering Kris's room, and Claire kicked the door shut.

"We'll work on that," Claire uttered as they collapsed on the bed.

About the Author

JM Dragon

JM Dragon is a New Zealand citizen, living in the beautiful Canterbury countryside. She loves to garden, travel, write, take care of her animals and family, and pursue her business interests—Affinity eBook Press and a Canterbury manufacturing company.

She is a keen reader of sci-fi, crime/mystery, classics, and romance, which helps to feed her imagination for her own stories.

Currently published by Affinity eBook Press NZ LTD, her books include *Do Dreams Come True*, *Fix It Girl*, *In Name Only*, *The Destiny Series*, *Circus*, and 2015 GCLS winner *The One*.

You can contact her by email at jm1dragon@yahoo.com or on Facebook at http://www.facebook.com/julie.dragon.

Other Books from Affinity eBook Press

The Review by Annette Mori
Silver Lining, a successful lesbian romance writer, has a contest for the first reader who posts a review of her new story will win a home-cooked meal. Jasmine, Silver's beta reader, hopes to be the winner. Bizarre messages from an unknown fan has Silver wondering if she has a stalker. Who will come out the winner, the past, the present, or the unknown stalker?

South of Heaven by Ali Spooner
Kendra Drake thinks her life is complete. She has taken over as captain of her father's shrimp boat. As a favor to her father, Kendra has agreed to give fellow shrimper Lindsey Bowen a chance to work on the boat. Kendra is fighting against Mother Nature, the open waters, and herself. Still, Lindsey finds a way into Kendra's heart. Will it only last for the summer?

Catch to Release by Lacey Schmidt

On the verge of finally releasing her own record label, lesbian folk-rock star, Shay Greenaura, finds herself caught up in more than just her music. Addison Weller, a former Diplomatic Security Services agent is called in to assess the threats against Shay. Follow this fast-paced adventure to its surprising romantic conclusion.

Ready for Love by Erin O'Reilly

Kylie Wilcox's life dramatically changed with the death of her husband. Dr. LJ Evans, a renowned archeologist, needed and wanted nothing but her work for her happiness. Their worlds are about to collide and lives will be altered forever.

Neptune's Ring by Ali Spooner

In the sequel to *Venus Rising*, Nat and Liz, owners of Venus Rising, invite Levi and Vanessa to join them in a venture for a new club on another island. They find the perfect place in an unfinished resort, Neptune's Ring. While on the island, Levi is drawn into a mystery involving secret compartments and a murder. Join the characters in this page-turning adventure, filled with steamy romance, intrigue, and an unsolved murder.

The Ultimate Betrayal by Annette Mori

Lara is a successful, beautiful, charming financier. She is also a total control freak, so whatever Lara wants, Lara makes sure she gets. Rachel is Lara's fun-loving, charming, irresistible wife. Sophia's surprise visit to see Lara sets in motion a number of life-changing events for them all. Hell has no fury like a woman scorned.

It's in Her Kiss by Various Affinity Authors
A collection of various holiday stories dedicated to anyone and everyone who reads it. Young, old, lesbian, gay, bisexual, and transgender. We are all the same inside and want the same things outside...love, happiness, and that special someone to spend all of our holidays with.

Keeping Faith by TJ Vertigo
Join the antics of Reece, Faith, Cori, Vi, and even The Animal, one last time in *Keeping Faith*. Faith has finally made the big screen, but how will Reece handle her success? Will the love that they share be enough to save their relationship and soothe The Animal?

Bound by Ali Spooner
A rogue master vampire threatens the existence of the New Orleans vampire clan. Lord Jordan enlists Devin Benoit, sister of the Baton Rouge Alpha, and her witch lover, Tia, to assist with cleansing the city from potential disaster.

The Circle Dance by Jen Silver
Jamie Steele has moved to another town, trying to forget the heartbreak of losing her lover of six years. Sasha Fairfield finds her thoughts taken up with her ex-lover and thinks she wants Jamie back. Follow this captivating romance as love dances through the lives of these women to its surprising conclusion.

Search for the White Moon by Natalie London
Kathryn Austin, a government agent, is given opera singer, Adriana Desi, as her new assignment. Their lives and futures are in danger as the White Moon terrorists hunt them. Immerse yourself in this fast-paced romantic thriller by debut author Natalie London.

Take Me As I Am by JM Dragon & Erin O'Reilly
When Jo Lackerly and Thea Danvers meet, an unexpected friendship develops, proving a catalyst for both women to change their lives irrevocably. Follow them on a journey of discovery that will have your heart smiling, blood boiling, and senses entangled in a wonderful romance.

Carved in Stone by Jen Silver
Join the characters from *Starting Over* and *Arc Over Time* in this final book from the Starling Hill trilogy. Ellie Winters thinks she might be going mad when the ancient queen wants a proper burial for herself and her consort. *Carved in Stone* has romance, adventure, a treasure hunt, and a happy endings for all, living and dead.

Anywhere, Everywhere by Renee MacKenzie
Gwen Martin's life in the Ten Thousand Islands area changes irrevocably when Piper Jackson comes into her life. Without trust, can the budding relationship between Gwen and Piper

survive? Or will the answers to the questions continue to haunt them?

Venus Rising by Ali Spooner
Levi Johnson arrives at Venus Rising, an exclusive lesbian-only tropical resort in the Virgin Islands and finds more than she expected—a sizzling hot love triangle. Torn between her attraction to two women, she struggles to choose the right woman to share her life.

The Devil's Tree by Ali Spooner
Torn between her love for the pack and her need to find what's missing in her life, Devin Benoit travels to New Orleans. Will the previous happenings at the Devil's Tree help or hinder Devin in the fight of her life, and the life of Tia, the woman who now owns her heart?

The Beggars' Coppice by Erica Lawson
Edda Case is a woman in crisis who discovers that things are not as they seem. Is it truly a message for her from beyond the grave or is something more sinister taking place? Can Edda solve the mystery of *The Beggars' Coppice*?

Locked Inside by Annette Mori

How much does the power of love matter to someone who must overcome obstacles far greater than most people face in a lifetime.

Line of Sight by Ali Spooner
Sasha and her lover Kara are back. Continue the thrilling adventures of this couple from the Sasha Thibodaux series.

Requiem for Vukovar by Angela Koenig
Requiem for Vukovar continues the Refraction series and the exploits of Jeri O'Donnell and her partner, Kelly Corcoran. In an epic siege largely ignored by the wider world, Kelly, who was prepared to give up comforts and certainties when she became part of Jeri's nomadic life, encounters more than physical danger. Her ability to maintain her core integrity is assaulted by the inevitable ugliness of war. For Jeri, the true battle is confronting her attraction to violence as she struggles against losing herself in the exhilaration of combat.

Against All Odds by JM Dragon
From award-winning and bestselling author JM Dragon, with significant updates by Erin O'Reilly, comes an original tale of romance where everything seems to be stacked against two women whose destinies bring them together. Life however takes a twisted path, setting both Steph and Louise in directions they never thought possible. Will love win out against all odds or will love be forever lost?

The Settlement by Ali Spooner
The outpouring of love and friendship toward Cadin helps her on her path to healing and learning to trust her heart to love once again. Join bestselling author Ali Spooner on this sensational journey that ends with a heartwarming romance.

Once Upon a Time by Alane Hotchkin
Raven only wanted to escape the blows that life had dealt her. She longed to be on the open sea and free. When she came upon a beautiful young girl sitting alone in the middle of a meadow, little did she know that her destiny would be changed forever. Will they become the pawns of the ancient vision or will both paths lead to the same port of destiny? Find out in this exciting high seas adventure that will capture your imagination.

Asset Management by Annette Mori
Follow the twists and turns to the explosive conclusion. Not everything is black and white. There are many shades of gray, and sometimes it's difficult to decipher who is good and who is evil. No one is all virtue or all malevolence, but sometimes love helps us rise above.

Do Dreams Come True? by JM Dragon

How do two people who really shouldn't get on end up in a relationship? Find out in this deliciously ordinary romance.

Return to Me by Erin O'Reilly
Will Salvation bring just that to Ellie, allowing her to find peace and happiness again, or will it have her questioning all that she believes in? A wonderful romance cloaked within an intriguing mystery.

Arc Over Time by Jen Silver
Book 2 of the Starling Hill Trilogy. This wonderful romantic continuation with the characters from *Starting Over* ties up loose ends. But the question is—does everyone have a happy ending? A must read.

The Presence by Charlene Neal
Can Rebecca and Kayleigh overcome ghosts from the past and their own insecurities, or will a presence from the past tear them apart?

A Walk Away by Lacey Schmidt
Sometimes chance brings you to the right person to help you resolve some of your baggage, and you learn to like yourself a little more. Kat and Rand are smart enough to recognize this chance in each other, but they also find that there is a catch

to every opportunity—walking toward something is always walking away from something else.

Possessing Morgan by Erica Lawson
The investigation has barely begun when Andrea becomes the target of a nearly fatal hit-and-run. But was it really aimed at her? Can she and Morgan find the common ground they need to solve the case and stop the attacks, or are the gaps just too wide to bridge?

Twenty-three Miles by Renee MacKenzie
This is a story about community, and how it comes together in dangerous and devastating times. When you don't know who to trust, you better have friends who will rally around you. Will Talia and Shay find the answers they need to the mystery of the murders on the parkway, or will justice be elusive? Will they survive their quest for the truth?

Reece's Star by TJ Vertigo
Under Faith's guiding, loving hand, will Reece successfully traverse the rocky road of emotion and embrace the positive changes in her life? Or will she panic and be unable to control that Animal part of herself? Will she take that next step to declare herself fully capable of love and devotion? This third installment in the popular series that began with *Private Dancer* continues the passionate and often

hilarious romance of Reece and Faith as they both grow in love and in trust.

The Chronicles of Ratha: Book 2 A Lion Among the Lambs by Erica Lawson
Can Jordana believe in herself like her Noorthi sisters do? Only then can she fulfill her destiny as The Chosen One. Follow the colorful cast of characters in this action-packed adventure sequel as they traverse the galaxy. Of course, nothing ever goes smoothly when Jordana is involved.

Starting Over by Jen Silver
Book 1 of the Starling Hill Trilogy. There's a mystery afoot— whose royal resting place is disturbed at Starling Hill? All is revealed in this classic romance of simmering passions, anguished loss, and the wonder of love.

If I Were a Boy by Erin O'Reilly
Will Katie and Helen be able to make a life together work or succumb to doubts and the pressures of family? This story will fill you with the thrill of passion and the tenderness of love.

Terminal Event by Ali Spooner
Will the killer be caught or continue to evade authorities? Can Tally and Blair's budding romance survive the

possibility? Read this intense murder mystery romance and find out.

Love Forever, Live Forever by Annette Mori
Fate intervenes and puts Nicky directly back into the path of her first love, Sara, and the corresponding events send her into a tailspin. Now she must decide—who will be the person she ends up living with and loving forever?

The One by JM Dragon
2015 GCLS Winner for Romance, Intrigue, and Adventure. The One is a romance with everything, love, intrigue, misunderstandings with a happy conclusion—the only question—who gets the girl?

Confined Spaces by Renee MacKenzie
Corporate politics, complicated romance, and long distances conspire to keep Andie and Kara all boxed in. Can love triumph despite the Confined Spaces?

Reflected Passion by Erica Lawson
Through a mirror, Françoise embraces life anew, while for Dale it is a powerful awakening, forcing her to discover not only her sensual nature, but the inner strength she possesses.

Flight by Renee Mackenzie

Some lives will be lost and others changed forever when the sisters' lives intersect. Will they be consumed by the wreckage, or will they be able to pick themselves up and take flight?

Cowgirl Up by Ali Spooner
Ride along with the MC2, for boot scootin', butt kickin', dirt eatin', rodeo adventures, with a love story thrown into the mix.

E-Books, Print, Free e-books

Visit our website for more publications available online.

www.affinityebooks.com

Published by Affinity E-Book Press NZ LTD
Canterbury, New Zealand

Registered Company 2517228